IN THE HEADLINES

Activist Athletes

WHEN SPORTS AND POLITICS MIX

THE NEW YORK TIMES EDITORIAL STAFF

Published in 2021 by New York Times Educational Publishing
in association with The Rosen Publishing Group, Inc.
29 East 21st Street, New York, NY 10010

First Edition

The New York Times
Caroline Que: Editorial Director, Book Development
Phyllis Collazo: Photo Rights/Permissions Editor
Heidi Giovine: Administrative Manager

Rosen Publishing
Megan Kellerman: Managing Editor
Michael Hessel-Mial: Editor
Brian Garvey: Art Director

Cataloging-in-Publication Data
Names: New York Times Company.
Title: Activist athletes: when sports and politics mix / edited by
the New York Times editorial staff.
Description: New York : New York Times Educational Publishing,
2021. | Series: In the headlines | Includes glossary and index.
Identifiers: ISBN 9781642823332 (library bound) | ISBN
9781642823325 (pbk.) | ISBN 9781642823349 (ebook)
Subjects: LCSH: Sports—Political aspects. | Sports and state. |
Sports and society. | Protest movements.
Classification: LCC GV706.35 A385 2021 | DDC 306.4'83—dc23

Manufactured in the United States of America

On the cover: Activist athletes challenge expectations of how
players should conduct themselves; Simone Noronha/The New
York Times.

Contents

7   Introduction

CHAPTER 1

Athletes as Workers: Organizing for a Voice

10   When a Players Union Doesn't Help the Players BY ARN TELLEM

14   Players Show Solidarity With Lockout Looming
     BY RICHARD SANDOMIR

16   In N.H.L. Negotiations, Union's Good Ideas May Not Matter
     BY JEFF Z. KLEIN

19   Unionized College Athletes? BY JOE NOCERA

22   Playing College Football Is a Job BY THE NEW YORK TIMES

24   A Threat to Unionize, and Then Benefits Trickle In for Players
     BY MICHAEL POWELL

28   College Athletes' Potential Realized in Missouri Resignations
     BY JOE NOCERA

33   Players Hold Power Over the N.C.A.A., if They Feel the Hunger
     BY MARC TRACY

CHAPTER 2

Taking a Knee: Athletes Fight Racial Injustice

37   Inside College Basketball's Most Political Locker Room
     BY MARC TRACY

44 The Awakening of Colin Kaepernick BY JOHN BRANCH

60 High Schools Threaten to Punish Students Who Kneel During Anthem BY CHRISTINE HAUSER

63 From the N.B.A., a Cautionary Tale on National Anthem Protests BY HARVEY ARATON

67 In a Busy Year, Malcolm Jenkins Raised a Fist and Checked All the Boxes BY KEN BELSON

73 Football Players Are Protesting Police Violence, Not the Anthem BY KASHANA CAULEY

CHAPTER 3

Fighting for Gender Equality, On and Off the Field

76 A Giant Leap for Women, but Hurdles Remain BY JERÉ LONGMAN

80 Understanding the Controversy Over Caster Semenya BY JERÉ LONGMAN

85 Gabby Douglas Says She Also Was Abused by Gymnastics Team Doctor BY MATT STEVENS

87 Billie Jean King Understands Colin Kaepernick BY ANA MARIE COX

90 8 Times Women in Sports Fought for Equality BY SARAH MERVOSH AND CHRISTINA CARON

95 The Best Women's Soccer Team in the World Fights for Equal Pay BY LIZZY GOODMAN

108 For Megan Rapinoe, Boldness in the Spotlight Is Nothing New BY JERÉ LONGMAN

CHAPTER 4

L.G.B.T.Q. Athletes Break the Silence

113 A Pioneer, Reluctantly BY GREG BISHOP

123 N.F.L. Prospect Michael Sam Proudly Says What Teammates
Knew: He's Gay BY JOHN BRANCH

129 Athlete to Activist: How a Public Coming Out Shaped a Young
Football Player's Life BY DAN LEVIN

135 Sprinter Dutee Chand Becomes India's First Openly Gay Athlete
BY MIKE IVES

138 At World Cup, U.S. Team's Pride Is Felt by Others, Too
BY ANDREW KEH

144 He Emerged From Prison a Potent Symbol of H.I.V.
Criminalization BY EMILY S. RUEB

CHAPTER 5

Other Outspoken Athletes, Past and Present

149 Magic Johnson and Public Opinion on AIDS and Sex BY JOHN SIDES

151 What the World Got Wrong About Kareem Abdul-Jabbar
BY JAY CASPIAN KANG

162 Muhammad Ali, the Political Poet BY HENRY LOUIS GATES JR.

166 Stephen Curry, on a 'Surreal' Day, Confronts a Presidential Snub
BY SCOTT CACCIOLA

169 Etan Thomas: Now a Different Kind of Player BY SOPAN DEB

173 Alejandro Bedoya Spoke Out on Gun Violence. It Helped Make
Him M.L.S.'s Player of the Week. BY VICTOR MATHER

177 Kenny Stills Criticizes Dolphins Owner Over Trump Fund-Raiser
BY KEN BELSON

CHAPTER 6

Sports Diplomacy in the International Arena

179 I.O.C. Names New President Amid Concern Over Possible Athlete Protests in Sochi BY JERÉ LONGMAN

183 Mandela Embraced the Power of Sports for Resistance and Unity
BY JERÉ LONGMAN

187 Flying 3 Flags and Seeking One Banner BY BILLY WITZ

192 Human Rights and the 2022 Olympics BY MINKY WORDEN

196 Palestinian Soccer Association Drops Effort to Suspend Israel From FIFA BY JODI RUDOREN

200 Egyptian Judo Athlete Refuses Handshake After Losing to Israeli
BY VICTOR MATHER

202 Under Fidel Castro, Sport Symbolized Cuba's Strength and Vulnerability BY JERÉ LONGMAN

207 Pan Am Games Protesters Get Probation. Olympians Get a Warning. BY JERÉ LONGMAN

211 Glossary
213 Media Literacy Terms
215 Media Literacy Questions
217 Citations
222 Index

Introduction

WE CELEBRATE MEGASTAR ATHLETES because they seem to be superhuman. They achieve feats of speed, strength, endurance and coordination in split-second moments that become legendary. Such athletes are celebrated for their often outsize personalities and lifestyles. But athletes are human, too. They have personal and family struggles, come from marginalized racial or gender identities, are workers with contract disputes and bring a wide range of interests and passions to their work.

But when athletes speak out on controversial topics, the public tends to respond with confusion and outrage. Why are they disrupting the game? Who do they think they are? Why don't they stick to sports? Shouldn't they be grateful? These common questions suggest that the public sometimes prefers athletes to be a little smaller, a little less noticeable. But activist athletes have existed as long as professional sports, raising a new question: How can we learn about some of the issues they care about?

The articles in this book begin with union efforts by athletes, as a reminder that the vast majority of professional players are workers with unique on-the-job difficulties. The risk of injury, grueling practice sessions and having a limited voice in their careers can help turn athletes into activists. While many professional players unions have already won the major battles, student athletes now call for unions of their own. Student athletes have yet to be recognized as workers, but their efforts link directly to other athlete protests on the larger political issues.

You may be reading this book because of one athlete in particular: Colin Kaepernick, who threw the N.F.L. into turmoil by refusing to stand for the national anthem. Kaepernick is not the first or most controversial activist athlete, but his act of "taking a knee" during the anthem was widely imitated, spreading to other professional sports. In the process, Kaepernick raised the ire of conservatives and liberals alike and jeopardized his career. Most importantly, his activism highlighted that for many athletes of color, racial oppression is a more pressing struggle than advancing to the playoffs. As former student athlete Nigel Hayes said, "I was black before I picked up a basketball, and when I retire, I'll still be black." Hayes reminds us that the human side of sports also includes the hard discussions about racism in America.

Many of the most outspoken women athletes have shown solidarity by taking a knee themselves, but women athletes face a struggle of their own. Though the last decade has seen professional women's sports become increasingly popular, female players face problems that reflect workforce gender disparities as a whole: pay gaps, limited resources, lower credibility and abusive working environments. Megan Rapinoe's fight for equal pay and Caster Semenya's fight

PETE KIEHART FOR THE NEW YORK TIMES

Amateur soccer player Jessica Bilo ties her cleats with rainbow laces, as a symbol of L.G.B.T.Q. pride. This action was inspired by activist players like Megan Rapinoe.

against unfair hormone testing suggest that among the barriers for women athletes, the most persistent come from unfairly high expectations of women compared with men.

The struggles of women athletes remind us that professional sports is still rooted in strict gender norms that aren't inclusive of all players. These norms have their greatest impact on gay, lesbian, bisexual and transgender athletes. For example, between 1975 and 2017, only six N.F.L. players publicly disclosed that they were gay, and they faced a great deal of social fallout for doing so. Recently, however, more athletes are beginning to play as their full selves, making it easier for younger generations to do the same. Like many activist athletes, these players don't necessarily choose to embrace controversy. Instead, some of the most important parts of themselves — their race, gender or sexual identity — are simply brought onto the field with them.

The coverage of outspoken athletes tends to focus on athletes as individuals and not on the solidarity among athletes that characterizes a more concerted activism. Athletes consistently stand up with and for one another. Indeed, political incidents during international sports like the Olympics and the World Cup especially highlight this tendency. International sports bring conflicts between nations and fights for human rights to a global stage. Such debates and activities even have a name: "sports diplomacy," the use of athletics as a channel for international relations.

How will contemporary activist athletes be remembered? Today, Muhammad Ali and Kareem Abdul-Jabbar are sports legends; during their playing careers they were seen as rabble-rousers. But such players always had something to teach us. Taking the broader view of sports over time, we see that activist athletes aren't just a 21st-century phenomenon. We will likely always debate the appropriateness of an athlete speaking out. But over time, we will just as likely look back fondly on the players who revealed their full selves, on and off the field.

CHAPTER 1

Athletes as Workers: Organizing for a Voice

As in other sectors, unions are often the first way athletes find their voice. Despite the money and prestige bestowed upon superstar athletes, professional sports remains a job. Among low-ranked players especially, athletes risk injury and financial instability after retirement. Athlete unions made the most gains long ago, resulting in common features such as revenue sharing, minimum salaries and free agency. But athlete union fights continue. Today, the sharpest athletic union debates concern whether student athletes count as workers given the hardships they face.

When a Players Union Doesn't Help the Players

OPINION | BY ARN TELLEM | MAY 7, 2011

HAVING GROWN UP during the New Deal, my parents made me keenly aware that unions gave workers what they lacked individually — a voice. My childhood hero was Marvin Miller, the labor economist who in 1968 negotiated the Major League Baseball Players Association's first collective bargaining agreement with team owners. Miller's own new deal raised the minimum salary to $10,000 from $6,000, the first increase since the 1940s. (It's now $414,000.)

Miller introduced the concept of salary arbitration, fought for stronger pensions and encouraged ballplayers to challenge the owners who, wielding the reserve clause, routinely treated players like chattel. The clause effectively bound players to one team in perpetuity at that team's discretion. With Miller at the helm, the reserve clause was abolished in 1975, paving the way for free agency.

Thirty-six years later, I wonder if unions in professional sports other than baseball have outlived their purpose. Pro football players voted to decertify their union in March immediately before the owners imposed a long-expected lockout. Faced with a similar situation, pro basketball players will almost certainly follow suit. As a player agent who represents 45 N.B.A. players, I think they should the moment the current season ends.

In the N.F.L. and the N.B.A., the noble ideal of solidarity has played itself out. Collective bargaining has proved ineffectual in protecting the rights of football and basketball players. The most that their union leaders can hope for is to minimize concessions. Enhancements to wages, benefits and working conditions are no longer even discussed. Meanwhile, team owners have set bargaining goals well beyond their needs and then demanded more than they could ever hope to achieve.

When the union inevitably balks, the owners feign indignation, complaining that the players won't compromise even though compromising would play into the owners' hands. Inevitably, the leagues' overreach achieves its desired effect, preventing the unions from advancing the players' legitimate concerns. The N.F.L. and N.B.A. players consistently allow the owners to define the issues. More often than not, management gets the concessions it seeks.

Pro football, the most profitable sport in the world, cries hard times and demands a longer schedule, a shrinking salary cap and a rookie scale that would include limits on length of contracts and guaranteed money. Team owners — who slice $1 billion out of the N.F.L.'s annual $9 billion pie before the remaining revenue is divided with the players — kicked off negotiations by insisting on an additional $1.3 billion a year for the next decade. The union countered by offering $550 million over four years without asking for financial verification. Today, the sides remain hundreds of millions of dollars a year apart.

Miller believed that a union should set minimum standards, not maximum salaries. Of the four major unions in pro sports, baseball's is the only one that has successfully pushed back management on this issue. (In 1999, the N.B.A.'s union agreed to a salary cap for individual players.) Interestingly, no commissioner, team executive or coach has a compensation cap. Nor have they been asked to take pay cuts despite the league's supposed financial troubles. Perhaps most tellingly, no owners have limits on the amount their clubs can appreciate in value.

Despite unparalleled revenue, the salaries of N.F.L. players are significantly lower than that of their counterparts in baseball and basketball. Football is the team sport with the shortest careers, averaging 3.5 years, and without the guaranteed contracts common in the other two.

Rather than address this reality, the N.F.L. wants to expand its schedule, which will no doubt result in more injuries, possibly more serious ones. Even more unconscionably, after an N.F.L. player leaves the game, he's entitled to only five years of health insurance. In such a brutal sport, adequate and permanent health care should be a given.

For years, the N.F.L. and the N.B.A. have found their players associations to be unwitting partners. Rather than compete in a free market, management has exploited the weaknesses of unions to inhibit competition. By shielding owners from the scrutiny of antitrust laws, the unions have effectively allowed collusion. More often than not, the result has been union retreat — on salary caps, salary scales and taxes.

Decertification has allowed N.F.L. players to sue the league on antitrust grounds, and could eventually force owners to open their books to scrutiny if the case proceeds. At the very least decertification allowed the players to get an injunction from a federal judge to stop the lockout, pending an appeal. Sure, the N.F.L. could attempt to impose whatever salary and free-agency restrictions it wishes, but it will have to tread carefully. If the league loses an antitrust suit, it will have to pay each player affected three times his actual economic loss.

Is it any wonder that N.F.L. and N.B.A. executives bewail decertification, and insist that agreements be reached through negotiation? The sad irony is that without a union, the courts and antitrust laws will level the playing field so that the risk is not borne solely by the players. Given the considerable risk of going to trial, the league commissioners will probably get what they want: a settlement negotiated by lawyers.

Something is fundamentally wrong when the only effective weapon in a union's arsenal is dissolution. The hard-won early victories — health benefits, minimum wage — have been overshadowed by the sacrifices that players are now not just asked, but also expected to make.

ARN TELLEM is an agent representing professional basketball and baseball players.

Players Show Solidarity With Lockout Looming

BY RICHARD SANDOMIR | JUNE 23, 2011

EIGHT DAYS BEFORE N.B.A. owners could lock them out, 52 players gathered for a show of strength at a Manhattan hotel on Thursday, united in their determination to reach a deal that is not a drastic leap backward.

Some were stars, like Kevin Garnett, Chris Paul and Blake Griffin. Others have had more modest careers, like Roger Mason Jr., Matt Carroll and Anthony Tolliver. Some wore suits. Others wore warm-up gear.

"We're not willing to accept an unfair deal," Derek Fisher, the president of the N.B.A. players union, said at a news conference. "We're unified in the sense of not being afraid" of a lockout.

The players, and Billy Hunter, the union's executive director, had just spent five hours in a strategy session at the New York Hilton, preparing for the resumption of negotiations with the league on Friday.

Then, in a room usually reserved for banquets, they stood three and four deep, flanking Fisher and Hunter.

"I wish you could have been in that room to feel the energy, sophistication and level of understanding," said Fisher, the Lakers' point guard. "There have been times in meetings with ownership where there's been an implication of our lack of understanding of the system." He called that "insulting."

He said some players feel the union had gone as far as it can; others wanted it to demand more.

Although Hunter said the "door is slightly ajar" to a new deal before the collective bargaining agreement expires Thursday, he seemed to doubt it. He inferred another goal to the owners, which sounded somewhat like standard labor-leader hyperbole.

"I think their real intention is to break the union," he said.

Michael Bass, a spokesman for the N.B.A., said in an e-mail: "A lockout is something that we are trying to avoid by making multiple offers that treat our players fairly. We are dismayed by the union's unfortunate rhetoric."

Hunter drew a parallel between the season-long 2004-5 lockout of N.H.L. players and the one that is looming over the N.B.A.'s 2011-12 season. He said the N.H.L. used the lockout to break the union and impose "the worst deal in professional sports," which included a hard salary cap.

Ted Leonsis, the owner of the Washington Wizards and the N.H.L.'s Washington Capitals, was fined $100,000 last year by Commissioner David Stern for advocating a hard cap like the one in the N.H.L.

The N.B.A. players union is displeased by the league's proposed "flex" cap, which it sees as no different than a hard cap, and the league's dismissal of its offer to reduce salaries by $500 million over five years. It is also upset at a league proposal to pay players a minimum of $2 billion annually over 10 years, which Hunter said amounts to a cut from the $2.17 billion that players received in salary and benefits last season.

Matt Bonner of the San Antonio Spurs, who is a union vice president, said that the owners "want everything."

"They want extreme financial givebacks in terms of salary and a hard salary cap," Bonner said.

To Garnett, the Boston Celtics' star forward, the owners' position "speaks of control."

But, he said: "There needs to be common ground. That's what we're trying to establish."

In N.H.L. Negotiations, Union's Good Ideas May Not Matter

SPORTS BLOG | BY JEFF Z. KLEIN | AUG. 16, 2012

COMMISSIONER GARY BETTMAN and the owners may be coming off as the villains in the eyes of the public in the N.H.L. labor negotiations, but that won't matter to them one bit, not while they have the chance to save hundreds of millions of dollars each year with a new collective bargaining agreement, and certainly not while they have the upper hand in these negotiations.

Right from the start of these talks there has been no mystery about what Bettman and the owners are after. They want a deal similar to the one the N.F.L. and N.B.A. owners got last year after locking out their players: a reduction in the players' share of earnings to about 50 percent — lower, if they can get it. N.H.L. players currently receive 57 percent of the league's revenue. Being liked by the public is a secondary concern for the owners, who would save $225 million a year by lowering the players' share to 50 percent. (They would save $450 million a year if they succeed in knocking it down to 43 percent, the owners' initial offer.)

Donald Fehr and the players' association are seen as the reasonable ones in this dispute, especially after the innovative offer they made Tuesday. Fehr has expressed himself using "the language of compromise rather than confrontation," as Stu Hackel noted Wednesday on SI.com, and that has helped ease hockey fans' concerns that Fehr is a teeth-baring union radical — an impression based on the baseball strike he led in 1994-95, not on the subsequent decade and a half of baseball labor peace he helped foster.

So favorable is the public perception of Fehr that it came as no surprise when reporters went over the moon for Fehr after he made the union's offer. "A forward-thinking stroke of genius," The Sporting News called his offer, the most rapturous among many favorable reports.

That proposal — a nimble agglomeration of temporary salary give-backs and revenue-sharing reforms that Fehr cast as a partnership between the players and the league's wealthy clubs meant to help the league's struggling clubs — contained many insightful ideas.

But to the owners, the plan was a nonstarter. It sidestepped what they want most: a big cut to players' salaries.

"It wasn't particularly responsive to our proposal," Bettman said flatly, and he wasn't just talking about the salary cuts.

The proposal did not address other key ownership concerns, like capping the length of contracts (the owners want a five-year limit; the players want to keep them unlimited), extending the length of entry-level contracts (the owners want five years; the players want to keep it at three), and making players wait 10 years before they can become restricted free agents (the players want to keep it at the current seven).

In a smart analysis of the union's offer, Sportnet's Michael Grange wrote Wednesday that there was "zero chance" the owners would accept it. Perhaps the biggest sticking point for the owners, Grange wrote, is that after three years of taking limited pay raises, the players can return to the current agreement and go back to earning 57 percent of league revenue.

The difference between the two plans is huge, Grange said: $435 million a year in total players salaries over the next four years.

While the owners may end up rejecting the union plan, there are still elements within it they may be willing to accept. Particularly intriguing is the concept of expanded revenue sharing, which may win favor among struggling teams like the Islanders, the Blue Jackets, the Panthers and the Stars.

The N.H.L. has by far the most limited revenue sharing among the big four North American sports leagues. According to rough estimates, the N.H.L. shares just 12 percent of the league's portion of revenue among its clubs — and according to union calculations, that figure is as low as 4.5 percent. Aspects of the union's proposal for a much broader revenue-sharing plan ($240 million in the first year) could find their way into a final agreement.

The union also proposed a way for rich clubs to pay over the salary cap, and for poor clubs to stay under the salary floor, TSN reported. Clubs in financial distress would be allowed to trade or sell up to $4 million in cap space to another team — so, for example, the struggling Islanders could deal $4 million to the Flyers, allowing them to add, say, another goalie, even though the Flyers are already at the cap ceiling.

Those pieces of the union offer may provide the owners with small islands of common ground to share with the players. Other slightly bigger islands are probably the players' acquiescence to the salary cap system and the players' volunteering to detach their earnings from overall league revenue, even for a short time.

But make no mistake: the owners are willing to lock out the players, and they will almost certainly do so on Sept. 15. Bettman and Fehr are scheduled to meet again next Wednesday, three weeks before the current agreement expires. N.H.L. owners want what N.B.A. and N.F.L. owners got, and that's all there is to it, no matter how many clever alternative proposals Fehr comes up with. The players are unwilling to take an enormous pay cut after having done so in the last lockout seven years ago, so they will not capitulate.

That leaves hockey fans, and perhaps the players, too, counting on the N.H.L.'s big TV contract with NBC and the size and prestige of its signature event, the Winter Classic, to act as a brake against the owners canceling the entire season.

Unionized College Athletes?

OPINION | BY JOE NOCERA | JAN. 31, 2014

KAIN COLTER IS a senior at Northwestern University, a pre-med stu-dent majoring in psychology with a 3.1 grade-point average. For the last two years, he has also been the starting quarterback for the university's football team, where he has shown himself to be a real leader and, in the words of his academic adviser, "a wonderful exam-ple of a true student-athlete."

One of the classes he took at Northwestern was about the mod-ern workplace. "We were talking about unions," he recalls. "About the steelworkers' union, and the professional sports unions. And the teacher said it was too bad you guys don't have the kind of protections a union can negotiate." By "you guys," of course, the professor meant college athletes. The lightbulb went on in Colter's head.

As an illustration of the power of an education, this story is downright heartwarming. But it could be a lot more. There is at least a chance — one doesn't want to get too carried away at this early stage — that it could wind up triggering a momentous change in the way big-time college athletics operates. On Tuesday, Colter and the majority of his teammates petitioned the National Labor Relations Board for the right to form a union.

Does a union for college athletes seem far-fetched? If it does, that's in large part because the N.C.A.A. has done such a good job over the decades of convincing America — and the courts — that because the athletes are students, they can't possibly also be employees.

The phrase "student-athlete" was, in fact, dreamed up in the 1950s by then-N.C.A.A. President Walter Byers, after it appeared that injured athletes in several states might be allowed to get workers' compensa-tion. The phrase, write Nicholas Fram and T. Ward Frampton in an arti-cle in the Buffalo Law Review, was meant to "obfuscate the nature of the legal relationship at the heart of a growing commercial enterprise."

Today, that commercial enterprise brings in not millions of dollars but billions. Yet the players not only don't participate in the spoils, they have no voice at all. "Players need to know that they will be taken care of if they are injured," said Ramogi Huma, the president of the National College Players Association, which is aiding the Northwestern effort. Guaranteed medical care is one of a number of issues that Huma thinks a union could help ensure.

The ultimate example, noted Huma, is the controversy over concussions. "It is terrifying to think of the damage concussions can do, and see the N.C.A.A. avoiding responsibility, while the N.F.L.P.A. has been making progress," he said. (The National Football League Players Association is the union for professional football players.) Indeed, in a recent court filing in a concussion lawsuit, the N.C.A.A.'s lawyers wrote that "the N.C.A.A. denies that it has a legal duty to protect student-athletes."

It's worth noting that neither Colter nor Huma is advocating that the players get paid a salary. "What we want is a seat at the table," said Huma. What college athletes need, more than money, is an organization that will push back against the all-powerful N.C.A.A. and their own athletic departments, which are so quick to throw their players under the bus at the first hint of a problem.

The question that the N.L.R.B. will have to grapple with is whether college athletes meet the criteria required to be labeled as employees. In their law review article, Fram and Frampton make the case that they do. The labor board, they note, defines employees as any "person who works for another in return for financial or other compensation." College athletes are compensated with a scholarship. They are also beholden to a coach who — to use the board's language again — "has the power to control and direct the employees in the material details of how the work is performed."

Still, Fram and Frampton note that the N.L.R.B. hasn't exactly shined in recent years. Scholars, they write, have described the board as being "largely ineffective." In the case of another class of student workers — graduate assistants — the board wound up ruling that they did not meet the definition of employee. (Yes, there are some graduate assistants' unions. But they were formed mostly without the help of the N.L.R.B.) Clearly, forming a union of college athletes will be an uphill struggle.

I always thought that the idea of a union for college players was unlikely, but not for legal reasons. Athletes enroll in universities when they are 18 or 19 years old. Their careers lie ahead of them. They don't want to do anything that might cause them to be viewed as trouble-makers. Even after they realize the way the system is stacked against them, they fear retaliation should they speak up. For that reason, I assumed they would never take that first step.

Sometimes it's nice to be proved wrong.

JOE NOCERA is an Op-Ed columnist for The New York Times.

Playing College Football Is a Job

EDITORIAL | BY THE NEW YORK TIMES | MARCH 27, 2014

BEFORE COLLEGE IS even in session, Northwestern football players spend up to 60 hours a week practicing at a one-month training camp. During the three- or four-month football season, they put in up to 50 hours a week preparing for games. That's more time than many full-time employees devote to their jobs.

Looking at these basic facts, the logic is clear. Football players at colleges like Northwestern with big-time sports programs are not "student-athletes," as the National Collegiate Athletic Association claims, but employees. Critics have been making this point for years. Finally, on Wednesday, a regional director of the National Labor Relations Board agreed, ruling that Northwestern football players on scholarships were eligible to form a union and bargain collectively.

"It cannot be said that the employer's scholarship players are 'primarily students,' " Peter Ohr wrote in his 24-page decision, noting that players were recruited for their athletic talents rather than academic ability, must undergo drug testing, and that they risked losing their scholarships if they did not follow team regulations.

This is a big deal, or at least the beginning of a big deal. Northwestern has already announced that it would appeal the decision to the N.L.R.B. national office. If it is upheld, Northwestern can still refuse to bargain with the players (assuming they actually vote to form a union), sending the case to a federal appeals court.

Still, Mr. Ohr's ruling gives weight to the argument that scholarship athletes are not amateurs who play merely "for the love of their sport" — as the N.C.A.A. said in a statement reacting to the decision.

The N.C.A.A. and athletic directors have fiercely resisted calls for change and argued that professionalization would ruin college sports. Naturally they are attached to the way things are because they benefit financially from capping compensation at the value of a scholarship. Northwestern football reported $235 million revenue from 2003 to 2012. USA Today revealed in September that the team coach, Pat Fitzgerald, made at least $2.2 million in 2011, making him the university's highest paid employee.

The college-sports establishment has brought this trouble on itself by not moving to address players' legitimate grievances. The group that brought the Northwestern petition to the N.L.R.B., the College Athletes Players Association, isn't seeking a specific share of football revenue or even salaries, but better medical protections for concussions and other injuries, guaranteed scholarships that cover the full cost of attending college and the establishment of a trust fund that players can use to finish their schooling after their N.C.A.A. eligibility expires.

Those are modest, reasonable goals. If Northwestern and other universities don't want to have to deal with unions, they should stop fighting their players and work with them to improve conditions.

A Threat to Unionize, and Then Benefits Trickle In for Players

COLUMN | BY MICHAEL POWELL | JAN. 12, 2015

BOULDER, COLO. — College football has gone on a roll that would bring a giggle to the lips of King Midas.

On New Year's Day, more than 28 million Americans watched the playoffs, and more still probably watched Ohio State's 42-20 victory over Oregon in the championship matchup on Monday night. And, good God, that glorious cascade of cash: College conferences expect to pull in hundreds of millions of dollars; ESPN executives take daily baths in their riches; professional gamblers are beside themselves.

The coaches, those fellows in sweatpants and headsets, are experiencing a hedge fund moment as their salaries make joyful, geometric leaps upward. Jim Harbaugh experienced a down year in the N.F.L., but no worries: The University of Michigan, a public institution wrestling with budget cuts in a fiscally straitened state, recently agreed to pay him $5 million next year, with millions of dollars of incentives.

Athletic directors are paid like potentates. University presidential suites at stadiums serve lamb roast and Cristal.

What, I asked Kain Colter, to make of this glorious bacchanal?

We sit in his living room on a high plains ridge outside Boulder. A lean, athletic 22-year-old man, he has the Cowboys-Packers game on the television and workout equipment around him. He made the Vikings' practice squad this season and hopes to join the team next season.

He also organized a players union movement at Northwestern, where he played quarterback for four years.

"I mean, as a fan, it's great fun, I love the college game," he said of college bowl madness. "But the incredible money underlines that we are truly the engines of a multibillion-dollar industry.

"Honestly, every guy in every college locker room in the nation talks about this."

Oregon and Ohio State possess fine quarterbacks, whirling dervish running backs, all-American defensive linemen and special teams that charge downfield like barbarian hordes.

Not a single one of these marvelously talented athletes makes a dime off his labor — sometimes as much as 60 hours a week — beyond a scholarship. In fact, if next season a coach recruits a better, more mountainous defensive lineman, there are no N.C.A.A. rules to prevent this season's version from losing his scholarship.

Most college football players practice longer and harder in pads and helmets than do the pros — the N.F.L. players union forced teams to set weekly limits on high-impact practices.

And those blown knees and concussions? Most players are on their own. Unlike the N.F.L., the N.C.A.A. has made no financial reckoning with the damage wrought on students by concussions.

Colter loved Northwestern, and 90 percent of its football players graduated, which is unusual for a major university. It came with compromises. Colter declared pre-med until it became an impossibility. His core classes conflicted with the football practices that were a condition of his scholarship.

Linemen gorged on food to keep their weight up. "It truly is a job," Colter said. "If you don't keep your weight up, you won't play or you won't start."

Colter and Ramogi Huma, president of the National College Players Association, the group seeking to represent college athletes, envision nothing like the high peaks of N.F.L. salaries. Minimum wage might be a nice start. Colter said he would like to see the colleges divert a small rivulet of their riches to establish endowments, which players could tap years after graduation.

"Even the players who graduate often don't really get an education," Colter noted.

Michigan offers a case in point. So high are its academic standards that it is often referred to as a public Ivy. Yet only 69 percent of football players graduate.

Michigan's new president, Mark Schlissel, a former provost at Brown University, recently committed the sin of talking honestly. "We admit students who aren't as qualified, and it's probably the kids that we admit that can't honestly, even with lots of help, do the amount of work and the quality of work it takes to make progression from year to year."

Such candor mortified alumni, who speculated that Schlissel was an Ivy League pinhead, or perhaps simply barking mad. The president soon backpedaled, proclaiming his allegiance to the athletic department, which — like those at Oregon and Ohio State — has budgets and revenues in the many tens of millions of dollars.

Michigan legislators took the role of blocking backs in protecting university gilt. In December, Al Pscholka, a Republican state representative in Michigan, pushed through a bill that forbids state college athletes to organize unions. Gov. Rick Snyder, a Republican, signed it into law about the time that Harbaugh signed his $5-million-a-year deal.

Michigan was once a proud union state, and labor leaders could have put up a fight. Nick Ciaramitaro, legislative director of the American Federation of State, County and Municipal Employees Council 25, which represents state workers, shrugged.

We didn't, he said, have plans to organize athletes anyway. He thus offered a study guide in the toothlessness of American labor.

Colter and his fellow players were tougher. A regional director of the National Labor Relations Board has ruled that players are, in fact, employees. And suddenly universities have begun making changes.

The Big Ten offered guaranteed four-year scholarships, and the Pacific-12 took it one step further, guaranteeing scholarships and postgraduate health care. There is more talk of health insurance for players after college, and bigger scholarship stipends.

Colter smiled. "They are taking steps to try to insulate themselves," he said. "That's good; that's what the threat of a union does."

New challenges loom. There is chatter about expanding the College Football Playoff to eight teams.

That would mean more hard games and hard practices, more time away from class and more opportunities to sustain season- and career-ending injuries. Ohio State won the national title with its third quarterback of the season.

Ohio State Coach Urban Meyer had pushed the N.C.A.A. to find a way to pay for players' families to travel to the championship game (an initiative that was approved last week). That's sweet. I'm guessing a few more dollars in players' pockets and the guarantee of degrees paid for by universities grown fat on football might have more meaning.

Meyer, another of the millionaire coaches, has stated that he is not a fan of unionization. Colter doesn't worry about that.

"If they can pay Harbaugh close to $8 million with incentives, they can put in place support programs for athletes," he said. "It's not really that complicated, is it?"

"Sports of the Times" is a collection of columns offering opinion and analysis from the world of sports.

College Athletes' Potential Realized in Missouri Resignations

COLUMN | BY JOE NOCERA | NOV. 9, 2015

WELL, *that* was fast.

When was it, exactly, that the African-American football players at the University of Missouri tweeted that they were going on strike until "President Tim Wolfe resigns or is removed" from office? It was Saturday night, around 9 p.m. Eastern time.

Now consider the following timeline, which The Columbia Missourian recently published.

On Sept. 12, Payton Head, the president of the Missouri Student Association, takes to Facebook to describe a campus incident during which the most vile of anti-black slurs was hurled at him. A second racial incident occurs on Oct. 5. By Oct. 10, dissatisfied by the administration's tepid response, a group called Concerned Student 1950 stages a protest during the homecoming parade. Ten days later, the group issues eight demands, including "an increase in the percentage of black faculty and staff," as well as Wolfe's removal from office.

A swastika drawn with feces is discovered in a bathroom on Oct. 24. Concerned Student 1950 has an inconclusive meeting with Wolfe three days later. Jonathan Butler, a protest leader, announces a hunger strike on Nov. 2. Another meeting with Wolfe takes place the next day, during which he promises, essentially, to do better.

In other words, nearly two months had gone by before the football players decided to get involved. Once they did, Wolfe lasted all of 36 hours. Later in the day, Chancellor R. Bowen Loftin said he would resign as well, effective at the end of the year.

In announcing his resignation Monday morning, Wolfe said he was motivated by his "love" for his alma mater. No doubt he was sincere. But it is hard to believe that his calculations didn't include money as

From left, the University of Missouri football players J'Mon Moore, Ian Simon and Charles Harris on Monday with members of Concerned Student 1950.

well: the $1 million that Missouri would be contractually obliged to pay Brigham Young University if the Tigers failed to play Saturday's game; and the mess it would create for itself — and the Southeastern Conference, which it joined only four years ago — if a players' strike lasted to the end of the season. Missouri's final SEC game in late November, against Arkansas, is scheduled to be televised by CBS, which pays the conference $55 million a year for television rights.

As Andy Schwarz, an economist who has been deeply involved in a series of antitrust lawsuits against the N.C.A.A., put it, "the issues at Missouri are far more important than college football, but the Missouri athletes showed that the color that matters most is green."

Will racism be eliminated from the Missouri campus now that the football players have succeeded in ousting Wolfe? Of course not. On a campus of about 35,000 students, only 7.2 percent are black. The school has worked to attract more students from urban centers, including outside of Missouri, which can create a cultural conflict with some in-state rural white students.

In addition to the incidents in which black students were called that repugnant name on a public street, there have also been several times recently when two trucks drove down a campus street with the occupants waving a Confederate flag.

"It's a very tense place, very racially tense," Stephanie Hernandez Rivera, the coordinator of the university's Multicultural Center, said in a video released by the Faculty Council Committee on Race Relations. Earnest L. Perry, an African-American journalism professor, told me that teaching a required journalism diversity course throughout the years opened him to "criticism and racism, both written and verbal; I am not immune."

No, it's going to take more than the resignation of its president to fix the racial problems affecting Mizzou.

On the other hand, Wolfe didn't do himself any favors. A former corporate executive, Wolfe possessed a command-and-control style that didn't jibe well with campus life. And he clearly didn't know how to respond to the protests.

Qiana Jade, a Missouri student, posted a video on Twitter showing an exchange between Wolfe and some protesters. It shows him clearly out of his element — and on his heels. Asked by the students to define "systematic oppression," he said, "I'll give you an answer, and I'm sure it will be a wrong answer." Pressed further, he said, "Systematic oppression is because you don't believe that you have the equal opportunity for success."

The students erupted in anger. As Wolfe walked away, a student yelled: "Did you just blame us for systematic oppression, Tim Wolfe? Did you just blame black students?"

Jade posted that video on Friday night. By Saturday night, most of her Twitter energy was devoted to spreading the word that black members of the football team had joined the protest.

"So proud of our young black men!!" she tweeted. "They are really stepping up."

And indeed they were. Which brings me to my second point. It turns out that the football players had something the other protesters didn't: power. There wasn't the slightest hint that Wolfe was considering resigning — until the football players got involved. Schwarz, the economist, told me that it was easy for the university administration to ignore the protesters because they were members of minorities and because they were young. But, he added, "The one place where young minority voices have economic power is sports."

As readers of my old Op-Ed column well know, I have long contended that the players in the revenue-producing sports — college football and men's basketball — are being terribly exploited by College Sports Inc. There are many players who feel that way, too, and who believe they deserve payment for the work they do beyond the cost of attending college. But they've always felt powerless to bring that about. After all, they are young and full of dreams of playing professionally — dreams that they fear might be dashed if they were to become involved in a strike or a protest.

And they are susceptible to pressure. In January 2014, when Kain Colter, the former Northwestern University quarterback, first informed the Wildcats' coach, Pat Fitzgerald, that the football team was trying to unionize, Fitzgerald said, "I'm proud of you guys for doing this." But Fitzgerald soon changed his tune and made it clear to the players that he viewed a vote for the union as a personal betrayal. At Missouri, Gary Pinkel, the football coach (he makes more than $4 million a year, by the way) openly supported his striking athletes. That was easy to do with the next game a week away and the team, at 4-5, unlikely to make a major bowl. How supportive would he have remained as we got toward Saturday?

That's why I have never considered it realistic that, for instance, college basketball players might one day boycott the Final Four to force the system to change. Or at least that's what I thought until this weekend. One wonders what athletes at other universities are thinking, now that they've seen a football team take down a university president in 36 hours.

"It is a monumental step," said Sonny Vaccaro, the former Nike marketing executive who now devotes his life to fighting the N.C.A.A. Vaccaro noted that the players took their stand not on their own behalf but for a larger cause, something, as he put it, "that affects their humanity."

Schwarz had a similar thought.

"Civil rights matter most," he said. "The next step is for athletes to realize that their economic lives matter, too, and that this power that they possess can also be used to push for justice on that front as well."

JOE NOCERA is writing a new "Sports Business" column that will appear in the print edition on Saturdays and at other times throughout the week. He previously wrote a column for the Op-Ed page.

Players Hold Power Over the N.C.A.A., if They Feel the Hunger

COLUMN | BY MARC TRACY | APRIL 8, 2019

MINNEAPOLIS — This Final Four is the fifth anniversary of one of the most effective, if inadvertent, instances of athlete activism in college sports.

This was when the Connecticut star Shabazz Napier, speaking to the news media shortly before the 2014 national championship game, said that he sometimes did not have enough to eat.

"There are hungry nights that I go to bed and I'm starving," he said.

Within weeks, the N.C.A.A.'s board of directors for Division I voted to lift restrictions on how much teams could feed their players. No longer would there be bizarre hairsplitting over what was and was not a meal (notoriously, serving peanuts did not count, while serving peanut butter did). Now teams can and do routinely give athletes feasts.

This common-sense reform had been in the works and probably would have occurred eventually. But the stark comments by a high-profile player at the N.C.A.A.'s signature event ensured the nearly immediate change and boatloads of attention on the N.C.A.A.'s power over college athletes.

It is fruitful to remember the efficacy of Napier's comments, because we are at a moment when it appears that further reform to college sports' much-maligned policy of amateurism will come only from within. The players will have the foremost and maybe even exclusive power to agitate for change.

What would have happened if Zion Williamson had said, after his Nike shoe exploded, jeopardizing his career, that enough was enough, that he no longer would wear a shoe for nothing while his coach was at least indirectly paid millions by Nike? And that no other player should put up with this hypocrisy, either?

"The power is with labor and the players," said Kain Colter, the former Northwestern quarterback who led a unionization drive among his teammates several years ago.

This was most obviously displayed in 2015, when Missouri football players threatened to sit out a game unless the university president stepped down or was fired. He stepped down. That the boycott concerned the campus's racial climate rather than the players' compensation ought not conceal the reality of what happened: The players — unpaid, un-unionized — flexed their muscles, and the system gave in.

Vesting power in athletes to reform sports is not historically aberrant. From Jackie Robinson withstanding taunts, threats and worse to break Major League Baseball's color line; to baseball players striking in the 1970s and '80s to gain and keep full-fledged free agency; to the track standout Edwin Moses devising benefits for Olympic athletes, athletes have often been the ones bringing about change. Their leverage is unmatched: They are the ones the fans pay to see, and therefore the ones who ultimately have the power over profit.

And they are the only ones with a steady interest in, well, their own interest.

Consider what else has happened since Napier's comments.

Colter's unionization effort, which a National Labor Relations Board regional director endorsed weeks before Napier's Final Four, was squashed by the overall board.

The antitrust lawsuit that might have allowed players to profit off the use of their likenesses in video games and other media ended in an extremely limited victory for players.

Last month, a second antitrust suit, which sought to explode the N.C.A.A.'s ban on compensation, concluded at the district-court level with a technical victory for players that looked as much like a victory for the establishment. A federal judge ruled that the N.C.A.A. could continue to limit payments to players that were not directly related to education.

"The courts are not a forum where you're going to get relief," said Don Yee, a sports lawyer and players-rights advocate.

For Yee, who also happens to be Tom Brady's agent, the solution is "private entrepreneurialism." He is planning a small professional football league that would field players not yet eligible for the N.F.L. (which generally requires players to be three years removed from high school). It would be developmental, like college football, but unlike college football, average pay would be $50,000.

A planned summer basketball league, the Historical Basketball League, would pay scholarships for its college-level players while enabling them to sell their names, images and likenesses to sponsors. The N.B.A.'s development league plans to offer higher salaries. The probable dissolution of the one-and-done rule in the next few years will again permit the most talented high school graduates to jump straight to the N.B.A. instead of having to spend at least a year in college.

A few states, notably North Carolina and California, have bills floating around that would allow athletes to be paid if, say, a video game uses their names and likenesses.

All these efforts are well intentioned. But if past is prologue, the system will not be successfully reformed in such patchwork fashion.

Nor is the college sports establishment likely to change its mind of its own volition.

At a news conference in Minneapolis last week, the N.C.A.A. president, Mark Emmert, said that he had sought to increase athlete participation in college sports' governance.

"I'm a lifelong academic," he said. "I grew up with that tradition, and I never worked at a school that didn't have students on their board, and they were full voting board members. They voted on my contract, and I think that's just perfectly appropriate."

There are athletes serving on several important councils, but there is not one on the N.C.A.A. Board of Governors. No athletes vote on Emmert's contract, which was extended late last year through 2023.

Tim Nevius, a onetime N.C.A.A. investigator whose experiences led him to turn on the system, believes the answer lies with player activism. Last month, he announced a new organization, the College

Athlete Advocacy Initiative, that plans to pair his business representing athletes before the N.C.A.A. with trying to advocate for broader reform in coordination with players.

He acknowledged in an interview the challenges, including the relatively short time spans that college athletes actually are college athletes, as well as their current lack of formal bargaining power. But he insisted that player action was the surest avenue to change.

"There are powers here that the athletes have," he said, "and we have to simply have them realize it and help them take the power into their own hands."

Ros Gold-Unwude, a Turner Sports analyst and former Stanford basketball player, said last month that she expected to hear more from college athletes about how they felt about their position in the pecking order.

"That's the way our culture is, where we all are telling our stories on social media platforms," she said.

"If you're really struggling or hungry," she added, "that experience will come out."

Apathy will come out as well, though. Beyond the structural obstacles to athletes deciding the system is unfair and determining to act to change it, a player could validly decide that he is happy receiving what he currently gets.

Napier, who is now a reserve on the Nets and who through a spokesman declined to comment for this article, said more during his "hungry nights" speech heard 'round the world, even though it received less publicity.

He noted that there were other wrongs. Players' jerseys were sold to fans, and the players did not receive a cut. More basically, he said, the players were not paid.

It was, he suggested, wrong. Probably.

"Something can change, something should change," Napier said five years ago. "But if it doesn't, at the end of the day, we've been doing this for so long."

CHAPTER 2

Taking a Knee: Athletes Fight Racial Injustice

Colin Kaepernick's refusal to stand for the national anthem is among the best known and most controversial examples of sports activism. However, Kaepernick is just one of many players to comment on contemporary racism. Many athletes who "took a knee," attended a protest or spoke out in some other form point out that while their careers may last a few years, their minority status will always be a part of their lives. The articles in this chapter highlight the motives behind the protests, as well as detail the criticism and professional fallout these athletes faced.

Inside College Basketball's Most Political Locker Room

BY MARC TRACY | NOV. 16, 2016

THE WISCONSIN BASKETBALL PLAYERS Nigel Hayes and Jordan Hill took a step behind their teammates during the national anthem before the ninth-ranked Badgers' season opener on Friday. It was another in a long series of visible protests from one of college basketball's most socially aware locker rooms.

Hayes, a senior who was named the preseason Big Ten player of the year, has lobbied for players to be paid, serving as a plaintiff in a lawsuit seeking a freer market for top athletes and once showing up to an ESPN "College GameDay" set sardonically identifying himself as a "broke athlete." Hayes has also posted about the Black Lives Matter movement to his more than 80,000 Twitter followers and recently joined other Wisconsin athletes in demanding university action after a fan appeared in a mask of President Obama and a noose at a Badgers home football game.

Hill, a redshirt junior, also writes provocatively on Twitter. And in September, Wisconsin's starting point guard, the senior Bronson Koenig, traveled to support protesters of the Dakota Access pipeline, many of whom are, like him, Native American.

On the eve of the presidential election, the three teammates sat in the locker room at Kohl Center in Madison, Wis., after practice and discussed the challenges and opportunities of being athletes — particularly college athletes — who want their voices heard. The interview has been edited for length and clarity.

LAUREN JUSTICE FOR THE NEW YORK TIMES

From left, Nigel Hayes, Jordan Hill and Bronson Koenig of the University of Wisconsin basketball team spoke about being athletes who want their voices heard on political and social issues.

Are you ever afraid to speak out knowing that you are not yet paid and could hurt your prospects?

HAYES I've had people tell me: "Hey, Nige, you need to stop. Be quiet. Stop voicing your opinion. It may hurt your draft stock next year. Teams may not want you." But at the end of the day, the quote I hang my hat on is, I was black before I picked up a basketball, and when I retire, I'll still be black.

I'll be black more of my life than I'll be a professional basketball player. It does not make sense for me not to say something at the point of my life when I can have the most impact. I'm playing basketball, and more of you are listening, which is why more of you are pissed and telling me to stop. So why would I not use this time to try to voice an opinion and bring about the most change?

HILL It's definitely a struggle. It would be stupid for me to say that I don't want to buy my mom a house, a car, want to make money doing what I love to do and travel and see the world. At the same time, I'm not going to feel good about myself with the knowledge that I've gained just holding my tongue.

KOENIG That's kind of selfish.

HILL Superselfish.

KOENIG I don't know why more people with the high profiles that they have don't speak up. I don't understand it. I get why they don't, but as he was saying, it's selfish.

You probably did not get into basketball to have more of a voice. What is it like discovering you have yours amplified?

KOENIG I think it's weird that in the United States, athletes have as big of a platform as they do. We don't really do anything that important. We're playing a sport.

It's odd to me that people want to hear what we have to say and care what we have to say, whether they agree with us or not. But I'm thankful for the platform that I have.

The position you're in as an athlete — you're kind of a role model whether you want to be or not. You have that voice. You have the right to choose whatever you want to do with it.

Colin Kaepernick really put himself out there.

HAYES What he's standing up for is obviously the right thing. His stance is that racial inequalities go on, particularly that occur with black people. You have a group of people that get upset about it, or a group of people that think he's stretching the truth or that racism isn't as prevalent as it is, and then you take a glance at Twitter, you see people calling him the N-word or saying, "Go back to Africa," or, "I hope you tear your A.C.L."

Do you think he has less credibility with the general public because he is an athlete?

HILL That would be the first inclination of people. But at the same time, he got up there and said what he said and was very, very eloquent. And he knows stuff to back it up. I don't know if you know all the stuff he's still doing now; he's having camps to help kids understand their rights.

They want you to come talk to their kids and come do this and help here and all that — as long as you're doing exactly what they want you to do, which is tell them to work hard and tell them to stay in school and so on. Not that those are bad things. But for you just to be boxed in to, "All right, just say this, but don't say anything on the issues that are actually plaguing the nation."

And even more, at that level, I respect it so much because he's risking money. There are people who I'm sure disagree with him who may have sponsored him or planned on sponsoring him. That's serious. That's his livelihood.

Jordan Hill, left, who uses Twitter to comment provocatively on social and racial issues, and Bronson Koenig, a Native American who has supported protesters of the Dakota Access Pipeline in person, in the players' lounge at the University of Wisconsin.

KOENIG You never know what's going on in his life, behind the scenes. The people in his corner even might be like, "No, don't say that because you're going to lose money, sponsorships, whatever." It's unfortunate that we have a voice, that people want to hear what we have to say, but when it's something they don't agree with, we're just dumb athletes.

Madison has a reputation for being very liberal. It is also, I'd imagine, whiter than the average place.

HAYES *(laughing)* By far.

Do you feel it is easier to take politically active stands there than it would be elsewhere?

KOENIG Kind of irrelevant. I've only seen the negative feedback around the comments of the articles that people write about me. Other than that, no one actually says anything to my face or even tweets at me. It's all positive feedback.

HAYES That makes one of us.

After the Missouri football players concluded a strike last year, a team captain said the experience had really connected them with the rest of campus. Is it difficult, as big-time athletes, to feel you are students like any others?

HILL I think there's going to be a natural disconnection because we do something that they can't do. I don't think we owe you anything other than to do the best we can when it comes to the court. Anything else we do is just a bonus — but for y'all, not for us. And we're not doing this because we're getting paid.

When did activism start for you guys?

KOENIG We all matured through the years. We were saying that we wouldn't have done this our freshman year.

HAYES My awakening period was sophomore summer. I have my A.A.U. coach, he's one of my greatest mentors, in Ohio. He gave me some books and some things to read, and it opened my eyes to things I'd never thought of or seen before.

Bronson, tell us about your North Dakota trip.

KOENIG I wanted to go out there and do something rather than just post an Instagram about it. Within five minutes of getting there, somebody recognized me. Two minutes later, someone handed me a microphone and said, "Speak to the whole camp."

We rolled into the reservation. There were some kids playing on the concrete court outside. It was dark by that time. We got out of the car to go ask them if they were coming to the basketball camp at the high school, and they recognized me. That was cool — in the middle of North Dakota.

What is the conversation like in the locker room when a teammate takes a prominent political stand?

HILL I was really proud of him. I think it's really important when people make the decision to stand behind their people.

Is there a temptation to dial back on the activism during the season?

KOENIG If anything, it's a better time.

HILL Just because that's here doesn't mean black people stop getting killed by police.

HAYES If anything, we're doing more. Bronson goes out and has 30 points Friday, and then Bronson at the news conference maybe says something that hits home about his Native American culture and people: what's going on, the amount of military they're sending up there.

KOENIG A group of people from here just went there. I know a couple girls who did, and they said they got tear-gassed and stuff.

HILL It's amazing what a country will do to its own people because of a difference of opinion.

HAYES It happens all the time. It's happened for a while now. Hundreds of years, actually.

The Awakening of Colin Kaepernick

BY JOHN BRANCH | SEPT. 7, 2017

In college, Kaepernick began a journey that led him to his position as one of the most prominent, if divisive, social activists in sports.

THE STANDOUT COLLEGE QUARTERBACK went to the meeting alone that winter night, looking to join. The fraternity brothers at Kappa Alpha Psi, a predominantly black fraternity with a small chapter at the University of Nevada, knew who he was. He was a tall, lean, biracial junior, less than a year from graduating with a business degree.

"When he came and said he had interest in joining the fraternity, I kind of looked at him like, 'Yeah, O.K.,' " said Olumide Ogundimu, one of the members. "I didn't take it seriously. I thought: 'You're the star quarterback. What are you still missing that you're looking for membership into our fraternity?' "

His name was Colin Kaepernick, and what he was looking for, Ogundimu and others discovered, was a deeper connection to his own roots and a broader understanding of the lives of others.

Seven years later, now 29, Kaepernick is the most polarizing figure in American sports. Outside of politics, there may be nobody in popular culture at this complex moment so divisive and so galvanizing, so scorned and so appreciated.

Attempts to explain who Kaepernick is — and how and why he became either a traitor ("Maybe he should find a country that works better for him," Donald J. Trump said as a presidential candidate last year) or a hero ("He is the Muhammad Ali of this generation," the longtime civil rights activist Harry Edwards said in an interview last week) — tend to devolve into partisan politics and emotional debates ranging from patriotic rituals to racial inequities.

Kaepernick is now (and may forever be) known for a simple, silent gesture. He is the quarterback who knelt for the national anthem before National Football League games last year as a protest against social injustice, especially the deaths of African-Americans at the hands of police.

Almost immediately, many of the complex real-world issues of the times — police violence, presidential politics and the foment of racial clashes that continue to boil over in places like Charlottesville, Va. — all flushed through the filter of Kaepernick's gesture. Time magazine put him on the cover, kneeling next to the words "The Perilous Fight."

With the N.F.L. season beginning in earnest this weekend, Kaepernick finds himself out of the league, either exiled or washed up, depending on the perspective.

The N.F.L. and its 32 franchise owners, none of them African-American, may be the most conservative fraternity of leaders in major American sports. They bathe their games in overtly patriotic ceremonies and discourage players, mostly hidden behind masks and uniforms of armor, from individual acts of showmanship. At least seven donated $1 million or more to Trump's inaugural committee, far more than any other sport's owners.

In Kaepernick's absence, other players will kneel. Demonstrators will protest. Some will boycott. His jersey will be seen, more as a political statement than a sporting allegiance, as the game goes on without him.

Living mostly in New York, Kaepernick has stayed out of the spotlight, friends said, because he wants the conversation to be not about him, but about the issues he has raised. (He declined several requests to speak to The New York Times for this article.) That is why he will, reportedly, stand for the anthem this season, if he joins a team.

Among those who will play this weekend is Brandon Marshall, a linebacker for the Denver Broncos. He was a teammate of Kaepernick's at Nevada, and it was his idea to join the fraternity. He was not sure Kaepernick would do it with him.

"He actually showed up to the meeting before me," Marshall said in an interview this week. "He's like: 'Where you at? I'm here.' He was real prompt. I was like, O.K., Colin's serious about it."

Kaepernick during media day ahead of his Super Bowl appearance. He eventually became very reluctant to say much in interviews.

Kaepernick's curiosity and worldview were expanding, growing inside him rather quietly. No one knew then that he would become one of the league's most thrilling players or that he would lead a team to the Super Bowl just a couple of years later. And they certainly did not expect that he would make even more noise with a now-famous silent gesture.

"Being part of that fraternity opens you to a new world," Ogun-dimu said. "I would not doubt that it is where he started becoming either more curious about his own background, or where he just started seeing more things — just realized that things weren't always so easy for the rest of us."

'HOW DARE YOU?'

Turlock is a pleasant and unremarkable place in California's flat, interior heartland. It is stifling hot in the summer and can be cool and rainy in the winter. Like many sprawling cities of central California, it features suburban-style neighborhoods and strip malls slowly eating the huge expanses of agriculture that surround it. And, like neighboring cities, the population of about 73,000 is overwhelmingly white and increasingly Latino. In Turlock, fewer than 2 percent of residents identify as African-American, according to the census.

Kaepernick moved there when he was 4. He was born in Milwaukee to a single white mother and a black father and quickly placed for adoption. He was soon adopted by Rick and Teresa Kaepernick of Fond du Lac, Wis., who were raising two biological children, Kyle and Devon. They had also lost two infant sons to congenital heart defects.

The family moved to California because Rick Kaepernick took a job as operations manager at the Hilmar Cheese Company, where he later became a vice president.

The boy became used to strangers assuming he was not with the other Kaepernicks. When anyone asked if he was adopted, he would scrunch up his face in mock sadness. "How dare you ask me something like that?" he would reply, and then laugh.

"We used to go on these summer driving vacations and stay at motels," Kaepernick told US magazine in 2015. "And every year, in the lobby of every motel, the same thing always happened, and it only got worse as I got older and taller. It didn't matter how close I stood to my family, somebody would walk up to me, a real nervous manager, and say: 'Excuse me. Is there something I can help you with?' "

Kyle nicknamed his younger brother Bo, after Bo Jackson, because Colin was good at football and baseball. Colleges were interested in him as a baseball pitcher and a football quarterback, but he made it clear that football was his priority. Kyle burned DVDs of Colin's high school highlights and sent them to college teams across the country. Only Nevada offered a scholarship.

It was in Reno that Kaepernick's potential as a quarterback was realized, and where his curiosity in African-American history and culture began to foment, mostly as he met teammates with vastly different experiences from his growing up.

"I saw him transform, develop, whatever you want to call it," said John Bender, an offensive lineman during Kaepernick's tenure and a frequent classmate. "Finding an identity was big for him, because in some aspects in life, he would get the racist treatment from white people because he was a black quarterback. And some people gave him the racist treatment because he was raised by a white family. So where does he fit in in all this?"

Kaepernick was a starter for most of four seasons. He became the first N.C.A.A. player to throw for more than 10,000 yards and rush for more than 4,000 yards. He scored 60 touchdowns and threw 82 more. In 2010, Kaepernick's final collegiate season, Nevada went 13-1, beat No. 3 Boise State in overtime and finished No. 11 in The Associated Press poll at season's end.

He never loved the attention that came with the success, but he was deft and polished with the news media, willing to do interviews and quick to share credit for successes. He was the rare player who never needed training in dealing with the media. Kaepernick said his father instilled in him the importance of manners and the proper way to conduct himself in front of others.

He once joined other players in calling season-ticket holders who were yet to renew for the upcoming seasons. An older woman told him that she enjoyed going to the games with her husband, but he had recently died. She said she couldn't afford the tickets and she couldn't imagine going alone.

Kaepernick's family already had 24 season tickets, and the four-hour drive from Turlock did not prevent a small army of supporters at every game. What's one more? Kaepernick thought. He bought the woman a season ticket.

"We're probably the only N.C.A.A. compliance office in the country that had to check to see if it was O.K. for a player to give a fan something," said Chad Hartley, an associate athletic director for Nevada.

Kaepernick excelled as a student. He graduated with a degree in business management. Some wondered when he slept.

When he showed up at Kappa Alpha Psi, members figured that Kaepernick would quit once he saw the commitment required: the time, the rituals, the community service, the all-night study sessions of the fraternity's history and liturgy. Marshall said that his own schoolwork suffered during the semester, but Kaepernick maintained perfect grades.

"The process is not easy," said Ogundimu, now a case manager for a rehabilitation hospital in Las Vegas. "It's definitely something that will shine a light on your weaknesses and shine a light on your strengths. He was all strength."

Kappa Alpha Psi, which says it has 120,000 members, has thrown its support behind Kaepernick, writing a letter to N.F.L. Commissioner Roger Goodell and joining a pro-Kaepernick demonstration at league headquarters recently.

THE 'ANTI-MANNING' PERSONA

Just four years ago, Kaepernick was a different type of sports phenomenon, "the anti-Manning," as the Sports Illustrated writer Peter King called him. He kissed his tattooed biceps when he scored, which turned his name into a verb: Kaepernicking. His jersey was spotted across the Bay Area. All lean muscles and corrugated abs, he posed nude for ESPN Magazine's Body Issue. He discussed his growing assortment of tattoos, the first of which were Bible verses inked in college. Active on Twitter, he mostly thanked fans, promoted appearances and kept opinions to himself.

"I want to have a positive influence as much as I can," Kaepernick told King in 2013. "I've had people write me because of my tattoos. I've had people write me because of adoption. I've had people write me because they're biracial. I've had people write me because their kids have heart defects — my mom had two boys who died of heart defects, which ultimately brought about my adoption. So, to me, the more people you can touch, the more people you can influence in a positive way or inspire, the better."

He had led the 49ers to the Super Bowl after Coach Jim Harbaugh inserted him as the starter midway through the 2012 season. Kaepernick dueled with and beat Tom Brady and the Patriots at New England on a brutally cold night in December, 41-34. ("He may have played the best game at quarterback, certainly one of the best games, that I've ever seen," the NBC analyst Cris Collinsworth said during an interview last week.) In a playoff game against Green Bay, Kaepernick had better passing statistics than Aaron Rodgers, and added 181 rushing yards.

A loss to Baltimore in the Super Bowl, after Kaepernick and the 49ers could not score a touchdown after having first-and-goal at the 7-yard line in the final minutes, did little to suppress the excitement over the quarterback.

"I truly believe Colin Kaepernick could be one of the greatest quarterbacks ever," the ESPN analyst Ron Jaworski said the following preseason. "I love his skill set. I think the sky's the limit."

But Kaepernick felt the barbs of stardom, too, often dipped in racial undertones. He (and later his mother) had to defend his tattoos after a columnist said that a quarterback is, essentially, the team's chief executive, "and you don't want your C.E.O. to look like he just got paroled."

In the midst of Kaepernick's growing fame, his birth mother, Heidi Russo, emerged and said that she wanted a relationship with her birth son, sparking a flurry of articles, including during Super Bowl week. Kaepernick expressed no interest. Columnists criticized him.

Kaepernick's public persona shifted, whether because of his distrust in the media or because he was following the lead of Harbaugh, often disdainful of reporters, seeing little value in sharing information. More and more in front of cameras and reporters, he was all sulking expressions and terse answers. In a running half-joke, reporters began to count the words in his responses. They were often comically short.

People who knew Kaepernick in Reno were surprised, and veterans of the N.F.L. were confused. But as long as the team was winning, few fans cared about his off-field demeanor.

But then the 49ers went 8-8 in 2014, and simmering disputes with the front office led to Harbaugh's departure at season's end. Kaepernick's playing career faded, here and gone like the trace of a comet. The 49ers were 2-6 under Jim Tomsula in 2015 when Kaepernick lost his starting job, then was placed on the season-ending injury list.

In 2016, Tomsula was replaced by Chip Kelly, who named Blaine Gabbert the starting quarterback for the first three preseason games. It was safe to wonder if most people had heard the last of Colin Kaepernick.

A QUEST FOR AN EDUCATION

Kaepernick's Twitter and Instagram feeds reveal his trajectory. There were a few football-related messages early in 2016, including a congratulatory note to Harbaugh, coaching collegiately at Michigan, for a bowl victory. Kaepernick posted a photo and quote of Malcolm X on the February anniversary of his murder. In June, he posted a video of Tupac Shakur, the rapper killed in 1996.

"I'm not saying I'm going to rule the world, or I'm going the change the world," Shakur said in the clip. "But I guarantee that I will spark the brain that will change the world. That's our job, is to spark somebody else watching us."

Kaepernick's next message was a thank you for supporting Camp Taylor, a charity for children with heart disease. Rick Kaepernick is on the board of directors.

By then, Colin Kaepernick was auditing a summer course on black representation in popular culture taught by Ameer Hasan Loggins at the University of California, Berkeley. He drove an hour each way to each class, took notes, did the readings and engaged in class discussions, Loggins wrote in a recent essay.

Kaepernick had been introduced to Loggins by Kaepernick's girlfriend, Nessa Diab, a syndicated radio host and MTV personality whom Kaepernick has dated since late 2015. (Diab previously dated Aldon Smith, another 49ers player, leading to a reported scrap between the two during training camp in 2015.)

Diab, known professionally as Nessa, has had a measure of influence on Kaepernick's views over the past two years.

Aside from her work on MTV, she is the host of a nationally syndicated show on Hot 97, an influential hip-hop station in New York, and supported the Black Lives Matter movement from that platform. She has been more active and overtly opinionated than Kaepernick on social media.

Loggins and Diab were classmates in Berkeley years ago, and she asked Loggins to recommend books for Kaepernick. It was not the first time Kaepernick sought reading material. As a rookie with the 49ers, he asked Edwards, the sociologist and civil rights activist who served as a consultant for the 49ers, for a reading list, Edwards said.

He recommended "The Autobiography of Malcolm X," James Baldwin's "The Fire Next Time," Ralph Ellison's "Invisible Man," and Maya Angelou's "I Know Why the Caged Bird Sings," Edwards said.

"He was willing to work and study to kind of understand what was happening with his teammates, with other people, and how this whole thing rolled out over 400 years," Edwards said.

The list from Loggins included "The Wretched of the Earth," by Frantz Fanon; "Black Feminist Thought: Knowledge, Consciousness, and the Politics of Empowerment," by Patricia Hill Collins; "Black Looks: Race and Representation," by bell hooks; and "The Mis-Education of the Negro," by Carter G. Woodson.

Before long, Kaepernick and Loggins were engaged in lengthy conversations, until the quarterback asked if he could sit in on the professor's upcoming summer class.

"People that trace our connection to U.C. Berkeley assume he became politicized in my class," Loggins wrote. "But Colin came in aware, focused, well-read and eager to learn. His decision was made on his own — from the heart. He came to me intellectually curious. The questions he asked me regarding my research, the lectures he attended, he was a sponge."

Kaepernick's social media posts flared with urgent intensity, though, when black men were killed by the police on back-to-back days in early July 2016.

Demonstrators confronted police officers as they protested the fatal police shooting of Philando Castile in July 2016 in St. Paul. On social media, Kaepernick reposted video of Castile dying in the passenger seat of the car he was riding in.

"This is what lynchings look like in 2016!" Kaepernick wrote on Instagram and Twitter when video of Alton Sterling's death became public. "Another murder in the streets because the color of a man's skin, at the hands of the people who they say will protect us. When will they be held accountable? Or did he fear for his life as he executed this man?"

A day later, Kaepernick posted video of Philando Castile dying in the driver's seat of his car after being shot by an officer, taken by a woman recording the aftermath from the passenger seat.

"We are under attack!" Kaepernick wrote. "It's clear as day! Less than 24 hrs later another body in the street!"

Kaepernick's rising anger online created little reaction, at least in football circles. He went to training camp to compete with Gabbert for the starting job. A sore throwing shoulder prevented him from playing in the first two preseason games. He was out of uniform, which is probably why no one in the media noticed that he sat on the bench during the national anthem.

It was not until the third game, at home on Aug. 26, that Kaepernick's gesture got attention. A reporter took a photograph of the San Francisco bench, unrelated to Kaepernick, and later spotted him sitting alone near the coolers.

Word of the protest did not spread. Steve Wyche of nfl.com was the only reporter to speak to Kaepernick about it after the game.

"I am not going to stand up to show pride in a flag for a country that oppresses black people and people of color," Kaepernick said. "To me, this is bigger than football, and it would be selfish on my part to look the other way. There are bodies in the street and people getting paid leave and getting away with murder."

He added that he had not sought permission from the team or sponsors.

"This is not something that I am going to run by anybody," he said. "I am not looking for approval. I have to stand up for people that are oppressed. If they take football away, my endorsements from me, I know that I stood up for what is right."

Many didn't like Kaepernick doing it during an anthem. Some said it was anti-military, a slap to those who served and died. (Kaepernick said on the first day that he had "great respect for the men and women that have fought for this country," including friends and family, but even veterans were not being treated right by this country.) Some thought it was disingenuous for a millionaire, especially one raised comfortably by a white family, to take a stance on black oppression. Some football fans saw Kaepernick as a second-string has-been looking for attention.

"The actual point of protest is to disrupt how we move about our daily lives," Wade Davis, a former professional football player and a black activist who often works with athletes, said in an interview last week. "What Kaepernick did was disrupt one of our most treasured sports. Whether you agree with his tactics or not is one type of conversation. The larger conversation is what he is protesting about. The fact that so many don't want to have that specific conversation speaks to the fact that they know what is happening in America is beyond tragic."

For the fourth preseason game, which Kaepernick started, he changed from sitting on the bench to taking a knee on the sideline. Safety Eric Reid joined him. The same night, Jeremy Lane of the Seattle Seahawks sat for the anthem, too. Then soccer player Megan Rapinoe did it before a professional game days later. On Sept. 9, Marshall, Kaepernick's teammate and fraternity brother from Nevada, was the first to do it in an N.F.L. regular-season game, with the Broncos.

The controversy slowly lowered to an uneasy simmer through the fall. Presidential politics took control of the national debate. Kaepernick kept kneeling before games but said little. The 49ers were awful, and Kaepernick retook the starting job. He went 1-10 as the starter for a team that finished 2-14. He threw 16 touchdowns and 4 interceptions, completed 59.2 percent of his passes and rushed for 468 yards. His passer rating of 90.7 was 17th in the N.F.L.

Kaepernick's teammates voted him the winner of the Len Eshmont award, the team's highest honor, "for inspirational and courageous play."

The coach and general manager were fired and replaced.

Kaepernick's contract with the 49ers was due to pay him $16.5 million for this season, according to ESPN, but was not guaranteed unless he made the team. Knowing that was unlikely, he opted out as a free agent on March 1, and he has been out of a job since.

His unemployment is a fuse on another debate, this one over whether Kaepernick is being willfully kept out of the league because of his politics, or if he is no longer good enough to play in it. The N.F.L's 32 teams each carry at least two quarterbacks, some three.

"It's really tough to make an argument that he's not one of the best 64," said Collinsworth, the NBC analyst. "Everybody has some reason that they haven't signed Colin Kaepernick. Maybe they have two or three quarterbacks they think are better. Maybe they don't want the distraction. Maybe they don't want to pay the money. But it's hard to say 'they,' like all 32 owners think exactly the same. That's ridiculous. That's what has made this really complex."

ACTIVISM OUTSIDE THE SPOTLIGHT

While Kaepernick waits to play, he has hardly been idle. Fulfilling a "million-dollar" pledge he made during the heat of the anthem flap last September, he has donated $100,000 every month since October to up to four charities, with little notice beyond Kaepernick's website.

The beneficiaries are usually small, relatively unknown and surprised.

"We had no idea how Colin Kaepernick heard about our organization," said Carolyn A. Watson, founder and executive director of Helping Oppressed Mothers Endure, or H.O.M.E., a foundation supporting single mothers in Georgia. Someone representing Kaepernick contacted the group, Watson said, "and before we knew it, we were giving them the appropriate information and received a $25,000 check in the mail."

Muhibb Dyer, a co-founder of the I Will Not Die Young Campaign in Milwaukee, thought the $25,000 donation was a prank.

"What is unique is that he identified grass-roots organizations like my own that are hanging on by a thread trying to do the work," Dyer said. "But a lot of the time we are face-to-face, in the trenches, with some of the most at-risk youth in this country. Having him reach out to us is like a lifeline to continue the work that we do that is oftentimes not highlighted, but very much essential to the life and death of youth every day."

The range of charities Kaepernick supports is broad. In January, for example, he gave $25,000 each to a Brooklyn group called Black Veterans for Social Justice, a clean-energy advocacy group called 350 .org, the Coalition for Humane Immigrant Rights of Los Angeles, and the Center for Reproductive Rights in New York.

Michelle Horovitz, a co-founder of Appetite for Change, which promotes healthy food through urban gardens and cooking seminars in Minneapolis, said the donation they received was "huge on an emotional level."

She added: "We are huge fans of him and I personally have decided to boycott the N.F.L."

Kaepernick has also held three "Know Your Rights" free camps for children. About 200 came to the one in Chicago in May, at the DuSable Museum of African American History, and others have been held in Oakland and New York. The goal, according to the website, is "to raise awareness on higher education, self empowerment, and instruction to properly interact with law enforcement in various scenarios."

Children received free breakfasts and T-shirts listing 10 rights: The right to be free, healthy, brilliant, safe, loved, courageous, alive, trusted and educated, plus "the right to know your rights."

There were seminars and sessions on black history, including segregation and Jim Crow laws. There were lessons on healthy eating and household finances. There was advice on speaking and dressing for respect, and for how to calmly handle interactions with the police.

Among the speakers were Eric Reid, Kaepernick's former teammate in San Francisco, and Common, the hip-hop star. Near the end, Kaepernick shared his personal story to campers in Chicago.

"I love my family to death," he said, according to Dave Zirin of The Nation. "They're the most amazing people I know. But when I looked in the mirror, I knew I was different. Learning what it meant to be an African man in America, not a black man but an African man, was critical for me. Through this knowledge, I was able to identify myself and my community differently."

He explained that he was giving the campers a kit to test their own DNA, to better understand their background, The Nation reported.

"I thought I was from Milwaukee," Kaepernick said. "I thought my ancestry started at slavery and I was taught in school that we were all supposed to be grateful just because we aren't slaves. But what I was able to do was trace my ancestry and DNA lineage back to Ghana, Nigeria, the Ivory Coast, and saw my existence was more than just being a slave. It was as an African man. We had our own civilizations, and I want you to know how high the ceiling is for our people. I want you to know that our existence now is not normal. It's oppressive. For me, identifying with Africa gave me a higher sense of who I was, knowing that we have a proud history and are all in this together."

Kaepernick traveled to Ghana this summer. On July 4 on Instagram, accompanying a video montage of the trip, he said that he made the pilgrimage to get in touch with his "African ancestral roots."

He sat in prison cells at "slave castles," the fortresses that detained people just before they were shipped across the ocean as slaves. He also visited the Kwame Nkrumah Memorial Park, schools and hospitals. Along with Nessa Diab, he also went to Egypt and Morocco.

"A part of the motivation was, if you have an awakening, then you start to want to have answers," Loggins, who was part of the travel group, said on a podcast with Zirin. "You start to become inquisitive at a level that can sometime be seen to others as obsessive."

On a day off last December, Kaepernick took the GRE, the standardized graduate-school entrance exam. "Just exploring all opportunities," he said.

It was about then that Kaepernick was introduced to Christopher Petrella, who teaches American Cultural Studies at Bates College in Maine. Petrella has since helped devise the curriculum and taught at the Know Your Rights camps and become part of Kaepernick's inner circle.

Their first conversation, Petrella said in an email interview, "unexpectedly morphed into a back-and-forth on Bacon's Rebellion, a late 17th-century political uprising in colonial Virginia that began to codify race and class hierarchies in the U.S. I was immediately struck by Colin's raw curiosity, historical fluency, and the sophistication with which he spoke of persistent forms of racial injustice and racialized forms of police brutality today."

He, too, has heard Kaepernick's name mentioned alongside other athletes who became civil rights icons. Petrella said the comparisons were apt, but Kaepernick's approach reminded him more of Ella Baker, a civil rights pioneer known for her work with the N.A.A.C.P., the Southern Christian Leadership Conference and the Student Nonviolent Coordinating Committee.

"Just as Colin tends to eschew the spotlight, Baker operated under the principle that 'Strong people don't need strong leaders,' " Petrella wrote. "Baker once said that 'People must fight for their own freedom and not rely on leaders to do it for them.' This approach seems consistent with Colin's principle of believing in the capacity of ordinary people to grow into leaders, to self-advocate and to lift as we climb."

What may be settled in the coming days and weeks is whether Kaepernick will once again experience the spotlight of the N.F.L. — whether a team will sign him, or whether it matters to the movement he has sparked.

"I'm so proud of him," said Marshall, his Nevada teammate and fraternity brother. "If people look at the real issue, and look at what he's doing in the community — the money he's donating, the time he's donating, the camps he's putting on — they'd be like: 'You know what? This dude's really a stand-up guy.' "

MALIKA ANDREWS contributed reporting.

High Schools Threaten to Punish Students Who Kneel During Anthem

BY CHRISTINE HAUSER | SEPT. 29, 2017

THE CONTROVERSY OVER kneeling in protest of racial injustice moved beyond the world of professional sports this week, when a number of schools told students they were expected to stand during the national anthem.

On Long Island, the Diocese of Rockville Centre, which runs a private Catholic school system, said students at its three high schools could face "serious disciplinary action" if they knelt during the anthem before sporting events.

Sean P. Dolan, a spokesman for the diocese, said on Friday that the letter, which was sent to principals, was intended to restate policy that the diocese already had in place.

But he added in an emailed statement: "Although the Diocese does not agree that demonstrations are appropriate in its schools during the playing of the National Anthem — which recognizes the tremendous sacrifices of Americans of all races, ethnicities and religions — it notes that students who seek to challenge racism and racial discrimination are firmly in accord with Catholic teaching."

In northwest Louisiana, Scott Smith, the superintendent of schools in Bossier Parish, said student athletes were expected to stand for the anthem. "It is a choice for students to participate in extracurricular activities, not a right, and we at Bossier Schools feel strongly that our teams and organizations should stand in unity to honor our nation's military and veterans," he said in a letter obtained by The New York Times.

Waylon Bates, the principal of Parkway High School in Bossier City, La., a municipality of more than 60,000 people near Shreveport, outlined the punishment students would face at his school. He sent a letter on Thursday to athletes and parents saying athletes were required to stand "in a respectful manner" during the anthem.

An image of the letter was posted online by Shaun King, a journalist at The Intercept.

"Failure to comply will result in loss of playing time and/or participation as directed by the head coach and principal," the letter said. "Continued failure to comply will result in removal from the team."

A call to Parkway High School on Friday was referred to the school board, which did not comment on Mr. Bates's letter.

In the past week, National Football League players have demonstrated during the national anthem in a show of solidarity against racial injustice and President Trump, who scolded the league and its players for protesting. Colin Kaepernick, the former quarterback for the San Francisco 49ers, spent much of last season either sitting or kneeling during the anthem, inspiring student athletes to recreate the gesture last year. But Mr. Trump's involvement has given the debate new momentum and helped push it beyond the sports world. This week, military veterans, actors and the singer Stevie Wonder took a knee.

When the issue is swept up into the public school system, as is happening in Louisiana, it runs up against students' First Amendment rights and a Supreme Court ruling in 1943, which said public school students could not be forced to salute the American flag or recite the Pledge of Allegiance if it conflicted with their religious beliefs. That ruling involved a case of Jehovah Witnesses who were expelled from school for not reciting the pledge.

"The law does not permit schools to forbid students from expressing their views, and all schools should be on notice that these policies are in fact unconstitutional," Marjorie Esman, the executive director of the American Civil Liberties Union of Louisiana, said in an interview on Friday.

The Supreme Court also touched on students' right to peaceful protest during public school hours in 1969, when it ruled in favor of students who wanted to wear black armbands to protest the Vietnam War.

The 1969 ruling essentially said that students do not lose their constitutional rights to free speech at the schoolhouse gate, said Francisco Negrón Jr., the chief legal officer of the National School Boards Association. If a protest is not disruptive, public schools have to allow it.

"That is the challenge for school districts in this scenario," he said in an interview. "They have got to balance that with the rights of students to protest in a way that is not disruptive." He said some school districts are "opting to use this as a teachable moment."

Private schools that do not rely on government funding have more flexibility in setting their own rules for student behavior. The Diocese of Camden in New Jersey said last year that any student who failed to stand for the anthem at a sporting event would be suspended for two games. Repeated offenses could get students dismissed from the team.

"The best approach is helping our young people understand that blood was sacrificed so that we all can enjoy the gifts of our faith and our country," the diocese said in a letter to its schools, NJ.com reported this week. "However, let me be clear. We are not public institutions and free speech in all of its demonstrations, including protests, is not a guaranteed right."

Ms. Esman said it was "troubling" that Louisiana school administrators "seem to not understand what they are supposed to be teaching their students — the right to protest peacefully."

The protests are "a statement about racial justice in this country," she added. "The fact that there are so many people who are publicly saying they are concerned about this means it is a problem that needs to be addressed."

From the N.B.A., a Cautionary Tale on National Anthem Protests

COLUMN | BY HARVEY ARATON | NOV. 6, 2017

IT HAS BEEN 21 YEARS since the N.B.A. punished a player for refusing to stand for the national anthem. And that player, Mahmoud Abdul-Rauf, paid a much greater price than the nearly $32,000 he lost for a one-game suspension.

A flashy 6-foot-1 guard and the Denver Nuggets' leading scorer for the 1995-96 season, Abdul-Rauf refused to stand because of personal and religious beliefs. He negotiated a fast truce with the league, acquiescing to its rule requiring players to stand for the anthem in an acceptable posture — while also cupping his hands and bowing his head in adherence to his Muslim faith.

He was also traded soon after to the Sacramento Kings, and by 1998, at 29, he was out of the league. He became, in essence, a cautionary tale as Colin Kaepernick pursues a case against the N.F.L. accusing it of colluding to deny him a job over his kneeling for the anthem last season.

Abdul-Rauf did not get much support from his peers.

"If you ask most players from that era, they'd say they regretted not supporting him more than they did," Buck Williams, who in 1996 was president of the National Basketball Players Association, said in a recent telephone interview. "He was kind of left out on an island."

That was then, a period largely defined by the soaring popularity of the famously apolitical Michael Jordan. This is now, an era of exploding social media leverage in which N.B.A. player and coaching personalities — more so than their N.F.L. counterparts — have established themselves as recognizable commentators.

So why haven't N.B.A. players — at least thus far in this young season — joined those among the N.F.L.'s rank and file who have lined up behind the now-unemployed Kaepernick in taking a knee as a means of protest?

It is not because they fear the wrath of President Trump, or even the punitive arm of the N.B.A.'s league office, according to Michele Roberts, the players union's executive director.

They haven't protested collectively, she said, because they can better do so individually.

"They don't need to take a knee when they can communicate their messages on their own," Roberts said in a telephone interview. "LeBron James, all he has to do is tweet and everybody knows exactly how he feels."

Or have "Equality" embroidered on the back of his sneakers, as James did before the Cleveland Cavaliers' season opener several weeks ago.

It is no secret that football, with its often anonymous foot soldiers in the trenches (many without fully guaranteed contracts), is a sport more designed for group expression. The N.B.A., said the former commissioner David Stern, has long been a laboratory focused on the behavior of individuals.

Asked why the league felt the need to impose a stand-for-the-anthem rule, in effect at least since the early 1980s, Stern said, "It was our minimal standard — when you come out on the court, please stand at attention — because the N.B.A. has always been something of a social cause, these great black athletes trying to work their way in what back in the day could be a hostile white environment."

He mentioned outsize players and personalities like Bill Russell, Wilt Chamberlain and Kareem Abdul-Jabbar, with far greater visibility and impact in their comparatively intimate workplace.

In the N.B.A., superficial issues like hairstyles and tattoos have for decades been part of the discussion, and judgment. Kaepernick basically hid his Afro under a helmet, but as far back as the 1970s, Julius Erving's could excite or aggravate.

By March 1996, when Abdul-Rauf was suspended, Jordan was arguably the world's most admired athlete and the N.B.A. was enjoying exponential domestic and global growth. Still, as Williams said,

"Race was the elephant in the room, and though I think David tried his best to deal with it, it was something that terrified the N.B.A."

Although Stern said he didn't believe Abdul-Rauf had been shunned by the league for his stance, and pointed out that he did return briefly with the Vancouver Grizzlies in 2000, Abdul-Rauf apparently believes otherwise.

Playing in the inaugural season of the Big3 league this year, his hair and beard speckled with gray, Abdul-Rauf, 48, continued to bow his head, close his eyes and pray during the playing of the anthem, which he maintains symbolizes oppression. In 2016, he told ESPN that he was at peace for keeping with his principles, despite career sacrifices.

It would be naïve to think that the elephant of race has left the room, but 21st-century N.B.A. players are riding and even steering it, Roberts said, and without much direction from her.

When James, Dwyane Wade, Carmelo Anthony and Chris Paul used measured tones at the 2016 ESPY Awards to decry violence against African-Americans as well as against the police, Roberts said she was among the last people to hear it was going to happen.

"I haven't had a single player ask me, 'What should we do?'" she said. "And I'm not intimidated or fearful of how they will be judged because I know whatever they do, they will do respectfully and with compassion."

Too sweeping a generalization, perhaps. In such a volatile or hostile environment, restraint or respect is not always possible. Stephen Curry of the Golden State Warriors tangled on Twitter with the president over the prospect of his team's visit to the White House, and James weighed in on the exchange rather inelegantly.

Tough rhetoric has been heard from coaches, too, such as Steve Kerr of the Warriors and especially Gregg Popovich of the San Antonio Spurs. But the residual effect, from the players' perspective, could be that they recognize they are no longer inhabiting the island that Williams said Abdul-Rauf was on 21 years ago.

Indeed, N.B.A. players share vivid memories of how swiftly and strongly Adam Silver, the current commissioner, dealt with the ramblings of Donald Sterling, the former Los Angeles Clippers' owner, in 2014. This September, Silver and Roberts signed a letter in support of the players' social activism.

"Adam was on the money with Sterling, and he's been on the money today," Roberts said. "But I don't think the players are behaving this way because the league supports them. They're acting based on how they feel, though they do appreciate the way the league supports them."

And if somebody kneels this season during the anthem? Silver has said he expects players to stand but declined to offer what he might do if they do not.

Roberts was also mum, though not completely.

"I'm not going to comment on what hasn't happened yet," she said. "Still, I can't imagine telling players that we support you but if you express yourself on an issue you feel strongly about, we're going to punish you."

That hypothetical, while not the elephant, is in the room.

"On Pro Basketball" is a regular analytical column focused on the National Basketball Association.

In a Busy Year, Malcolm Jenkins Raised a Fist and Checked All the Boxes

BY KEN BELSON | JAN. 25, 2018

He led protests, was called a traitor, persuaded the N.F.L. to spend nearly $100 million on social causes, made the Super Bowl and had another child.

PHILADELPHIA — Malcolm Jenkins, the Philadelphia Eagles' star safety, was dragging Monday afternoon, and for good reason.

The previous night, he helped the hometown team earn a trip to the Super Bowl with a 38-7 thumping of the Minnesota Vikings. He left the stadium at 11 p.m. After a brief appearance at a team party, he went home and played poker with some college fraternity brothers until 3 a.m. His alarm went off at 6 a.m., as it always does. He looked in on his 5-day-old baby and got ready to take his 4-year-old daughter to school. Then it was off to the Eagles' training facility for rehab, Super Bowl planning and to discuss his other full-time job — fighting for criminal justice reform and addressing racial inequality.

"There's a huge emphasis for me on time management," Jenkins said with a shrug. "Sometimes it requires burning the candle on both ends."

Jenkins, 30, has been burning that candle since the summer of 2016, when the killing of several African-Americans by the police became his call to action. Since then, he has used every waking hour he isn't spending on football or family to work with the Players Coalition, a group of N.F.L. players seeking solutions to seemingly intractable problems facing African-Americans.

His raised fist during the playing of the national anthem before games in October and November became one of the enduring images of this most political of N.F.L. seasons. Beyond that gesture, though, Jenkins and the Players Coalition have met with leaders of police departments, public defenders, bail officers and lawmakers. They have visited prisons and courts to learn about problems, and pushed for legislation to address them. They also met with top N.F.L. executives repeatedly throughout the season.

After some prodding, the N.F.L. announced in December that it would spend up to $89 million over seven years to help grass-roots groups fight inequality. On Tuesday, the league said that the owners of the Browns, the Cardinals, the Dolphins, the Falcons and the Jaguars, along with three current players and two retired players, would form a committee to choose programs and initiatives to support.

Jenkins is not on the committee, but he remains the public face of the Players Coalition. He says he is happy with the league's commitment, but he will not declare victory. The problems are unrelenting.

"When I look at our communities, our country, our justice system, those are things I want to change and I'm committed to changing, and that's going to take sacrifice," Jenkins said, a gold chain with a pendant in the shape of a fist around his neck. "Laying the foundation is the hardest part, and requires a lot of sacrifice and time."

TRAITORS OR HEROES?

The 2017 season will probably be remembered more for what happened off the field rather than on it. For large parts of the season, the coast-to-coast debate over whether players should all stand during the playing of the national anthem drowned out any discussion of X's and O's.

President Trump ignited a full-throated shouting match in September, when he urged owners to fire players who did not stand for the anthem. His fury turned the N.F.L. — traditionally a unifying force — into a mosh pit of competing agendas and emotions, pitting owners, players and league officials mostly against the president, at least initially, and longtime fans against the league.

The dispute with Trump overshadowed the original intent of the protests. The former San Francisco 49ers quarterback Colin Kaepernick, who was the first not to stand for the national anthem in 2016, did so to shine a light on police brutality and what he saw as the unfairness of the criminal justice system.

Some tarred Kaepernick and other protesting players as traitors. Others hailed them as heroes. Amid the storm, Jenkins and about three dozen other players formed the Players Coalition and got to work on finding solutions to the problems they cared about most. During the spring and summer, and then on their days off during the season, they visited lawmakers on Capitol Hill and in statehouses, went to prisons and bail hearings, and met with activists trying to help the incarcerated get back on their feet. They wrote op-ed pieces and letters to legislators and spoke on television.

Jenkins; his Eagles teammate Chris Long; the former wide receiver Anquan Boldin; Michael Bennett and Doug Baldwin of the Seattle Seahawks; Devin McCourty of the New England Patriots; and players on every other team also lobbied their bosses, the 32 team owners and Commissioner Roger Goodell, to use the N.F.L.'s deep pockets to help fight these issues.

It was a delicate dance, and some owners wondered whether the league should be expanding its mission far beyond football.

"Institutionally, we are not here for a lesson in civics," Jerry Jones, the owner of the Dallas Cowboys, said in December. "Institutions — churches, businesses — have all been slow to act. When they act, they usually overreact, and then they have to come back and back the adjustment."

Also, while the players wanted the league to help, they did not want to be seen as asking for its permission. Some players worried that the league might co-opt their message, or demand they stop protesting in return for support. Other players felt that the league could do a lot more than it ultimately did.

Jenkins and the majority of his group were simply glad the owners and the league heard them out.

"Listening to the players, giving us a seat at the table, it was something we wanted," Boldin said.

Philadelphia Eagles safety Malcolm Jenkins has been at the center of N.F.L. players' protests this season, fighting for criminal justice reform and addressing racial inequality.

In fact, by the time Trump lashed out at the league, Goodell, the Eagles owner Jeffrey Lurie and league officials had already spent an entire day in Philadelphia with Jenkins and other players. They met with the police commissioner and public defenders, sat in on bail hearings and heard from former prisoners about the challenges of getting back on their feet.

Jenkins said the afternoon was the group's opportunity to explain why players had chosen to demonstrate, sacrifice their time and "put our necks out there, because these are things happening every day and happening in N.F.L. cities."

Just days later, the league was trying to dance around the political third rail of the anthem protests and the president. The league's sponsors and television partners were jittery. Through the fury, the Players Coalition became a way to approach the issues productively, and the league and the group had established a degree of trust.

"One of the things you come away with is, they are incredibly knowledgeable, articulate and passionate about these issues," the Atlanta Falcons' owner, Arthur Blank, said of the members of the Players Coalition.

GETTING TO WORK

In an odd way, the president may have done the Players Coalition a favor. His obsession with the anthem protests accelerated the discussion about the issues the group was trying to highlight. Those discussions were awkward for some owners, but also for the players who were being branded unpatriotic. Jenkins said the group was determined to seize the moment.

"I realized I could have a far greater impact than I ever had," said Jenkins, a nine-year veteran.

All he needed was time, and Jenkins already had a lot on his plate. His foundation, which provides leadership and life skills to young people in underserved communities, had expanded to four states. He had also recently opened a high-end clothing store in Philadelphia. The baby was on the way, and the Eagles were suddenly one of the league's top teams.

Holly Harris, the executive director of the Justice Action Network, enlisted Jenkins to write a letter of support for a program in Ohio that diverts nonviolent drug offenders from prison to community treatment programs. In no time, Jenkins, who played at Ohio State, sent a letter to legislators. Harris said the letter helped save the program.

Bill Cobb, the deputy director of the A.C.L.U. Campaign for Smart Justice, which tries to reduce racial disparities in the criminal justice system, took Jenkins and other players to Graterford Prison, in Collegeville, Pa., about an hour's drive from Philadelphia, to talk with officers and inmates, including juveniles who received life sentences. Jenkins recorded a video and wrote an op-ed column to publicize Cobb's program. He gave Super Bowl tickets to a man who was released from the prison after serving 30 years of a life term, which he received as a 15-year-old.

Jenkins credited players on the Coalition, his wife, Morrisa, and Lurie for helping to shoulder the workload.

Among N.F.L. owners, Lurie is uniquely sympathetic to what the Players Coalition has been trying to achieve. Long before he bought the Eagles, he earned a doctoral degree in social policy and lectured on topics like incarceration rates. In the lobby at the Eagles' training facility, there are large photos of Martin Luther King Jr., Nelson Mandela and Jonas Salk, rather than sepia-tone images of the team's best former players.

While he supports Jenkins and the players, Lurie told them they needed to better publicize their goals so they were not sidetracked by people accusing them of being unpatriotic, like those protesting the Vietnam War in the 1960s.

"They had to understand that the message is really important, and if the message is not being received, it hurts their ability to take action," Lurie said.

At one point, Jenkins received criticism from those against the protests and those in favor of them. After the league and the Coalition announced their plan to support grass-roots groups, Jenkins said he would no longer raise his fist during the playing of the anthem. Critics, including some players who quit the Players Coalition, said he had cut a deal to get support from owners who wanted the protests to end.

But Jenkins said the protests had succeeded in shining a light on social injustice and the need for action, and the N.F.L. had made a commitment to help, even if it meant working under a bright and sometimes harsh light.

"The goal is not to make everyone comfortable and happy," Jenkins said. As players, we had "to understand the noise is just part of the deal, and if you're going to get involved, you have to be tough enough to ignore that, and eventually our words and actions will answer all the questions people have."

Then he was off to get back to his new baby.

Football Players Are Protesting Police Violence, Not the Anthem

OPINION | BY KASHANA CAULEY | AUG. 25, 2018

There are consequences to mischaracterizing the reason players aren't standing.

NOW THAT THE N.F.L. preseason has begun, some of the league's players are again refusing to stand during the national anthem in protest of police brutality. A number of news organizations have mischaracterized the protests as "anthem protests," and President Trump has gone further, saying they just "wanted to show their 'outrage' at something that most of them are unable to define." He keeps coming back to this issue over and over.

Most of those players are black men. They have lived with the reality of police brutality their whole lives. This slander is an insult to them. But even if everyone who frames the kneeling as "anthem protests" is unintentionally making a mistake, it's a harmful one.

The protests have always been intended to draw attention to police brutality and the economic and social oppression of people of color. "I am not going to stand up to show pride in a country that oppresses black people and people of color," said Colin Kaepernick, who started the protests, after a preseason game in 2016. "To me, this is bigger than football and it would be selfish to look the other way. There are bodies in the street and people getting paid leave and getting away with murder." Calling the protests "anthem protests" is a dishonest way to change the conversation from systemic issues that the protests have raised again and again.

The false claim that they are "anthem protests" also implies that protesting police violence is inconsistent with patriotism. In fact, African-Americans have a long history of staging protests during the national anthem because of a deep understanding and internalization of the anthem's patriotic significance.

In 1892, at a meeting in a Chicago A.M.E. church after a lynching in Memphis, a pastor asked the 1,000 black people in the audience to sing "My Country, 'Tis of Thee," the de facto national anthem of the time. But everyone refused. One man argued, "I don't want to sing that song until this country is what it claims to be, 'sweet land of liberty.' "

Kevin Kruse, a history professor at Princeton, told me in an email:

> At the 1968 Olympics, medalists Tommie Smith and John Carlos raised their fists during the playing of the anthem to draw attention to a variety of concerns, including black poverty and the legacy of lynching in America. While their stance was dismissed by some as radical at the time, more mainstream black athletes understood their stance and agreed with it. A few years later, Jackie Robinson wrote in his memoir "I Never Had It Made": "I cannot stand and sing the anthem. I cannot salute the flag; I know that I am a black man in a white world."

Wayne Collett, the African-American silver medalist in the 400-meter dash in the 1972 Munich Olympics, also refused to face the flag while the anthem played at the medal ceremony. "I couldn't stand there and sing the words, because I don't believe they're true," he is reported to have said. "I believe we have the potential to have a beautiful country, but I don't think we do."

Last year, the football player Richard Sherman echoed this sentiment: "There isn't liberty and justice for all. I think guys for a while — at least a year now — have been protesting that by taking a knee, sitting down, putting up a fist."

These are the words of people who love their country, who have thought long and hard about the national anthem and what it says, and simply wish to hold America accountable to the promises it makes in its anthem.

If we have to stand and honor a song about freedom, why can't all our country's citizens be free, instead of subject to state violence and extrajudicial killings?

There's one last reason to avoid calling the N.F.L. protests "anthem protests." In an era where people are worried that they're getting fake news, and also possibly tempted to dismiss the reality of racism in the United States, it's important that people who comment on or cover the N.F.L. protests tell their audiences the truth of what the protests are really about.

So don't call them "anthem protests." Call them what they are — "protests against racist police violence."

KASHANA CAULEY is a television and freelance writer and a contributing opinion writer.

CHAPTER 3

Fighting for Gender Equality, On and Off the Field

The last decade has seen women's athletics reach unprecedented levels of popularity, especially in American institutions like the W.N.B.A. and the women's national soccer team. However, beneath those successes are structural barriers to full equality in sports. Along with discrepancies in pay and airtime, there remain severe instances of abuse and unhealthy training standards behind the scenes. At the most extreme, South African runner Caster Semenya's fight against hormone testing represents a sports body putting unfair burdens on women who don't conform.

A Giant Leap for Women, but Hurdles Remain

BY JERÉ LONGMAN | JULY 29, 2012

LONDON — During Friday's opening ceremony, Jacques Rogge, the president of the International Olympic Committee, drew loud and sustained applause when he said: "For the first time in Olympic history, all the participating teams will have female athletes. This is a major boost for gender equality."

It is true that women have come light-years from the first modern Games, held in Athens in 1896, when their presence was welcomed only as spectators. Women, too, have made significant gains even since the Atlanta Games in 1996, when 26 nations did not send female athletes.

Yet the fight for true equality is far from being won. For the first time, Saudi Arabia sent two female athletes to compete in London, along with at least one sports official. But the three women who participated in the opening ceremony walked behind the men, not among them.

For some Westerners, this has been viewed as a reminder of the subordinate place of women in the conservative Islamic monarchy, where sport is forbidden for girls in schools and women are effectively not allowed to drive cars.

The moment was undoubtedly scripted, but it would have been unrealistic to expect anything else in a society where men and women are generally separated, said Christoph Wilcke, an expert on Saudi Arabia for Human Rights Watch, which has forcefully pushed for inclusion of the country's women in the Olympics.

"If they were walking together and holding hands, that would not have been cool for the domestic audience," Wilcke said.

The participation of Saudi women remains complicated, even as the Games are under way. On Friday, Wodjan Ali Seraj Abdulrahim Shahrkhani is scheduled to compete in judo. She is required by Saudi officials to wear a hijab, or head scarf. But the international judo federation said last week that Shahrkhani could not compete with a head covering for safety reasons and to preserve the "principle and spirit of judo."

On Sunday, a Saudi newspaper, quoting Shahrkhani's father, said she would withdraw from Friday's competition if she could not wear a hijab. Olympic officials said Sunday that they were trying to resolve the situation. Soccer once banned hijabs, too, but approved them last month. Granted, judo is a different sport; the use of hands is critical. Safety should be paramount. But surely a remedy can be found. Otherwise, it will be hugely embarrassing to the I.O.C. and to the Saudis.

"The judo situation seems to be a debacle," Wilcke said. "Participation of Saudi women has been one of the I.O.C.'s major issues. It seems strange the I.O.C. wouldn't have contemplated clothing. That would be one of the first things on the checklist."

Perhaps Shahrkhani could compete without a head scarf if the event were not televised, but that seems unlikely, Wilcke said. He suggested a head covering like the one in soccer could be used. Failure to resolve the matter, he said, would result "in hurt feelings on both sides, for the Saudis who tried and feel betrayed, and the I.O.C., which tried to find the right balance line."

The other Saudi athlete competing, beginning Aug. 8, is an 800-meter runner named Sarah Attar. She grew up and lives and trains in Southern California, where she attends Pepperdine. Her family asked the university to remove photographs of Attar from her online biography. And the only photographs and video issued of Attar by the I.O.C. showed her hair, arms and legs fully covered. She has also declined interviews, further seeming to confirm that hers is but a token presence in London.

Yet, small steps can be important ones. Qatar also entered its first female athletes in the Summer Games. One of them, a shooter named Bahiya al-Hamad, carried her country's flag in the opening ceremony. Beforehand, she said on Twitter that she was "truly proud and humbled."

About 45 percent of the 10,500 athletes competing are women. Restrictions are falling away, stereotypes are being turned on their head. NurSuryani Mohamed Taibi, a shooter from Malaysia, became one of the few Olympic athletes to compete while pregnant when she participated Saturday in the 10-meter air rifle event.

"I felt her kicking," NurSuryani, who is scheduled to give birth to a daughter next month, told reporters. "But I said to her, 'O.K., be calm; Mummy is going to shoot now.' "

Ten or 15 years ago, it would have been unheard-of, and possibly career threatening, for any member of the United States women's soccer team to publicly announce that she was a lesbian. But midfielder Megan Rapinoe did so just before the Games, and the response has been widely supportive.

"As athletes, we live our lives in the public eye and have a platform to be positive role models," Rapinoe wrote in a blog on espnW. "I'd like to help create more tolerance and acceptance across the board. That means more people talking about it, more people coming out and, at the end of the day, making less of a massive deal about being gay."

Not that discrimination, or slights, have exactly ended. Japan's women's soccer team is the World Cup champion. But its players were forced to fly coach, while the men's team rode in business class, on a 13-hour flight to Paris from Tokyo before the Games.

On Wednesday in the women's Olympic soccer tournament in Glasgow, organizers infuriated the North Koreans by placing South Korean flags next to their faces and names on the scoreboard.

Yet female soccer players have also gained praise for performing without the diving, theatrical writhing and complaining inherent in the men's game. A British reader named Geoff Cooling wrote to The Daily Mail on Sunday that he had watched an entire match devoid of excessive preening and whining.

"Was I dreaming?" he wrote.

Understanding the Controversy Over Caster Semenya

COLUMN | BY JERÉ LONGMAN | AUG. 18, 2016

RIO DE JANEIRO — Caster Semenya of South Africa, heavily favored to win the Olympic women's 800 meters, ran a quick opening round this week and then breezed past reporters.

Who could blame her?

Perhaps no female athlete has faced such brutal scrutiny by fellow competitors, sports officials and journalists.

When Semenya, then 18, dominated the 800 at the 2009 world track and field championships, winning by more than two seconds, a fellow competitor called her a man. Pierre Weiss, the general secretary of the International Association of Athletics Federations, track and field's world governing body, said, "She is a woman, but maybe not 100 percent."

Semenya was barred from competition and subjected to sex tests. She returned months later, but the insensitivity shown toward her was sad.

Katrina Karkazis, a Stanford University bioethicist, said Semenya was punished simply for "being too fast and supposedly too masculine" by Western standards.

The questioning of Semenya's success led to a policy enacted in 2011 by the I.A.A.F., the sport's governing body, that restricted the permitted levels of testosterone, which occur naturally high in some women. That condition is called hyperandrogenism.

Female athletes above the testosterone threshold of 10 nanomoles per liter — considered at the lower end of the male range — faced the prospect of invasive, humiliating and potentially risky measures if they wanted to continue competing. These included hormone-suppressing drugs and surgery to remove internal testes, which can produce testosterone.

It is not known for certain what, if any, procedures were undergone by Semenya, who won a silver medal at the 2012 London Olympics.

CHANG W. LEE/THE NEW YORK TIMES

Caster Semenya ran a 1:58.15 in the semifinals of the 800 meters on Thursday night.

Nor could it be verified, as reported in 2009 in The Daily Telegraph of Australia, that Semenya had internal testes and three times the testosterone level of a typical woman.

At this point, it does not matter. Last year, the Court of Arbitration for Sport, the Swiss-based high court for international sport, suspended track and field's testosterone policy for two years.

The court said it had been "unable to conclude that hyperandrogenic female athletes may benefit from such a significant performance advantage that it is necessary to exclude them from competing in the female category."

Did elevated testosterone provide women with a 1 percent competitive advantage? Three percent? More? Available science could not say, the court ruled. It gave the I.A.A.F. two years to try to discern that advantage. The ruling was based on the case of Dutee Chand, a sprinter from India.

The court ruling was the correct one.

As the arbitration panel noted, science has not conclusively shown that elevated testosterone provides women with more of a significant competitive edge than factors like nutrition, access to coaching and training facilities, and other genetic and biological variations.

All Olympians have some exceptional traits. That is why they are elite athletes. A level playing field for everyone remains elusive, perhaps unattainable.

Kenyan and Ethiopian marathoners live and train at altitude, naturally enhancing their oxygen-carrying capacity. And they tend to have long, thin legs that make running more energy efficient. Kevin Durant and Brittney Griner are great basketball players in part because they are nearly 7 feet tall.

Eero Mantyranta, a Finnish cross-country skier who won seven Olympic medals in the 1960s, including three golds, was found to have a genetic mutation that increased his hemoglobin level to about 50 percent higher than the average man's.

There is "no fundamental difference" between a congenital disorder that produces high testosterone levels and a genetic mutation that produces elevated hemoglobin levels, according to a recent commentary, "The Olympic Games and Athletic Sex Assignment," in The Journal of the American Medical Association.

Yet elevated levels of naturally occurring hemoglobin do not disqualify athletes. In any case, the Journal commentary said, "all of these biological differences are minuscule compared with the suspected use of performance-enhancing substances."

If elevated testosterone provided an overriding competitive advantage, said Karkazis, the Stanford bioethicist, why did Chand, the Indian sprinter, not advance beyond the first round of the Olympic 100 meters?

"If you believe this is jet fuel, then what's going on?" said Karkazis, who testified on Chand's behalf before the arbitration court.

The I.A.A.F. does not investigate further if atypically high levels of testosterone in men are determined to occur naturally, an editorial in Scientific American recently noted. It added, "Fairness and science both dictate that women should be treated exactly the same."

There are reasonable people on both sides of the testosterone debate. And there is deep emotion, too. It is an extremely complex issue, which includes the Olympic participation of transgender athletes.

Experts do not suggest that Semenya has taken banned substances. No one serious is calling her a man. No prominent voices suggest that separate categories should not exist for women's and men's sports.

But many remain concerned that women's sports will be threatened if some athletes are allowed to compete with a testosterone advantage, even if athletes are reluctant to address the testosterone issue during the Olympics.

Semenya easily advanced out of the semifinals on Thursday night; the final is Saturday. Ajee Wilson of the United States, who finished second to Semenya in their opening heat, said, "It is something that should be revisited." But Wilson also said: "At this point, what I think doesn't really matter. We're all on the track. Whoever's on there is racing."

Dr. Eric Vilain, a medical geneticist from U.C.L.A., told my colleague Juliet Macur last year that "if we push this argument, anyone declaring a female gender can compete as a woman."

He added, "We're moving toward one big competition, and the very predictable result of that competition is that there will be no women winners."

Paula Radcliffe of England, the retired world-record holder in the women's marathon, told BBC Radio last month that it was "no longer sport" when a victory was so seemingly assured as Semenya's appeared in Rio.

Radcliffe also suggested that some unnamed countries might actively recruit hyperandrogenic athletes to win more races.

But this feared "gender apocalypse," as Karkazis calls it, seems unlikely. We are talking about a very small number of women. And male impostors exist in myth more than reality. It appears that

Semenya's case is being used to make wider assumptions based more on supposition than evidence.

The notion that women's sports need to be protected is paternalistic, Karkazis said, calling it "the mantle under which all kinds of discriminatory and sexist ideas enter."

In a sport once dominated by white Europeans, said Madeleine Pape of Australia, who competed against Semenya in the 2009 world championships, women who have fought so hard for the right to compete and for sustainable financial support can feel threatened by the rising success of a faster competitor. Especially, Pape said, if that athlete is non-gender-conforming and is married to another woman, as Semenya is.

In truth, Radcliffe is more of an outlier than Semenya. Radcliffe's marathon record of 2 hours 15 minutes 25 seconds is about 10 percent slower than the fastest men's time of 2:02:57. Meanwhile, Semenya's best performance at 800 meters of 1 minute 55.33 seconds, which is not the world record, is about 12 percent slower than the men's record of 1:40.91.

Radcliffe and gold medal athletes in Rio, like the American gymnast Simone Biles and the swimmer Katie Ledecky, have been as dominant as Semenya or more dominant, but their gender has not been openly questioned, Pape said.

"When we look at it objectively, Caster Semenya is no more exceptional than they are," Pape, who is a doctoral student in sociology at the University of Wisconsin, said in an email. "So why do we celebrate them while persecuting Semenya?"

The Journal of the American Medical Association said it was appropriate for athletes who were born with a disorder of sex development and were raised as female to be allowed to compete as women.

That sounds like the right call. Let athletes compete as who they are.

"God made me the way I am, and I accept myself," Semenya told You, a South African magazine, in 2009. "I am who I am, and I'm proud of myself."

It would seem unfair to tell her, Sorry, you can't run in the Olympics because of the way you were born.

Gabby Douglas Says She Also Was Abused by Gymnastics Team Doctor

BY MATT STEVENS | NOV. 21, 2017

GABBY DOUGLAS, the Olympic gymnast who was criticized last week for placing some of the onus on women to avoid sexual harassment, apologized again on Tuesday and said that she, too, had been abused by a team doctor.

Ms. Douglas, 21, drew angry responses on Friday after she wrote on Twitter that it was a woman's responsibility "to dress modestly" so as not to attract "the wrong crowd." She later apologized for that comment, noting that "regardless of what you wear, abuse under any circumstance is never acceptable."

In a statement she posted on Instagram four days later, Ms. Douglas reiterated that "no matter what you wear, it NEVER gives anyone the right to harass or abuse you."

Then, in drawing an analogy, Ms. Douglas suggested she was one of the many gymnasts who contend that they had been abused by Lawrence G. Nassar, a former team doctor for U.S.A. Gymnastics.

"It would be like saying that because of the leotards we wore, it was our fault that we were abused by Larry Nassar," Ms. Douglas wrote. "I didn't publicly share my experiences as well as many other things because for years we were conditioned to stay silent and honestly some things were very painful."

Responding to an email from The New York Times on Tuesday, Jeff Raymond, Ms. Douglas's publicist, said that through her Instagram post, "Gabby is confirming that she too was a victim of Larry Nassar." He would not detail the abuse Ms. Douglas alluded to in her statement.

In addition to Ms. Douglas, at least six other former members of the United States' national gymnastics team have publicly said they were abused by Dr. Nassar: Jeanette Antolin, who competed at the 1999 world championships; Jamie Dantzscher, who won a bronze team medal at the 2000 Olympics; Jessica Howard, a three-time national champion in rhythmic gymnastics; Mattie Larson, a silver medalist at the 2010 world championships; McKayla Maroney, a star of the 2012 Olympics; and Aly Raisman, who won six medals at the 2012 and 2016 Olympics.

More than 140 women have said that Dr. Nassar had touched them inappropriately during medical appointments.

Dr. Nassar is in jail in Michigan, facing 22 counts of first-degree criminal sexual conduct involving at least seven victims. He has so far denied the charges.

But this week, multiple news media reports said that Dr. Nassar would plead guilty to multiple charges of sexual assault and face at least 25 years in prison. Dr. Nassar has a court hearing scheduled for Wednesday in Michigan's Ingham County.

Ms. Douglas had been responding to a statement made by Ms. Raisman on Friday when she made the controversial remark about how women should dress and behave.

Ms. Raisman had said on Twitter that women dressing "sexy" does not entitle men to shame or sexually abuse them.

Ms. Douglas's initial response — in which she said "dressing in a provocative/sexual way entices the wrong crowd" — drew rebukes from many, some of whom accused the gymnast of blaming the victims of sexual harassment for the abuse.

Simone Biles, the Olympic gymnast and former teammate of Ms. Douglas, was among those who publicly criticized Ms. Douglas and expressed support for Ms. Raisman.

In her statement on Tuesday, Ms. Douglas insisted that she did not support "victim shaming/blaming in any way, shape or form!"

"Please forgive me for not being more responsible with how I handled the situation," she wrote, adding, "I have learned from this and I'm determined to be even better."

On Wednesday morning, Ms. Raisman responded to Ms. Douglas's latest statement on Twitter, saying: "I applaud your bravery. I support you."

MAGGIE ASTOR contributed reporting.

Billie Jean King Understands Colin Kaepernick

INTERVIEW | BY ANA MARIE COX | SEPT. 13, 2017

EMMA STONE PLAYS YOU *in "Battle of the Sexes," a new film about your 1973 tennis match against Bobby Riggs. You gently corrected her during the promotional tour after she overlooked the racial component in the wage gap. That was very, if you'll excuse the term, woke of you. How do you keep yourself educated on civil rights issues?*

I never think I can catch up. Coretta Scott King used to talk about how each generation has to start the fight for freedom over, and I think that's true, because the pendulum goes back and forth. You can fight for a lot of things and have it all undone 20, 30 years later and have to start over.

Are you more surprised by the progress we've made since then or the lack thereof?

I don't think it's ever enough. When I was 12, I had an epiphany: Everybody in tennis wore white shoes, white socks, white clothes, used white balls, and everybody who played was white. And I asked myself: Where is everybody else? I figured if I were good enough, maybe I could help change not only my sport but also the world. Sports are a microcosm of society.

You were outspoken in your support of Colin Kaepernick's protest last year.

I support him, but I personally wouldn't do it the way he does it. My dad was in the Navy; he used to cry every time he'd see the flag, O.K.? So I personally couldn't have done that when our anthem is on. Personally. But I understand what he's doing, and I would stand by him.

You've written that your own parents were unaccepting of your homosexuality.

You have to understand, this was the '50s. My mother was always very kind to others, no matter what. They were homophobic because it really was an indicator of their generation more than anything. They figured it out eventually. It was a long, hard trip, and I didn't get comfortable in my own skin until I was 51, when I went through an eating disorder.

I didn't know you were in treatment for an eating disorder.

I was a binge eater. For me to be overweight, I felt like I was protected. I pushed my emotions down as far as they could go, trying to get them to the bottom of my stomach, so I didn't have to think and feel. It was a relief. Once I figured out why I was doing that, that was the start of getting well.

You were outed by a woman you had an affair with, who gets very sympathetic treatment in the movie. Was that hard to watch?

I can tell you that every gay person I know who has seen this movie gets so tense when they're watching these scenes, because it reminds them of themselves. But I asked how they felt, and they said it was fantastic. They remember their first experience, or how they felt about being gay, and how everything was so shame-based, and they recognize that.

It must have been weird to watch a sex scene based on your life.

It was! Totally bizarre to watch the whole thing. I've only been able to watch it two or three times, and it's really hard on me because it brings back so much emotion and shame. I was pushed and pulled in every direction, and I don't know how I made it physically or emotionally, looking back now.

Sports have changed a lot since your day. One of the more shocking things in "Battle of the Sexes" is that you went on a tour sponsored by a cigarette company.

Those were some of the best people we worked with, at Philip Morris. They were fantastic people. But did I like it? Absolutely not.

Aside from the disappearance of tobacco sponsorships, what are some of the biggest social changes you've seen since the time of the film?

We've made a lot of advances in the L.G.B.T. community. We still have a long way to go, and I think we're starting to go backward a bit, especially with the ban on trans people in the armed forces. We have to keep pushing. We have to have equality in every way. Everyone deserves to belong.

Interview has been condensed and edited.

8 Times Women in Sports Fought for Equality

BY SARAH MERVOSH AND CHRISTINA CARON | MARCH 8, 2019

ON FRIDAY, all 28 players on the United States women's soccer team filed a gender discrimination lawsuit against the United States Soccer Federation, an escalation in their increasingly public battle for equality.

The players have said that they play more games than the men's team — and win more of them — yet still receive less pay. They said "institutionalized gender discrimination" affected not only their paychecks, but also where they played and how often, how they trained, the medical care and coaching they received, and even how they traveled to matches.

They are not alone in their fight for fairer pay and better treatment. Here are eight times in recent memory when women fought for equality in sports.

FINISHING THE BOSTON MARATHON DESPITE AN ATTEMPT TO EJECT HER

Experts claimed for years that distance running was damaging to women's health and femininity.

In 1967, women weren't allowed to officially enter the Boston Marathon, so Kathrine Switzer entered that year as "K.V. Switzer" to hide her gender.

Two miles in, an official tried to eject her from the course, a moment captured in dramatic photographs. She finished anyway, becoming the first woman to complete the race as an official entrant.

"We learned that women are not deficient in endurance and stamina, and that running requires no fancy facilities or equipment," Switzer wrote in The New York Times in 2007.

Women were officially allowed to enter the race in 1972. Women's marathoning joined the Olympics in 1984.

A FEMINIST TENNIS CHAMPION WINS THE BATTLE OF THE SEXES

The year 1973 was a big one for Billie Jean King, the trailblazing tennis star.

She founded the Women's Tennis Association. She led a movement for female players to earn equal prize money in tournaments that featured players of both sexes.

And, on a September night at the Astrodome in Houston, she epitomized her crusade for gender equality when she handily beat Bobby Riggs, a self-described male chauvinist pig, in the Battle of the Sexes.

King went on to receive the Presidential Medal of Freedom in 2009 for her work championing the rights of women and gay people. She is considered to be one of the most important athletes of the 20th century.

"Everyone thinks women should be thrilled when we get crumbs," King once said. "I want women to have the cake, the icing and the cherry on top, too."

YALE ROWERS STRIP TO PROTEST LACK OF WOMEN'S SHOWERS

Chris Ernst is a two-time Olympic rower. But in the spring of 1976, she was the captain of Yale University's women's crew team — and sick of not having proper showers to use after practice.

She led 18 teammates in an eye-catching protest at Yale's athletic office. The athletes stripped to their waists, revealing the words "Title IX," which had been drawn in blue marker on each woman's back and breasts.

The Times ran an article in the next day's paper, and a photograph of the history-making event also ran in The Yale Daily News.

Within two weeks, the female rowers had new locker rooms. And, across the country, educators began viewing Title IX — which had been in effect for just four years — as a law that required compliance.

VENUS WILLIAMS WINS A VICTORY FOR WOMEN OFF THE COURT

In 2007, after pressure from the tennis great Venus Williams and others, Wimbledon announced that women's tennis players would receive prize money equal to the men's.

Williams had made a failed plea to Wimbledon's governing body the night before she won the title in 2005. And in 2006, she wrote an op-ed essay in The Times of London titled "Wimbledon Has Sent Me a Message: I'm Only a Second Class Champion."

"Have you ever been let down by someone that you had long admired, respected and looked up to?" she wrote. "Little in life is more disappointing, particularly when that person does something that goes against the very heart of what you believe is right and fair."

After the policies changed in 2007, she was awarded $1.4 million for her fourth Wimbledon victory, the same amount as the men's champion, Roger Federer.

A FIRST FOR WOMEN'S HOCKEY

In March 2017, the women's national hockey team announced that it would boycott the coming world championship if U.S.A. Hockey, the sport's national governing body, did not increase the women's wages.

"It's hard to believe that in 2017, we have to fight so hard just to get equitable support," Meghan Duggan, the team's captain, said at the time. "We want to do the fair thing, and the right thing — not just for hockey but for all women."

They put their careers on the line, but the risk paid off.

Less than two weeks later, the team reached a four-year deal with U.S.A. Hockey. It provided the female players a $2,000 training stipend each month from the United States Olympic Committee and larger bonuses for winning medals. The team also received the same travel and insurance provisions that the men's national team did, and a pool of prize money to be split each year.

FEMALE SURFERS RECEIVE EQUAL PRIZE MONEY

Four prominent female big-wave surfers, Bianca Valenti, Andrea Moller, Keala Kennelly and Paige Alms, spent years fighting for equal pay in the largely male sport where they regularly risk their lives.

Last July, the Committee for Equity in Women's Surfing, an organization formed by six women, sent letters to the California Coastal Commission arguing that by treating women unequally, the World Surf League was in violation of state civil rights law.

Months later, in September, Valenti and other female surfers earned a victory when the World Surf League announced it would offer equal prize money to men and women.

Valenti, along with Sabrina Brennan, the president of the San Mateo County Harbor Commission, and Karen Tynan, a labor lawyer, also successfully pushed for women to be included in the Maverick's Challenge, a big-wave surfing competition that had traditionally invited only men.

"Some people would tell me that by trying to get the (prize) pie redistributed I was ruining it for everyone," Moller said in December. "But I would just say: 'That's wrong. We're fighting for the industry. People love watching women surf big waves, so the whole sport will grow.' "

W.N.B.A. PLAYERS SPEAK UP

In the world of professional basketball, pay disparities are well-documented: In the N.B.A., a multibillion-dollar industry where players often make millions, the *minimum* starting salary is about eight times what the average W.N.B.A. player makes.

And female players are speaking up, on social media and on TV.

Skylar Diggins-Smith, the W.N.B.A. All-Star who plays guard for the Dallas Wings, recently appeared in a commercial to raise awareness about pay inequity.

The commercial, by the investment adviser Wealthsimple, contrasts the paths of two young players, a boy and a girl. Each lists their basketball dreams and accomplishments, but only one will grow up to receive a multimillion-dollar rookie contract.

A'ja Wilson, a star rookie who was the first overall W.N.B.A. draft pick in 2018, has also weighed in: "must. be. nice," she wrote about LeBron James's $154 million contract with the Los Angeles Lakers. "We over here looking for a M but Lord, let me get back in my lane."

Wilson earned about $53,000 that season. The top N.B.A. draft pick last year, Deandre Ayton, was expected to earn about $6.8 million in his first year playing for the Phoenix Suns.

THE BEST FEMALE SOCCER PLAYER BOYCOTTS THE WORLD CUP

Ada Hegerberg, a 23-year-old Norwegian, was recognized as the best female soccer player in the world last year when she became the first person to win the women's Ballon d'Or, a prestigious individual honor in soccer that had previously been reserved for men.

Despite the big award, she has decided not to play on the biggest stage of all, the Women's World Cup, in France this summer.

Hegerberg quit the Norwegian national team in 2017 in protest of what she said was a lack of support for women's soccer in her home country.

"I was quite clear with them about what I thought needed to be better," she said in an interview after winning the Ballon d'Or. "I gave them the reasons. I wish my national team all the best. I love my country. I wish I could play for them. In this case, I had to move on."

MAYA SALAM and **MIHIR ZAVERI** contributed reporting.

The Best Women's Soccer Team in the World Fights for Equal Pay

BY LIZZY GOODMAN | JUNE 10, 2019

As the U.S. women's national soccer team defends its World Cup title in France, its members are preparing for a courtroom battle.

IN SPRING 2018, Abby Wambach, the most decorated soccer player in American history, gave a commencement address at Barnard College that went viral. The player who had scored more goals than any other, male or female, in international competition described standing onstage at the ESPYs the year after she retired in 2015, receiving the Icon Award alongside two peers, Peyton Manning and Kobe Bryant. "I felt so grateful," she recalled. "I had a momentary feeling of having arrived; like, we women had finally made it." As the athletes exited the stage, each having, as Wambach put it, "left it all on the field for decades with the same ferocity, talent and commitment," it occurred to her that while the sacrifices the men made for their careers were nearly identical to her own, their new lives would not resemble hers in one fundamental way. "Kobe and Peyton walked away from their careers with something I didn't have: enormous bank accounts," Wambach said. "Because of that, they had something else I didn't have: freedom. Their hustling days were over; mine were just beginning."

The United States women's national team is the best in the world and has been for decades. Since the FIFA Women's World Cup was inaugurated in 1991, the United States has won three of the seven titles, including the most recent one in 2015. Since women's soccer became an Olympic sport in 1996, it has won four of six gold medals. The team has been ranked No.1 by FIFA for 10 of the last 11 years and has produced some of the biggest female sports stars of the last several decades, from Mia Hamm to Wambach to the current starting center forward, Alex Morgan. The squad playing at the World Cup this month in France includes Morgan; her accomplice on the left wing, the

Tilda Swinton doppelgänger Megan Rapinoe; and the previous World Cup's hat-trick-scoring hero, Carli Lloyd; along with newcomers like the elegant but deadly Mallory Pugh and the ingenious, bruising midfielder Lindsey Horan. The American team is favored to successfully defend its title, despite a field of opponents whose depth, fitness and all-around sophistication improved drastically even in the past four years, reflecting the rapid growth of women's soccer globally. "This is the first World Cup where I feel like — and I'm rejoicing over this — I can count potential World Cup winners on more than one hand," the former player and current ESPN commentator Julie Foudy said when calling a recent match between the United States and Mexico.

It was particularly important, then, in the months leading up to this moment, for the American women to keep their focus, minimize distractions and avoid drama at all costs. Which they did, with one enormous exception. On March 8, they sued the United States Soccer Federation, claiming "purposeful gender discrimination." "The bottom line is simple," the star defender Becky Sauerbrunn said in a statement. "It is wrong for us to be paid and valued less for our work because of our gender." Rapinoe, also in a statement, mentioned the responsibility the team feels to advocate "on behalf of our teammates, future teammates, fellow women athletes and women all around the world." This was 95 days before the team's first World Cup match in France and mere weeks before the beginning of its next training camp — a weeklong blend of intense practice and tryouts aimed at enabling Coach Jill Ellis and her staff to get the alchemy just right. But the players felt they could not wait. "We don't always want to be patient," Morgan tells me. "You have to seize the moment."

The lawsuit's timing may be dramatic, but it was the natural next step in a continuing dispute that centers on equal compensation. Members of the U.S.W.N.T. have been pursuing fair compensation for years, with only marginal improvement: The lawsuit asserts, for example, that from 2013 to 2016, if a male and a female national team player each played 20 exhibition games in a year, members of the men's squad would have earned an average of $263,320, while members of the women's squad would have earned a maximum of $99,000. The suit also claims that "during the period relevant to this case," the women's team earned more for U.S. Soccer than the men's team did. It cites numbers from the 2016 fiscal year that indicate that the federation had expected a combined net loss for the national teams of $429,929, but that largely because of the women's team's successes it revised its pro jections to a $17.7 million profit.

In a response filed on May 7, U.S. Soccer denies many of the specifics provided in the lawsuit, including those mentioned above, but it doesn't dispute that the men's and women's players are not paid equally. Instead, it asserts that those inequities are a result of "different pay structures for performing different work." It characterizes as "misleading and inaccurate" the claims that the women's team generates more revenue than the men's, while also framing the women's and men's teams as so different from each other that they can't legitimately be compared at all. This is true in at least one sense: The women are way, way better. The men's national team lost in the round of 16 at the 2014 World Cup and didn't even qualify for the 2018 World Cup. American men haven't won an Olympic medal in more than a century. Partly as a consequence of their superior results, from 2015 to 2018, the women's team played 19 more matches than the men. In other words, the women aren't working as hard as their male counterparts for less money; they're working *harder* for less money. For the record, the men's team's players association released a statement of full-throated support for their women's team compatriots and the mutual goal of equal pay.

In her Barnard speech, Wambach said she regretted being so caught up in gratitude for what she and her peers did receive that she "missed opportunities to demand equality for all of us." Her former teammates do not intend to make that same mistake. They are better paid than any women's sports team in history, and at least as well known, but it's not enough. Not only because by the players' calculations they are making as little as 38 cents to their male counterparts' dollar, but because these players feel a responsibility to fight, in public, on the biggest stage possible, while they can. "It's wonderful to be a professional athlete and feel fulfilled, but at the same time, what sort of legacy do you want to leave?" Morgan wonders. "I had this dream of being a professional soccer player, and I never knew it entailed being a role model, being an inspiration, standing up for things I believe in, standing up for gender equality. But now I don't know a world where I just play soccer. It goes hand in hand."

ON A GLITTERING APRIL evening in Los Angeles, 20,941 fans crowded into the Banc of California Stadium, home to Major League Soccer's Los Angeles F.C., to watch the American women trounce the 20th-ranked Belgians, 6-0, in a match of no real consequence. (This was one of several exhibition matches, known as "friendlies," the women's team played before leaving for France.) Three teenage girls gathered on the south end of the stadium near the Belgian goal. Two wanted to head up to the mezzanine to see if they could get a glimpse of the Hollywood celebrities in the house — Natalie Portman, Jessica Chastain, Jennifer Garner, Eva Longoria and Uzo Aduba were all in the V.I.P. box, hanging out with Megan Rapinoe, who was not playing because of a mild injury. But one of the teenagers, a tall brunette in jean shorts and a cropped T-shirt, wasn't ready to go actress hunting yet. She stood staring at the action on the pitch, mesmerized. "Let me just see this last play," she pleaded — and right then, Carli Lloyd cut back behind her defender and threaded a perfect pass to Alex Morgan, who chipped it into the back of the net.

The official Time's Up Instagram account later posted a photo of the actresses, all Time's Up supporters, in their U.S.W.N.T. jerseys, with the caption "It's time for U.S. Soccer Federation to pay their women players what they deserve." That Time's Up is choosing to formally align itself, and its quest for equal pay in Hollywood, with the women's national team is particularly gratifying for the players.

They consider their fight to be in keeping with the larger social-justice stories of this era, from the rise of explicitly feminist movements like Time's Up and #MeToo to Black Lives Matter and L.G.B.T. advocacy. "It's one and the same," Rapinoe says. "I get asked this question a lot, like, 'Where does this come from?' or 'Why do you stand up for these things?' To me, it's literally all the same, insofar as I want people to respect who I am, what I am — being gay, being a woman, being a professional athlete, whatever. That is the exact same thing as what Colin did." Rapinoe began kneeling during the national anthem in sol- idarity with Colin Kaepernick in September 2016; in March 2017, U.S. Soccer instituted a policy requiring players to "stand respectfully." (Rapinoe now stands but does not place her hand over her heart.) "Who do you want to be?" Rapinoe says. "What kind of person do you want to be for yourself, but also in the larger context of the country and in the world?"

Serena Williams, asked by reporters to comment on the women's soccer team's lawsuit after a second-round victory at the BNP Pari- bas Open in Indian Wells, Calif., called the pay discrepancy "ludi- crous," adding, "I think at some point, in every sport, you have to have those pioneers, and maybe it's the time for soccer." Indeed, American women's soccer has its original class of pioneers: the so-called 99ers, members of the 1999 World Cup-winning team. At the Los Angeles friendly, Jennifer Garner wore one of their names — Mia Hamm — on her jersey, Aduba wore the legendary goalkeeper Briana Scurry's number and Jessica Chastain wore the jersey of a player with whom she happens to share a surname: Brandi Chastain. It was Brandi Chastain who became a kind of aesthetic allegory for the spirit of the national team when, after sinking the winning penalty against China in the 1999 final, she whipped off her jersey in celebration. The image of Chastain in her sports bra, six-pack on display, triumph on her face, is one of the most famous in the history of sports, both because it cap- tured a huge moment in soccer and because it launched a backlash against Chastain, who was accused of being disrespectful by critics who appeared to believe it was cool for male players to celebrate in this way but uncouth for women to do the same.

Many of the 99ers were in attendance at the friendly to celebrate the 20th anniversary of their World Cup victory. It was that win that established the Americans as women's soccer's first true global stars, the first group of players with the clout to move the needle on issues big (better pay) and small (getting uniforms in women's sizes). Before that World Cup, which was held for the first time in the United States, the team was accustomed to playing to crowds of 5,000, but the 1999 World Cup final at the Rose Bowl drew 90,185 people, still the record for a women's sporting event. After they won, the players toured the country like rock stars, visiting the White House, Disneyland and "The Late Show," where David Letterman referred to them as "babe city." When the dust settled, however, America's newest sweethearts discovered that they were out of work. There was still no viable professional league in the United States.

The 99ers were determined to use the leverage gained by their victory to start a fully professional league, the W.U.S.A. But by the time the national team (including a young Abby Wambach) was defending its title four years later, the league had already folded. And so it went for the next decade. The women's national team continued to be among the most elite in the world, but it returned home after major victories (Olympic gold in 2004, 2008, 2012) to a succession of professional leagues that never stabilized, all the while clawing out incremental financial advances in a series of collective-bargaining agreements with U.S. Soccer.

The National Women's Soccer League, now in its seventh season, is the longest-running professional women's soccer league ever in the United States, but its players still do not make a living wage: The minimum salary was just bumped up to $16,538. Major League Soccer pays male players a minimum salary in the $50,000-a-year range.

The women's national team's lawsuit will play out in a Los Angeles courtroom on a date yet to be set by the Federal District Court, where U.S. Soccer will need to show that the pay disparities between their two teams exist for some reason, any reason, other than sex. According to the women's lawsuit, U.S. Soccer has said it can't grant economic parity because "market realities are such that the women do not deserve to be paid equally to the men." Then there's the "But you agreed to be paid less" argument, which appears to be central to U.S. Soccer's strategy: In April 2017, the women's national team and U.S. Soccer signed a new collective-bargaining agreement in which the women gained ground but did not receive the equal pay they were hoping for. "It was the best deal we could get at the time," Rapinoe says.

The previous agreement had been in place since 2013. As the 2016 Olympics loomed, the female players were reportedly considering striking — hoping to leverage their position as defending gold medalists to increase their shot at earning equal compensation in their next collective-bargaining agreement — when U.S. Soccer sued to prevent them from doing so and won.

Shortly before that ruling came down, five members of the team — Megan Rapinoe, Carli Lloyd, Becky Sauerbrunn, Alex Morgan and Hope Solo, the goalkeeper at the time — filed a federal discrimination complaint with the Equal Employment Opportunity Commission, which is required before you can sue. This February, when the team was between training camps, the five original players named in the 2016 complaint finally received a response in the form of "right to sue" letters, meaning that no determination had been reached one way or another and that they had 90 days to file suit in federal court. So they did.

The 2019 Women's World Cup is expected to be the most watched in history. In the United States, these matches will most likely be among the highest-rated soccer games ever played. (The 2015 final in Canada, between the United States and Japan, averaged 23 million English-language viewers in the States, six million more than the 2014 Men's World Cup final.) Yes, the Americans are favored, but they have never won Women's World Cup titles back to back, and the United States has lately shown some vulnerability. The last major tournament it won was the 2015 World Cup. In 2017, it failed to perform as well as expected in two invitational events hosted on home soil, coming in last in the SheBelieves Cup and finishing second to Australia in the Tournament of Nations. At that point, several senior players, in what Sports Illustrated called a "player revolt," initiated conversations with U.S. Soccer about replacing Coach Jill Ellis.

This unrest came in the wake of the most psychologically gutting performance in team history, at the 2016 Olympics in Brazil. For the first time ever, the team failed to make the Olympic gold medal match; they lost on penalty kicks to Sweden in the quarterfinals. To say the humiliation of this defeat still stings is to put it mildly. "A lot of the players on this team that have never been to a World Cup did go to the Olympics and were a part of the team that didn't perform as well as we should have and had the worst exit that we've ever had in the Olympics, and we never want to replicate that ever in this program, but especially this World Cup," Alex Morgan told me in an unusually breathless burst. "That's definitely in the back of my mind." At the end of 2017, U.S. Soccer made it clear that Ellis was staying, and by 2018 things had stabilized a bit; the team went undefeated last year. But in their first match of 2019, they lost 3-1 to France, a rising power that will no doubt be emboldened this summer, playing on its home turf.

In filing suit when they did, the players set themselves up for a very tense few months — in part because they believe that their performance on the pitch holds the key to their progress off it. "Always and forever, how well the team does on the biggest stage is probably the most important thing," Rapinoe says. "That's what I stress to these kids," she continues, referring to the younger players like Pugh and Horan, who walked into the national team's world believing that their job was merely to play the best soccer of their lives and are now learning that's only part of it. "Everything is more and better," Rapinoe says. "I want them to understand that it's better because we earned it; but it's also better because we won. The most important thing is continuing to win."

IN THE LOBBY of a boutique hotel in downtown Santa Barbara, where the national team stayed during its World Cup training camp in March, well-heeled tourists poured cucumber water from glass vats and discussed where to lunch. The whole place smelled like expensive candles. "No more Marriott Residence Inn for us," Rapinoe said with a grin after settling into an overstuffed love seat next to a stunning bouquet of flowers.

About an hour earlier, the 28 athletes who were in contention for the World Cup team (23 would make the cut) finished practice. As some traipsed through the lobby, sweaty and joking with one another, a few sang the chorus to Lil Nas X's "Old Town Road" ("Can't nobody tell me nothin'/You can't tell me nothin'"), which had been a fixture in camp. Soon they would shower and have group lunch. The day before, the players also had morning training followed by lunch, then a meeting with the team's sports psychologist before group dinner. After training, there are ice baths and other recovery work. This is how the players' lives are programmed: Eat, train, recover, eat, sleep, repeat. "Soccer is like 'Groundhog Day,'" Rapinoe says. "It's great, it's fine, but it's not that exciting all the time."

"We know the sacrifices we make; it's no different than what men make," Carli Lloyd says. "We're away from our families. We're away from our friends. We're spending every waking hour dedicating ourselves to this." If an international squad is a collection of roles filled by a rotating cast of actual human beings, Lloyd is currently in the "seasoned veteran in the twilight of her career" spot, the one Wambach was in during the last World Cup. A two-time FIFA player of the year, Lloyd scored a hat trick in the first 16 minutes of the 2015 final against Japan, topping off an already remarkable run of play. Lloyd is 36 now. She feels as sharp as ever, she says, and has been playing largely as a second-half substitute in these recent friendlies, scoring thrilling clutch goals. But she is not likely to get a ton of playing time in France, and even if she does, this is almost certainly her last World Cup.

When I joked about how it would be amusing to try to train with her, she snickered and told me about one reporter who tried that and tore her A.C.L. — "You could hear the pop" — and another who broke her wrist trying to block a Lloyd shot. But Lloyd turned wistful when she shared that she and her husband are planning to start a family in the next few years, but in looking at their bank account she realized: "I can't just say, 'O.K., this is my last game, and I've made tens of millions of dollars and it's stashed away and we're good.'" For the moment, Lloyd has no interest in retiring. She remains committed to the lawsuit — though she acknowledges she "may be done playing by the time this gets resolved" — and to winning in France. She also deeply enjoys the rigorous two-a-day training sessions she does when home in New Jersey. This is all part of what Lloyd calls her eternal addiction to "chasing something I need to improve on."

They all talk like this, about a state of permanent dissatisfaction and a pleasure taken in pursuing the very perfection they know is unattainable. The one thing every of them has is this superhuman drive. "Players come in all the time, great players, sometimes more talented players," says the forward Christen Press, the squad's resident "What does it all mean?" existential philosopher, who first played on the team in 2012. "The players that survive here are the most competitive ones. No one on this team has been here for more than two years and not felt like they had their face planted on the ground. Many just don't get up. The people that last here get up." She continues: "It's such a small, elite group that you're filtered out if you don't have that."

If Lloyd represents one role in the life cycle of a national team player, Lindsey Horan represents its opposite: the young-gun rising star and one of the picks to emerge from this World Cup a newly minted superstar. Her path is itself a testament to the progress that has been made in opportunities for American women who love to play soccer. When Lloyd made her debut on the team in 2005, there was still no viable professional league in the United States. Lloyd played all four years at Rutgers, then came to the national team "right when they were negotiating stable salaries and contracts," she remembers. Horan, on the other hand, went straight to the pros from high school. This is a controversial move. Press calls it "crazy" for most players, laughing and shaking her head. "The league is not stable enough," she explains. "If you're playing in the N.B.A., you can make two years of your salary and pay for your college anytime you want to go back. But that's not the case with the N.W.S.L."

Advisable or not, by 2012, when Horan got on the plane to France to begin her time at Paris Saint-Germain, professional women's leagues were prominent enough, in the States and in Europe, that such a move was possible. It was her dream, so she went for it. Horan is not much for keeping her cards close to her chest. Getting called up, training, playing well in international tournaments, then focusing on showing her best game in camp these last months has been enough of a challenge, she says, without the added pressure to become a civil rights activist overnight. "It has been very hard," Horan says. "I've always just been like: Oh, I love soccer. I love being here. I'm so happy to be a part of this team." But lately, that has shifted. "I've always wanted to just stay out of that and focus on the game, but now I think that is almost selfish, because we do have a voice, and so many people watch us, and we're their inspirations, and we're their idols, and us speaking up is huge."

The "four or five girls that are very vocal" who Horan says helped her reach this conclusion — the team leaders when it comes to advocacy — have a knack for instilling a sense of social responsibility in others. "We try, first of all, education," Rapinoe says. "We break down the inequities. We tell them: This is why we are choosing to take this stance, for these reasons. We try to show specifically how it affects each individual player, but then also the team as a whole." Could someone have declined to join the lawsuit if she wanted to? "Yeah," says Rapinoe, slowly. "It's always possible, and we had some players that took longer." But, she says, "If you want the door open, you have to open it."

ON A WELCOME bright April day after a very wet stretch in Denver, 10-year-old Lilli and her 9-year-old friend, Reese, sat in their soccer kits, legs dangling off white folding chairs, in front of City Hall. This was a school day, but Reese's mother brought them to watch two of their heroes, Lindsey Horan and Mallory Pugh, receive an honorary street sign and a "challenge coin," the equivalent of a key to the city. Pugh and Horan are both Denver-area natives, and both came up through the hypercompetitive ranks of Colorado youth soccer. They are models for what Lilli and Reese plan to become when they grow up: pro soccer players. "It's educational!" Lilli insisted of this field trip for two. Then she showed off the ball, shoes, shin guards and backpack she had brought to have signed. By which player? "Both of them!" Lilli plays offense, and this kind of game-day aggressiveness will come in handy for her on the field, for sure, but it may be even more important off the field if she's serious about a career in professional soccer.

Watching Horan and Pugh stand only somewhat awkwardly next to the mayor, with their parents snapping pictures and a local news crew on hand to document the quaint pageantry, felt like watching the opening scene in a biopic. Each is already a groundbreaker: Pugh is the youngest American player, at 17, ever to play in an Olympic-qualifying match, and Horan is the first American woman to go straight from high school to the pros. They now play for top teams in the N.W.S.L. — Pugh for the Washington Spirit, Horan for the Portland Thorns — and they have high-profile endorsement deals (Pugh with Nike, Horan with Adidas). Pugh and Horan didn't know this yet, but they would each make the World Cup squad — another milestone reached. But the question remains: Will one or both of these players break the record so many of her predecessors could not and become the first in women's soccer history to retire without having to worry about her next paycheck? And if not Pugh or Horan, how about by the time we get to Lilli or Reese?

The 28 women suing U.S. Soccer have, in some cases, very little in common other than their sport. Avowed Christians and atheists, gay and straight, politically active and not, they have nonetheless rallied behind this collective cause. "You really do need everyone," Rapinoe says. "It's a crazy intimate environment. We're not all really, really close, but we're extremely intimate." At the hotel in Santa Barbara, she brought up the concept of "the double earn," a reference to the unpaid labor taken on by women, especially at home, that goes largely unacknowledged; Rapinoe was drawing a parallel between that work and the work that she and her teammates are having to do to secure equal rights that should already be theirs. The soccer players, differences aside, have something powerful in common besides competitive drive: They are, every one of them, from 20-year-old defender Tierna Davidson to 36-year-old Carli Lloyd, pulling a double shift. "We really don't want to be doing all of this all of the time," Rapinoe says. "We'd much prefer to not be engaging in litigations. We'd much prefer not to have to be the nag in the room. We'd prefer to be thought partners and business partners." Rapinoe sat up a little straighter in her seat. "But obviously that's not the case."

LIZZY GOODMAN is a journalist and the author of "Meet Me in the Bathroom," an oral history of music in New York City from 2001-11. She last wrote about the musician Kacey Musgraves.

For Megan Rapinoe, Boldness in the Spotlight Is Nothing New

BY JERÉ LONGMAN | JUNE 27, 2019

PARIS — The interview room was packed with reporters and television cameras. Fox Sports went live with a telecast, as if it were covering a presidential news conference. In an indirect way, it was.

Then Megan Rapinoe, the star forward for the United States women's soccer team and a social activist, stood her ground. At a regularly scheduled news conference for the team on Thursday, she reiterated that she would refuse to visit the White House if the Americans won the Women's World Cup, regardless of President Trump's criticism of her via Twitter on Wednesday.

That move probably didn't surprise anyone. It is difficult to imagine an athlete who appears more assured in her views and comfortable in the spotlight than Ms. Rapinoe. She has, after all, dyed her hair lavender for the tournament, a sign of her willingness to stand out.

Recently, she became the first openly gay athlete to appear in the Sports Illustrated swimsuit issue. She and her partner, the basketball star Sue Bird, last year became the first gay couple to be featured in ESPN's Body Issue, in which athletes pose without their clothes.

Ms. Rapinoe has led the way in the women's national team's lawsuit against U.S. Soccer, accusing the federation of gender discrimination. She has referred to herself as "a walking protest" of the Trump administration. On the field and off, she has relished the big stage and has sought to use the public platform provided by the success of the national team to advance both women's soccer and broader social issues.

"If you want to be in this profession, it's best to embrace those big moments," Ms. Rapinoe said Thursday. "That's where all the goods are."

In a statement before the news conference — held to discuss Friday's much-anticipated quarterfinal match in Paris between the World

Cup's two favorites, the United States and France — Ms. Rapinoe apologized for having used an obscenity when dismissing the idea of a White House visit. That comment came in a videotaped interview with the soccer magazine 8 by 8 earlier this year.

She even doubled down on Thursday, suggesting that she would encourage her teammates not to visit the White House, either. She said she did not want a decades-long fight for equality and inclusivity by the American team to be "co-opted by an administration that doesn't feel the same way and doesn't fight for the same things that we fight for."

Ms. Rapinoe did not directly address Mr. Trump's criticism of her, in which he wrote on Twitter that she "should never disrespect our country, the White House or our flag."

He also wrote: "I am a big fan of the American Team, and Women's Soccer, but Megan should WIN first before she TALKS! Finish the job!"

Ms. Rapinoe, who will be 34 next week, was asked Thursday whether her jousting with Mr. Trump might distract her team at such an important moment in the World Cup, or destabilize the American locker room. She said emphatically that it would not. "I think, if anything, it just fires everybody up a little more," she said.

Ms. Rapinoe has been heavily influenced as an athlete and as an activist by an older brother, Brian, who is 38. When Ms. Rapinoe and her twin, Rachael, were growing up in Redding, Calif., it was their brother who led them into soccer and vigorously challenged them in two-on-one pickup basketball games, instilling in the sisters an unrelenting approach.

In his adult life, Brian Rapinoe has struggled with drug addiction, and both he and Megan have spoken openly of his issues. On Thursday, Ms. Rapinoe acknowledged that her brother's struggles had influenced her social conscience, her views on drug reform and her desire to help protect society's most vulnerable people.

Brian Rapinoe has been in and out of jail for a series of drug-related crimes. According to the California Department of Corrections, he is in custody in a community re-entry program in San Diego and will be eligible for parole in August.

Ms. Rapinoe said she had come to realize that those incarcerated for drug addictions were "just normal people; they're your brothers and your friends and your family." In influencing her sense of social justice, she said, her brother's story "has a lot of ramifications outside of drug abuse."

Most notably, Ms. Rapinoe began kneeling during the national anthem in 2016 to protest systemic racism and police violence in solidarity with Colin Kaepernick, then the San Francisco 49ers quarterback. U.S. Soccer later began requiring players to "stand respectfully."

Now Ms. Rapinoe stands for the anthem but does not sing or place her hand over her heart. On Thursday, she declined to detail exactly what her protest entails. But earlier this month, Ms. Rapinoe told Lizzy Goodman for a story in The New York Times Magazine that her involvement in social issues reflected the work of movements like Time's Up, #MeToo, Black Lives Matter and L.G.B.T.Q. advocacy.

"To me, it's literally all the same, insofar as I want people to respect who I am, what I am — being gay, being a woman, being a professional athlete, whatever," Ms. Rapinoe said in the article. "That is the exact same thing as what Colin did."

She added: "What kind of person do you want to be for yourself, but also in the larger context of the country and in the world?"

Ms. Rapinoe's breakout occurred during the 2011 World Cup, when she scored a goal against Colombia, grabbed an on-field microphone and began singing Bruce Springsteen's "Born in the U.S.A."

In that same tournament, she made one of the greatest plays in the history of American soccer, lofting a crossing pass to Abby Wambach for a headed goal in the 122nd minute of an eventual victory in a penalty shootout against Brazil.

In the next match, Ms. Rapinoe came off the bench to deliver two assists in a semifinal victory over France. Afterward, she said blithely,

Ms. Rapinoe scored both American goals in the round of 16 win over Spain on Monday.

"I believe I'm a fantastic player, and I try to go out there and do those things."

Jill Ellis, the U.S. coach, has long agreed with that assessment. She said Thursday she was not worried about any increased pressure on the American women, noting that they thrived under pressure.

"I think we all support Megan," Ms. Ellis added. "She knows that."

Ms. Rapinoe also appears to have the support of FIFA, soccer's world governing body. FIFA has historically been lacking in support for women's soccer, but at Friday's match and at other quarterfinal games it plans to campaign publicly for inclusivity and against discrimination of any type.

Ms. Rapinoe was not always so comfortable in the spotlight.

In middle school, Ms. Rapinoe told Yahoo Sports in May, she felt "lost" and "really alone." But she began to flourish once she started understanding her sexuality, her twin sister told Yahoo.

"Maybe part of the reason she was quiet growing up was because she felt a little different," Rachael Rapinoe said. "She didn't quite feel comfortable in her skin. But once she realized who she was and why she felt the way she felt," that's when "she found strength in her voice."

On a national team that, for two decades, has been publicly standing against what it considers inequalities in pay, travel and playing conditions, Ms. Rapinoe's assertiveness has helped give broad, fearless license to her teammates to also demand equitable treatment and social justice.

She spoke Thursday, as she often has, of using the platform of soccer "for good and for leaving the game in a better place, and hopefully the world in a better place."

Julie Foudy, a former captain of the national team and a two-time World Cup winner, said of Ms. Rapinoe and her teammates: "In a way that I have never seen before, this team seems to unapologetically own their voice. It's O.K. to be confident. I no longer need to apologize for saying I want to win. I don't need to say I'm sorry because I'm competitive."

Ms. Foudy added: "I haven't heard that before in such a way, across the board. Maybe that's because you have examples like Megan, who does it so authentically."

SUSAN BEACHY contributed reporting from New York.

CHAPTER 4

L.G.B.T.Q. Athletes Break the Silence

Because athletic ideals are often tied to social expectations of gender, professional sports have progressed more slowly in accepting L.G.B.T.Q. players. Previously, athletes who publicly expressed their sexuality or gender identity have risked public support of their careers. But recent years have shown more acceptance. Many prominent athletes have "come out" and in the process inspired other L.G.B.T.Q. athletes. However, the stories in this chapter show the daily struggle many athletes face to simply live as their full selves.

A Pioneer, Reluctantly

BY GREG BISHOP | MAY 10, 2013

SCHAUMBURG, ILL. — Fallon Fox climbed inside the steel cage, past the sign that read "The Beating Will Continue," and onto a black mat. She followed right jabs with left hooks and kicks flung at imaginary kneecaps, safe, if only for a moment, from the questions and insults and the suffocating fame that descended overnight.

Inside the cage, Fox was free.

Outside, she was caged.

The past month had plunged Fox back into depression, after she became the first openly transgender athlete in mixed martial arts and the most prominent in a professional sport since the tennis player Renée Richards in the 1970s. Fox did not control the timing of the revelation, which came in a Sports Illustrated article, and could not control the backlash that resulted, the harsh words from Hulk Hogan, the hateful comments of the fighter Matt Mitrione, the confusion voiced by the Ultimate Fighting Championship women's champion Ronda Rousey.

In April, Fox watched the basketball players Brittney Griner and Jason Collins tell the world they were gay and receive what seemed like overwhelming public support. Collins's announcement, Fox wrote in an e-mail, left her "proud and happy" and a "tad bit envious." That was more like what she had expected for her experience, and she lingered on the topic of reporters who dug into her fighting licenses and personal background, who asked what has become her story's fundamental question: should someone born a man be allowed to fight women?

At a restaurant in the Chicago suburbs, strangers approached Fox, recognizing her from a recent CNN appearance, and their words, which were supportive, only added to a discomfort that commingles with fear. On one hand, Fox does not want anybody to know where she lives or what her daughter's last name is. And on the other, she has accepted this ambassadorship, even if it means she is less a sports pioneer than a symbol to be analyzed and debated, thrust into a spotlight that singes her psyche.

"I want the public to know how it feels, the fear of being scrutinized, of being outed," Fox said. "The fear of what happens when you come out and the media puts you under a microscope. It's crippling. You get lost."

That was most apparent at a Panda Express restaurant last month near her training center, where Fox, 37, fought back tears as she tried to explain what she did not yet understand. She wanted her life back, but her recent declaration rendered that impossible and resurrected emotions she had for years tried to bury along with her past.

As music played softly in the background, a soothing blend of harps and whistles and violins, Fox pulled her green hat low over her eyes. "I don't even want to talk about it, really," she said. "I don't want to. I never set out to do this. But I have to."

Fallon Fox had gender reassignment surgery in 2006. She fights against women, and her record is 2-0.

She continued, "I'll stand here, for my community, because I have no other choice."

Her story, no matter how much she wanted to command it, was no longer her own.

FINDING HERSELF AND A PURPOSE

Fallon Fox was born Boyd Burton, the middle of three children, in a conservative, religious, mixed-race household in Ohio. Her father, also Boyd Burton, compiled a long list of arrests and citations from Toledo Municipal Court, including one for failing to restrain a "vicious dog" and another for domestic violence. (Fox declined to discuss this part of her childhood, or her relationship with her family now.)

The family attended church service every Sunday and most Mondays and Wednesdays. Fox said they regularly spoke in tongues. They believed they could heal through prayer and "cure" lesbians and gays. Sometimes, Fox borrowed clothes from her mother's and sister's closets when no one was around.

Art gave Fox an avenue through which to explore the larger world, beyond Ohio, away from church. She spent hours in her room, drawing and painting and studying comic books and anime. Jim Lee was her favorite artist, his work for Marvel Comics crisp and detailed. She appreciated the new worlds he created.

Fox often pictured herself in New York City, in a loft downtown, an easel in the corner, her artist apron on. When she told her parents of her plans, they told her she would find the devil there.

She first heard the word "transgender" when she was 17, on daytime television, and realized that there was a term for what she had been feeling inside. As Boyd Burton, she took a year off after high school, married and had a daughter. She said she married because of the pregnancy. She did not divorce her wife until 2007, according to public records, after she had become Fallon Fox. She served four years in the Navy. She went to technical college and enrolled at the University of Toledo.

All the while, she felt trapped, confined, and she started to research gender dysphoria. She read about other transsexuals who waited years, even decades, to transition, about how it became harder over time. Then her hair started to fall out.

"Looking in the mirror, it was destroying me," Fox said, before pausing to compose herself.

To tell this part of her story was difficult because it is not easily understood and would inevitably be translated into the cookie-cutter version of her life. She took a deep breath and dived back into her tale: to the two years she drove an 18-wheeler across the country, saving money and researching transitions and taking hormones in "this in-between stage"; to the gender reassignment surgery in Thailand in 2006.

Upon her return, the odyssey continued, the search for meaning, for her place in the larger world, more heightened than before. She drove a school bus and worked as a diesel truck mechanic. She lifted weights and studied jujitsu and stumbled across a video on the

Internet of Megumi Fujii, a female mixed martial artist. She consumed videos of Fujii and her opponents for days on end.

"It was like, wow, women are fighting," Fox said. "I remembered watching the first U.F.C. You couldn't get it on TV. They were doing it bare knuckles. No gloves. I wanted to do that."

In 2010, Fox landed at Midwest Training Center here, owned by Alex Trujillo and home over the years to hundreds of M.M.A. fighters of every ethnicity and social status. One of Fox's training partners is a 42-year-old pediatrician with a 2-0 record, like Fox's. Others have advanced to the U.F.C., the sport's highest level; Fox fights at a lower level.

The first time Trujillo trained Fox, he believed she could fight professionally. He said "it became very quickly very hard to find opponents who would fight her." She turned pro in 2011, complete with a nickname, the Queen of Swords. Before bouts, she pretended to unsheathe a sword, and in victory, she replaced it.

Her first fight paid less than $700, and expenses, but it provided Fox with far more than monetary gain. The gym became her home, the fighters her replacement family, the cage the place far removed from the relatives who shunned her and the world that did not understand her. At the gym, she could control what happened, and she showed up twice a day almost every day, for years. Her absences were notable, the trainer Dan Finnegan said, because there were so few.

As Fox watched video of her first fight on her cellphone recently, her eyes danced, and she said: "There's the triangle. Then I punch her in the face. Into arm bar. She's already out."

That escape never proved more than temporary. As Fox left the gym each day, her secret resurfaced, always there, always looming, and she agonized over whether "somebody would say something" or "somebody from my past would recognize me." She felt certain she would be forced to reveal her transgender status at some point.

Last August, she met with the National Center for Lesbian Rights, a legal group that has been active in sports issues. Helen Carroll, the director of the center's sports project, walked Fox through potential

strategies for coming out. Fox preferred to keep private her medical history, to reveal it to commissions when it came to licensing but not to opponents or the public. That seemed unrealistic, even to her, and yet she held out hope that she could control her announcement, her medical records and her career.

Then a reporter called.

VITRIOL AND SUPPORT

Prompted by that inquiry, Fox took her story to Sports Illustrated. In that instant, her life changed, far more than she initially expected. The article came out. The Web site TMZ published photographs from a former girlfriend of Fox as Boyd Burton. CNN called. Doctors sought medical records. Commissions reviewed applications for her to fight.

Joe Smith, an assistant trainer and gym manager at Midwest Training Center, patrolled mixed martial arts message boards, even as he implored Fox not to. What he found there turned his stomach. He wondered how his own fighters would react to Fox.

Fox showed up, day after day, same as always, but now her story was already all over the Internet, her face on television. She was no longer just a mixed martial artist, no longer simply Fallon Fox. She was the first transgender M.M.A. fighter, and she felt as if she walked around underneath a giant, blinking neon sign announcing that to the world.

The topic was avoided at the gym. No one voiced complaints. Her coaches and trainers said they knew little of her background before the article. They decided that if states would license Fox to fight women, they would train her to do the same. And if there were problems with her licenses, she would be welcome at the gym anyway.

In her role at the National Center for Lesbian Rights, Carroll has worked with 30 to 40 transgender athletes. Those who declared themselves publicly could count on vitriol and support. They faced many of the same questions and criticisms that Richards, the tennis player, did decades earlier when she went to court to overturn the United States Tennis Association's attempts to prevent her from playing in women's events at the United States Open.

"It has been harsher for transgender athletes," Carroll said.

"There has been more public education and acceptance around L.G.B.," she said, referring to lesbian, gay and bisexual issues. She added: "Gay marriage has really brought that up front and personal to all people. There's not that base of knowledge in the general public for transsexuals."

Fox's experience embodied that. First, she became the target of hatred and confusion, the worst of it from Mitrione, who called Fox a "lying, sick, sociopathic, disgusting freak." He was briefly suspended by the U.F.C. and was later denounced by the champion fighter Jon Jones. In the interim, Mitrione's words were rebutted by doctors, who wished to raise awareness and clear up misconceptions about transsexuals.

They pointed to policies enacted by the Association of Boxing Commissions, the International Olympic Committee, the N.C.A.A., and other sports leagues and organizations that have allowed transgender athletes to compete under certain guidelines, like gender reassignment surgery and hormone therapy for a minimum amount of time, usually one or two years.

Dr. Eric Vilain, a medical geneticist and the director of the Institute for Society and Genetics at U.C.L.A., helped formulate some of those policies. He reviewed Fox's medical records and said she "clearly fulfilled all conditions." Rousey, the U.F.C. women's champion, ventured that because Fox went through puberty as a male, she retained greater bone density, an assertion dismissed by doctors.

Fox did what seemed like hundreds of interviews. She answered the kind messages she received on Facebook. She cleared up remaining license issues. But all this clarification and education robbed Fox of her gym time and delayed her next fight. For a month, she hardly ventured to the place where she felt safest.

Lost in the scientific viewpoints — and in the not-so-scientific ones — was Fox herself, not the symbol but the human now on international display. She struggled with that. She still struggles with that. The portions of her story she considered footnotes became headlines, the questions less about whether she could fight and more about whether she should.

Kye Allums sympathized. A friend of Fox's, Allums was the first transsexual to play on an N.C.A.A. Division I women's basketball team. When he came out as a transgender man at George Washington University in 2010, Allums conducted interviews for two hours a day for two weeks straight. This strained his relationship with teammates, who remained supportive but grew tired of the continual barrage of questions. He felt irritated for them. A "lose-win," Allums called it.

Gabrielle Ludwig's first month in public view unfolded in a similarly chaotic fashion, after she came out as a transgender basketball player last season at Mission College in California. Two radio hosts derided her as "it." She received death threats, including against her children.

"I had to come to grips that I would no longer be looked at as a basketball player," she said. "I would be looked at first as a transsexual basketball player. You want to keep your anonymity, but it's gone. You have to embrace it. Fallon has to embrace it. You have to say: 'We're not transvestites. We're not cross-dressers. We are in fact women who were once men.' "

A LIFE IN TRANSITION

Back inside the gym, Fox all but collapsed at the end of another practice, after the treadmill and the heavy bag and the harness drills. Her toenails were painted with purple polish. She wore a black tank top that revealed sculptured biceps and wide shoulders, her frame devoid of fat and muscled at 5 feet 6 inches. Her brown hair fell in curls to her shoulders.

Jay-Z's "99 Problems" played over the sound system as Fox interacted with the other fighters, men with triceps the size of cantaloupes and ears that looked like cauliflowers.

Fox, whose license plate frame reads "I'd rather put you in a chokehold," who says casually, "Getting choked out feels a lot better than getting knocked out," caught the eye of one training partner across the room.

"What are you looking at?" Fox said.

She winked.

The reply came, "Not you."

On this day, Fox worked on her transitions, using jabs and crosses to shoot in close and grapple opponents into submission. She dipped under her trainer Trujillo's punches, shot elbows toward his chin, small transitions amid larger ones.

Here, the cage was real, and the pain was inflicted on someone other than herself. She understood the world here, where there are rules, winners and losers, where hard work nets results, where the only question is whether she can fight.

Fox is competing in the Championship Fighting Alliance featherweight tournament. Her semifinal is scheduled for May 24 in Coral Gables, Fla. Trujillo said he believed Fox would win the tournament and its $20,000 prize, and he said he could envision a time when Fox would be ranked among the top female mixed martial artists in the world, age willing. If only that were her only fight, a matchup with

Father Time, not with bigots and those on the Internet who make death threats and cruel jokes at her expense.

After practice, Fox climbed into her car as she left the gym, her hat back on, her eyes sullen, perhaps the product of the public glare. She drove home, where one side of her house was boarded up from a recent fire, where two swords rested atop a shelf that held the books from the "Twilight" series and the Bible.

She said she loved to fight because she could do so at an elite level, because she could define herself by accomplishments instead of by sexual identity, because she loved to train, because "it does make me feel safe." She was later asked if she feared for her safety or that of her daughter, and she snapped back not to ask her that again.

She paused for 30, 40, 50 seconds. Tears came to her eyes.

She continued: "The danger is you never know if people are actually saying what they mean. I've learned you never know how someone will react. I've lost relationships over it."

In an e-mail late last month, Fox said she was "feeling better lately" and "feeling positive" and had been temporarily depressed. Thus continued her latest transition, from a fighter with a secret to a symbol without privacy, from someone who sought control to someone who lost it when she told her story to the world. There is no turning back now, no way to change the narrative.

Only, she hopes, acceptance. For her, certainly. And from her, too.

JACK BEGG contributed research.

N.F.L. Prospect Michael Sam Proudly Says What Teammates Knew: He's Gay

BY JOHN BRANCH | FEB. 9, 2014

COACHES AT THE University of Missouri divided players into small groups at a preseason football practice last year for a team-building exercise. One by one, players were asked to talk about themselves — where they grew up, why they chose Missouri and what others might not know about them.

As Michael Sam, a defensive lineman, began to speak, he balled up a piece of paper in his hands. "I'm gay," he said. With that, Mr. Sam set himself on a path to become the first publicly gay player in the National Football League.

"I looked in their eyes, and they just started shaking their heads — like, finally, he came out," Mr. Sam said Sunday in an interview with The New York Times, the first time he had spoken publicly about his sexual orientation.

Mr. Sam, a senior who was listed at 6 feet 2 inches and 260 pounds, had a stellar season as Missouri finished 12-2 and won the Cotton Bowl. He was a first-team all-American and was named the Associated Press defensive player of the year in the Southeastern Conference, widely considered the top league in college football. Teammates voted him Missouri's most valuable player.

Now Mr. Sam enters an uncharted area of the sports landscape. He is making his public declaration before he is drafted, to the potential detriment to his professional career. And he is doing so as he prepares to enter a league with an overtly macho culture, where controversies over homophobia have attracted recent attention.

As the pace of the gay rights movement has accelerated in recent years, the sports industry has changed relatively little for men, with no publicly gay athletes in the N.F.L., the N.B.A., the N.H.L. or Major League Baseball. Against this backdrop, Mr. Sam could become a symbol for the country's gay rights movement or a flash point in a football culture war — or both.

Mr. Sam, 24, is projected to be chosen in the early rounds of the N.F.L. draft in May, ordinarily a path to a prosperous pro career. He said he decided to come out publicly now because he sensed that rumors were circulating.

"I just want to make sure I could tell my story the way I want to tell it," said Mr. Sam, who also spoke with ESPN on Sunday. "I just want to own my truth."

But the N.F.L. presents the potential for unusual challenges. In the past year or so, it has been embroiled in controversies ranging from antigay statements from players to reports that scouts asked at least one prospective player if he liked girls. Recently, Chris Kluwe, a punter, said that he was subject to homophobic language from coaches and pushed out of a job with the Minnesota Vikings because he vocally supported same-sex marriage laws. And last week, Jonathan Vilma, a New Orleans Saints linebacker, said in an interview with NFL Network that he did not want a gay teammate.

"I think he would not be accepted as much as we think he would be accepted," said Mr. Vilma, a 10-year league veteran.

In a statement Sunday night, the league said: "We admire Michael Sam's honesty and courage. Michael is a football player. Any player with ability and determination can succeed in the N.F.L. We look forward to welcoming and supporting Michael Sam in 2014."

At a showcase game for seniors last month, several scouts asked Mr. Sam's agent, Joe Barkett, whether Mr. Sam had a girlfriend or whether Mr. Barkett had seen him with women.

The league, which has a policy prohibiting discrimination based on sexual orientation (among other things), is the largest of the major sports leagues in the United States, with about 1,600 players on rosters at any time during the season. But it has never had a publicly gay player.

Over the decades, some players in the major sports leagues did little to conceal their sexual orientation, but they were not out to the public during their careers. A few players have come out upon retirement, like the N.F.L. player Dave Kopay in the 1970s and the N.B.A. player John Amaechi in 2007, both considered pioneers by many gay people.

Last spring, Jason Collins, a 12-year N.B.A. veteran, mostly as a little-used reserve, came out after the season. A free agent, he has not been signed by another team.

Also last year, Robbie Rogers, a former member of the United States national soccer team who later played professionally in England, revealed that he was gay after he announced his retirement. Encouraged by the supportive response, he resumed his career, playing for the Los Angeles Galaxy of Major League Soccer.

While Mr. Sam's pro prospects are far from certain, several N.F.L. draft forecasters have predicted that he will be chosen in the third round. (Thirty-two players are selected in each round.) Rarely are players who are drafted that high cut by teams; they often become starters, sometimes as rookies.

Between now and the draft, Mr. Sam plans to attend the scouting combine, where players are put through a gantlet of physical and mental tests to judge their readiness for the N.F.L. Mr. Sam might be considered too small for an N.F.L. defensive end, meaning he would have to learn to play as an outside linebacker. But it is reasonable for Mr. Sam to wonder what sort of effect — positive or negative — his declaration will have on his prospects.

"I'm not naïve," Mr. Sam said. "I know this is a huge deal and I know how important this is. But my role as of right now is to train for the combine and play in the N.F.L."

Mr. Sam graduated from Missouri in December, the only member of his family to attend college. He grew up in Hitchcock, Tex., about 40 miles southeast of Houston, the seventh of eight children of JoAnn and Michael Sam. It was a difficult childhood; three of his siblings have died, and two brothers are in prison, Mr. Sam said. He was raised mostly by his mother, and he spent some years with another family. All have been supportive of his coming out, he said.

Mr. Sam said he began to wonder if he was gay in his early teens, though he had a girlfriend in high school. It was after he arrived at Missouri in 2009 that he realized for certain that he was gay. Teammates increasingly suspected as much, and some knew that he dated a man on the university's swim team, but it never prevented Mr. Sam from being one of the most popular players on the team. He was known for his intensity on the field and his booming voice off it.

"When I first met him, you could be downstairs and you could hear Mike all the way on the second floor of the dorms," said receiver L'Damian Washington, who met Mr. Sam on a recruiting trip and quickly became a close friend. "He's just a loud guy. Everybody knows when Michael Sam is in the building."

Mr. Sam came out to two of his friends on the team, Mr. Washington and Marvin Foster, about a year ago. It was not a huge surprise. Mr. Washington was with Mr. Sam when Mr. Sam said he needed to go pick up a friend. He told Mr. Washington that the friend was gay and asked Mr. Washington if that would bother him. Mr. Washington said no, and Mr. Sam came out to him.

"Michael is a great example of just how important it is to be respectful of others," Missouri's football coach, Gary Pinkel, said in a statement released Sunday night. "He's taught a lot of people here firsthand that it doesn't matter what your background is, or your personal orientation, we're all on the same team and we all support each other."

Last April, the Missouri athletic administration held diversity seminars for all athletes, part of the You Can Play project, focused largely on lesbian, gay, bisexual and transgender issues. Mr. Sam was one of several athletes to approach Pat Ivey, the associate athletic director for athletic performance, to compliment him for the lesson. But Mr. Sam was the most effusive, Mr. Ivey said, as if trying to tell Mr. Ivey something.

"When Mike finished the conversation, he said, 'Coach, I know I can play,' " Mr. Ivey recalled. "And we kind of had an understanding of each other, that this wasn't just him saying, 'Good job.' This was him saying: 'Coach, I'm involved in it. I'm a part of what we just discussed.' "

During practices in August, Missouri mixed players from different position groups on the team and put them into small meetings of 8 or 10. Mr. Washington, a wide receiver, happened to be in the same group as Mr. Sam.

"I knew that something was about to come because of the way he was balling up the paper in his hands," Mr. Washington said. "He kept rolling it up. So I kind of knew something was coming, but I didn't think it was that."

Mr. Sam was a senior and a longtime friend to other team leaders. Younger players looked up to him. But on a team with about 100 players, of different backgrounds and beliefs, there was varying discomfort.

"I think there were, just like in society, there are people who don't understand, and don't want to understand, and aren't accepting," Mr. Ivey said. "And we worked through those issues."

Mr. Sam played down any repercussions, saying he had the full support of teammates, coaches and administrators. One teammate, he said, accompanied him to a gay pride event in St. Louis last summer, and others went with him to gay bars.

"Some people actually just couldn't believe I was actually gay," Mr. Sam said. "But I never had a problem with my teammates. Some of my coaches were worried, but there was never an issue."

One lingering issue, Mr. Washington said, was trying to get players to change casual language in the locker room. Loosely lobbed homophobic remarks suddenly had a specific sting.

Mr. Sam played down that, too. For him, coming out to his team was a positive step, on a path that seems as if it will lead to the N.F.L.

"Once I became official to my teammates, I knew who I was," Mr. Sam said. "I knew that I was gay. And I knew that I was Michael Sam, who's a Mizzou football player who happens to be gay. I was so proud of myself and I just didn't care who knew. If someone on the street

would have asked me, 'Hey, Mike, I heard you were gay; is that true?'
I would have said yes."

No one asked.

"I guess they don't want to ask a 6-3, 260-pound defensive lineman
if he was gay or not," Mr. Sam said. And he laughed.

Athlete to Activist: How a Public Coming Out Shaped a Young Football Player's Life

BY DAN LEVIN | DEC. 1, 2018

In a very public speech last year, Jake Bain, now a college athlete, became an accidental activist determined to change the national conversation about gay teenagers.

TERRE HAUTE, IND. — Jake Bain's dorm room is a typical college crash pad, right down to the rumpled bedsheets and hampers overflowing with dirty laundry. Less common, for a space shared by two Division I football players, is the photo collage taped above his bed: Jake and his boyfriend kissing at their high school graduation; a romantic selfie of Jake resting his head on his boyfriend's shoulder; the young couple holding hands at sunset.

The Indiana State University athlete's very public coming out last fall — during a 13-minute speech inside an auditorium to his entire Missouri high school — was an act that continues to shape his life in ways he could not have imagined back then.

"If a future Division 1 football player can be openly gay," Jake, at the time the popular square-jawed captain of the John Burroughs high school football team, said to those who had assembled, "then so can you."

With that speech, in which he implored his classmates to be themselves, Jake became an accidental activist determined to change the national conversation about gay youths. His sharpest weapon? Social media, where he receives as many as 50 messages a week from as far away as Australia and from teenagers in countries where it is illegal to be gay.

His life, as it unfolds on the football field and before nearly 13,500 Instagram followers, has inspired many others to come out, their own stories often left in comments on his page. It also has been the focus

Jake Bain, a freshman at Indiana State University, keeps a photo of himself and his boyfriend in his dorm room.

of taunts and protests, as recently as this month. But Jake's narrative, at turns harrowing and triumphant, is playing out in heartland towns and conservative state universities across the country, as gay and transgender teenagers emboldened by the power of social media are stepping into the limelight and demanding acceptance and equality.

"Show everyone that it is O.K. to be who you want to be, to love who you want to love," Jake said in the speech that elicited a standing ovation, wide news media coverage and its own hashtag, #StandWithJake. "Nothing ever changes without people showing that it is O.K. to be different."

Declaring his difference, though, came at a painful cost. He received anonymous and hateful texts. Ugly insults piled up on Instagram and on the high school football field, with opponents shouting slurs during games. And members of the virulently homophobic Westboro Baptist Church traveled to Ladue, Mo., to picket outside his high school.

In the end, Indiana State University offered him a full scholarship to play football, and gay rights activists joined friends and strangers at a counterprotest that vastly outnumbered those from the Westboro group. Admiring messages began to pour into his social media accounts, eventually exceeding the taunts. And last spring, he attended his senior prom with his boyfriend, both of them wearing tuxedos with matching pink bow ties.

Still, Jake and others like him face formidable headwinds from activists invigorated by the Trump administration's efforts to roll back transgender and gay rights and a Supreme Court newly dominated by conservatives. Three months ago, the parents of a Division 1 cross-country and track runner on a partial athletic scholarship to Canisius College in Buffalo told her that they would no longer support her after they found photos of her and her girlfriend online. More than 2,400 people donated money to a GoFundMe account, approved by the NCAA, raising nearly $100,000 for Emily Scheck, a sophomore, so that she could stay in school. And earlier this month, the Westboro Baptist Church targeted Jake again, this time on the campus of Western Illinois University as that school's football team played against Indiana State in their final game of the season. And again, counterprotesters significantly outnumbered them, with more than 100 of Jake's supporters to the five or so Westboro members.

At 19, Jake has already accomplished a lot. In high school, he scored 41 touchdowns, rushed more than 3,400 yards, led his team to a district championship and one state championship, and was named offensive player of the year for the state of Missouri.

Jake was born and raised in St. Louis, the son of a white mother and black father. They divorced when he was 2, but football was always part of his family. His grandfather was the head football coach at his high school for more than three decades, and his two older brothers also played the sport there.

As he was growing up, America was changing around him. When Michael Sam, an All-American defensive lineman from the University of Missouri, came out publicly in 2014, Jake's football coach shared the news as an opportunity to tell his players that he would always have their backs, regardless of their sexuality.

"I was really young when I heard that speech, but I thought if I ever come out, he'd be a good person to talk to," recalled Jake, who is thinking of becoming a clinical psychologist for teenagers and their families.

But he continued to struggle with his sexuality for years, telling himself it was just a phase. "Had I not have been an athlete, I think I would have come out a lot sooner," he said. Instead, he hid behind the persona of a stereotypical jock. He dated girls and began going to therapy and taking antidepressants.

"I spent so long acting overly macho, trying to mask who I was, knowing I was living a lie," he said.

In the summer before his junior year, his secret weighing on him, he quietly told a few close friends, then his family, his coach and teammates. Their support gave him the courage to ask out a red-haired, rosy-cheeked varsity swimmer named Hunter Sigmund, who is now a freshman at the University of North Carolina.

They are still a couple, despite the nearly 700 miles between them. Their shared struggle of coming-of-age as young gay men has motivated Jake to stand up for lesbian, gay, bisexual and transgender rights.

Across the country, a record seven current college football players are openly gay or bisexual, according to Outsports, a website that showcases L.G.B.T. athletes. Yet Jake almost failed to make that roster, and his experience may help explain why so few college football players are out. When he was a sophomore, Jake was named Class 3 offensive player of the year in Missouri, the same year his high school won the state title. The following season he became the team captain. College coaches had flocked to Ladue to watch him play.

"After I came out," he said, "everything kind of went radio silent."

He said he tried reaching out to the coaches but never heard back, and when his own coach sought to get answers, he was told they had decided to go in a different direction.

Indiana State, though, still wanted him to play. During a campus visit in the summer of 2017, he met with the head coach, Curt Mallory, accompanied by his mother and grandparents. "I told him I'm openly gay and that before I committed, I needed to know if that was an issue," he recalled. Mr. Mallory told him he would do everything in his power to make sure Jake was accepted.

"We just treat him like everybody else," Mr. Mallory said in an interview. "He fit right in. I never thought twice about it."

The traumatic ordeal of publicly coming out made it easier for Jake to be open with his teammates. He sent his future roommate his Instagram profile, which spotlights a mosaic of romantic photos, football game snapshots and gay pride flags. He told the rest of the team over a group chat.

"Jake wrote 'hey guys I'm gay,' " said Chris Childers, 18, a running back from Chicago. "We didn't believe it at first. It was definitely new for me, but nothing about him being gay will ever affect us being friends or teammates."

A redshirt this year, like most freshman players on his team, Jake appeared in four games, and recently switched from defense to wide receiver. Over the season, which ended after the team's victory against Western Illinois, he befriended several of his teammates. They bonded during grueling football practices and over nachos at Applebee's, where Jake didn't hesitate to share stories about his boyfriend.

Still, in some ways his sexuality has made him an outsider in the testosterone-infused world of college football and in the middle of conservative Indiana. He avoided showering with his teammates out of concern for what they might think, and he kept his gay pride tees on a shelf and quit wearing his rainbow-splashed "love is love" hat on campus because, he said, "you get stared at."

He won't take off two bracelets, though, a rainbow one he got on the day of the first Westboro protest, and geographic coordinates engraved in metal that mark the exact location where he and Hunter officially became a couple. Taking them off, he said, would make him feel like he is hiding a part of himself, and that would be "hypocritical."

Counterprotesters supporting Jake during the demonstration outside of Western Illinois University.

For now, Jake said he has found solace in helping the closeted gay teenagers who contact him on Instagram.

In April, he received a message from a closeted Irish teenager who described the relentless bullying he experienced at his Catholic all-boys school. "I just admire your bravery and I need someone to guide me on what to do," the boy wrote.

Jake offered some advice and months later, he received a new message: "Jake, one week ago I came out to my family," wrote the boy, who explained that he had shared Jake's story with his religious parents, which ultimately helped them accept him for who he is.

"Thank you so much," the boy wrote. "You were the reason I decided to come out."

DAN LEVIN covers American youth for the National Desk. He was a foreign correspondent covering Canada from 2016 until 2018.

Sprinter Dutee Chand Becomes India's First Openly Gay Athlete

BY MIKE IVES | **MAY 20, 2019**

A CHAMPION SPRINTER with village roots has become India's first openly gay professional athlete, less than a year after the country's top court overturned a longstanding ban on gay sex.

A member of India's national track and field team, Dutee Chand, 23, was previously known for fighting for the right to race against other women. She has hyperandrogenism, a condition that naturally produces high testosterone levels, and which in 2014 prompted the sport's governing body to ban her from competition. The decision was reversed a year later after she challenged it in court.

On Sunday, Ms. Chand was quoted by an Indian newspaper as saying that she was in a same-sex relationship with a woman from her rural village in eastern India. She said she was inspired to go public after September's ruling by the Indian Supreme Court that unanimously struck down a colonial-era ban on consensual gay sex.

"I have always believed that everyone should have the freedom to love," Ms. Chand said in an interview with The Sunday Express. "There is no greater emotion than love and it should not be denied."

Many Indians are socially conservative, and go to great lengths to arrange marriages with the right families or castes. Countless gay people there have been shunned by their parents and persecuted by society, and few think that a same-sex marriage law is on the near horizon.

Ms. Chand said in the interview that she hoped to settle down with her partner sometime after the upcoming World Championships and the Olympic Games in Tokyo. She declined to name her partner, saying that she did not want her to become the object of undue attention.

Ms. Chand's announcement — which came amid news that the country's conservative prime minister, Narendra Modi, appeared headed for re-election — prompted jubilant responses from her long-time supporters.

"I have always been proud of @DuteeChand and admired her courage," Payoshni Mitra, an Indian researcher who has advocated on behalf of Ms. Chand and other intersex athletes, said on Twitter.

"It is not easy to come out in certain societies," Ms. Mitra added. "This is huge for India!"

Adille J. Sumariwalla, the president of the Athletics Federation of India, described Ms. Chand's announcement as a personal matter that the federation "has nothing to do with."

"We support our athletes in every way to perform better without getting into their personal lives and totally respect their privacy," he said in an email on Monday.

Ms. Chand was raised in Gopalpur, a village in the eastern Indian state of Odisha, by illiterate parents who earned less than $8 a week as weavers. Her legal fight for the right to race against other women — at a moment when biology is no longer seen as the sole determinant of gender — has been closely watched as a bellwether of how sports bodies should set boundaries between male and female competitors.

The dispute began in 2014, when the Athletics Federation of India gave Ms. Chand an ultrasound and told the government that it had "definite doubts" about her gender.

Further tests showed that Ms. Chand's natural testosterone levels were above what track and field's governing body, the International Association of Athletics Federations, deemed acceptable at the time for female competitors. Officials banned Ms. Chand from competition for a year, and said she could return to the Indian national team only if she medically reduced her testosterone level.

But Ms. Chand refused and filed a case at the Swiss-based Court of Arbitration for Sport, a kind of Supreme Court for international sports, arguing that the I.A.A.F.'s testosterone policy was discriminatory. Many saw the rule as yet another example of international sports organizations policing women for having "masculine" qualities.

In 2015, a three-judge panel in the case struck down the I.A.A.F.'s rule, saying that the exact role natural testosterone plays in athleticism remained unknown. Ms. Chand promptly returned to competition, and last year won silver medals at the Asian Games in the 100-meter and 200-meter races.

But a new I.A.A.F. rule requires female athletes who have male-patterned chromosomes to regulate their hormone levels if they wish to compete in middle-distance races.

In May, the Court of Arbitration for Sport dismissed an appeal against that rule by Caster Semenya, a two-time Olympic champion runner from South Africa.

Ms. Semenya had called the rule, which went into effect this month, "discriminatory, irrational, unjustifiable." But the court said that while she had "done nothing whatsoever to warrant any personal criticism," the rule was necessary to maintain fair competition in female athletics.

Ms. Chand, who had supported Ms. Semenya's appeal, criticized the rule.

"This is a wrong policy of the I.A.A.F. and whatever reason they are giving, it is wrong," she was quoted as saying at the time.

At World Cup, U.S. Team's Pride Is Felt by Others, Too

BY ANDREW KEH | JUNE 29, 2019

The United States women's team has been a source of inspiration to L.G.B.T. soccer players in France, who say they do not enjoy the same freedom to be themselves.

PARIS — Like many French fans at the Parc des Princes stadium on Friday night, Marine Rome was heartbroken as her team spiraled out of the World Cup in a quarterfinal matchup against the United States.

But for her, at least, there was some consolation.

Rome, 32, is the co-president of Les Dégommeuses, an amateur soccer team in Paris primarily made up of lesbian and transgender players. For many soccer fans, Friday's game exposed the gap in talent that remains between the French and American teams. But to Rome and others in France's L.G.B.T. community, the juxtaposition highlighted a different gulf: one in inclusion, in diversity.

In the American players, Rome observed a walking, running, kicking representation of L.G.B.T. pride and acceptance — a kind she and many others said was still lacking in France.

"In France, with the idea of universalism and equality, when you're a minority you're supposed to be silent, because they say we're all the same, even though we're not," Rome said. "I think that's the main difference with the U.S."

The difference, she said, felt stark. Five members of the American team and the coach, Jill Ellis, are publicly out, and the team as a whole has worked in recent years to engage with L.G.B.T. communities in the United States. One of the viral moments of the team's 2015 World Cup championship was striker Abby Wambach's kissing her wife after the final only a week after the United States Supreme Court had legalized gay marriage.

Frederique Gouy, a member of Les Dégommeuses, with her girlfriend, Amandine Denise, during last week's tournament. "It feels like family because I don't have one," one player said of the team.

Such things are nearly unheard-of in France, many people in the French sports community said. Marinette Pichon, the career goals leader for the French team, said in an interview that gay players in her country would not dare come out publicly.

"There is still homophobia in French football today," said Pichon, who is considered the only player in the country to ever publicly identify as gay.

Attitudes toward L.G.B.T. rights vary widely among the nations involved in the World Cup this summer, and the United States is not the only team that has been so openly welcoming to gay players. But it has the highest profile.

After the game on Friday, American winger Megan Rapinoe was asked about playing during Pride Month, and on a weekend when many cities around the world were holding their annual Pride events.

"Go gays!" said Rapinoe, who scored two goals on Friday. "You can't win a championship without gays on your team. It's never been done before. That's science right there."

Rapinoe soon had everyone around her laughing.

"To be gay and fabulous during Pride Month and the World Cup is nice," she said.

Then she smoothly transitioned back to answering questions about soccer.

The moment, in Rome's view, embodied everything a French player could not do, and the reason she and many of the 20 members of Les Dégommeuses, a nickname that translates roughly as the Smashers, at the stadium on Friday were cheering for players on both teams.

The organization, created in 2012, has about 100 players and two primary aims: to create a safe space — at weekly practices and games in Paris — for people who might otherwise be excluded from French soccer culture, and to press for greater inclusivity in the country's sports landscape.

"It feels like family because I don't have one," said Marko, a lesbian who is a refugee from Chechnya, where the government has arrested people simply for being gay. Marko asked that her full name be withheld for safety reasons. "My only family is Les Dégommeuses."

Going back to the early 20th century, sports have provided a haven and positive space for many lesbians, according to Susan Cahn, a professor of gender and sexuality in sports at the University at Buffalo. The playing field offered an environment, she said, where many sensibilities — physical contact, intensity, aggression, muscularity — can take on positive connotations.

Over time a stereotype developed that good female athletes must surely be lesbian, leading organizations to an overcorrection, a sort of hyper-feminization that academics refer to as "the feminine apologetic." Many players felt forced to erase their identity.

The importance of a team like the United States, then, is not only

Marine Rome, 32, is the co-president of Les Dégommeuses.

in seeing straight and gay players side by side, but also debunking notions of what a lesbian player might look like.

"The fact that these women are out, explicitly or casually, lets people know that lesbians are in sports, and they come in all shapes and sizes," Cahn said.

In France, the problem can be deceptively acute. Rome cringed as she recalled a marketing campaign unveiled by the French soccer federation some years ago that reductively revolved around high heels, glitter and the color pink. (She said the team's marketing promoting the team has improved significantly around this World Cup.)

She pointed to more subtle things, too. In December, Jess Fishlock, a Welsh midfielder playing at the time for the French club Olympique Lyonnais received one of Britain's highest civilian honors for her services to women's soccer and the L.G.B.T. community. But the club's news release about the honor, Rome noted, stated only that the award had been for her commitment to "various causes."

"In France, you can't be yourself, you have to hide," said Frédérique Gouy, 34, a civil engineer from Paris who came out four years ago and joined Les Dégommeuses shortly afterward. "It's a big difference from the United States and many other teams at this World Cup. We are still at the beginning of the fight."

Pichon, 43, who scored 81 goals in 12 years playing for France, said she experienced the situation in French soccer firsthand.

"You don't dare to say that you are homosexual in the locker room because you fear the consequences on the image of your team, of your club, but also on yourself," Pichon said. "You may well become a punching bag for other players. I know many people who refused to come out because they feared the consequences."

Pichon saw something different in two stints playing professionally in the United States. She said the American approach to welcoming and integrating L.G.B.T. players into their women's teams was "the approach we should work toward in France." And she said she was amazed to see television commercials and marketing content in the United States that featured positive images of gay people.

Pichon did not broadcast her sexual orientation during her playing career. She said she was not desperate for anyone's acceptance. But many say there are positive effects when professional athletes feel personally comfortable enough to express themselves that way.

Rome, for instance, recalled watching the French tennis player Amélie Mauresmo come out as gay 20 years ago. Rome was 12 and was having trouble articulating why she felt she was different than her peers.

"I realized, thanks to her, that I was not a monster, basically," Rome said.

Being honest to oneself can have an effect on performance, activists said.

Rapinoe realized the power, and the positives, of being more open about who she was years ago. While she had been out to friends and family since college, she did not come out to the broader public until after starring in the 2011 World Cup.

"When you're out, it's only one part of who you are," she told Yahoo Sports earlier this year. "But when you're not out, it's just this all-consuming thing."

These are the ideas that Les Dégommeuses and others are hoping will be voiced as the United States maintains its platform at the World Cup.

Les Dégommeuses have tried to do their part. They smuggled an enormous rainbow flag into the opening match of the tournament and waved it joyfully for several minutes before putting it away to watch the game. They commissioned posters to hang around Paris depicting diverse images of women's soccer players. On Saturday, they marched in the Paris Pride parade.

Before the game on Friday, Rome had hoped a French victory would make their players superstars who would feel emboldened to express themselves publicly.

"Maybe they have the next Megan Rapinoe on their team," Rome said.

That did not happen. France lost, and the United States advanced.

For now, cheering for the real Megan Rapinoe will have to do.

CONSTANT MÉHEUT contributed reporting.

He Emerged From Prison a Potent Symbol of H.I.V. Criminalization

BY EMILY S. RUEB | JULY 14, 2019

Michael L. Johnson, a gay athlete convicted of not disclosing his H.I.V. status to sexual partners, was released 25 years early and has become a galvanizing force to overhaul laws.

LAST WEEK, MICHAEL L. JOHNSON, a former college wrestler convicted of failing to disclose to sexual partners that he was H.I.V. positive in a racially charged case that reignited calls to re-examine laws that criminalize H.I.V. exposure, walked out of the Boonville Correctional Center in Missouri 25 years earlier than expected.

Mr. Johnson, 27, was released on parole on Tuesday after an appeals court found that his 2015 trial was "fundamentally unfair." His original sentence was longer than the state average for second-degree murder.

Reached by phone two days after his release, Mr. Johnson said he was rediscovering freedom through convenience store snacks, cartoons and his cellphone.

"I'm feeling really, really good," he said.

But there were periods when he felt intimidated by people who did not believe he had a right to stand up for himself, he added.

His case, which encompasses a half-dozen years of court appearances, unflattering headlines and stints in solitary confinement, has galvanized advocates working to update laws that they say further stigmatize and unfairly penalize people with H.I.V.

Mr. Johnson, who was a black, gay athlete at Lindenwood University in St. Charles, Mo., has become a public face of people who are disproportionately affected by the virus and entangled in the criminal justice system. (If current trends continue, about half of all black men who have sex with men in the United States will eventually learn they have H.I.V., according to the Centers for Disease Control and Prevention.)

Mr. Johnson's legal troubles began in 2013, when he was arrested after a white man he had had consensual sex with told the police he believed that Mr. Johnson had given him the virus.

Five other men, three of them white, would later testify that Mr. Johnson had not only failed to disclose his H.I.V. status before engaging in consensual sex, but had willfully lied about it.

Mr. Johnson has publicly maintained that he informed all six men he was H.I.V. positive before having sex without a condom.

After a weeklong trial in 2015 in St. Charles County, a conservative, predominantly white area northwest of St. Louis, Mr. Johnson was convicted on multiple felony counts, including recklessly infecting another with H.I.V., which carries a 10-year minimum sentence.

The jury sought the maximum penalty of 60 ½ years even though prosecutors offered no genetic evidence that Mr. Johnson had infected any of his partners, according to BuzzFeed News.

The judge ultimately sentenced him to 30 years in prison.

Today, some of the people who put him in prison say the sentencing and parts of the prosecution were mishandled.

"We're still operating under laws that were based on views that are outdated and are proven inaccurate by science," said Tim Lohmar, the St. Charles County prosecuting attorney, whose office's handling of the trial has been criticized.

Missouri is one of about 34 states with laws that make it a crime to expose another person to the virus without disclosure or add additional penalties for people with H.I.V. who are convicted of separate offenses, such as sex work, according to the nonprofit Center for H.I.V. Law and Policy. In six states, a person may be required to register as a sex offender if convicted of an H.I.V.-related crime.

Many of these laws were written in the 1980s and 1990s under a fog of fear about the virus and how it was transmitted, and before the advent of effective treatments. In those years, Magic Johnson's sweat on the basketball court and Greg Louganis's blood on a diving board panicked fans and teammates. Parents pulled children from school

Originally sentenced to 30 years, Michael L. Johnson has galvanized advocates working to update laws that they say further stigmatize and unfairly penalize people with H.I.V.

in 1985 because an H.I.V.-positive boy with hemophilia was in their seventh-grade class.

Back then, an H.I.V. diagnosis meant debilitating symptoms and almost certain death.

For the last five years, Steven Thrasher, a journalism professor at Northwestern University, has chronicled Michael L. Johnson's case for BuzzFeed News and recently completed his doctoral dissertation on race and H.I.V. criminalization.

Dr. Thrasher, who greeted Mr. Johnson outside the correctional facility on Tuesday, said he was first drawn to the case because of its parallels with the history of black sexuality and lynching.

"Black men would just get lynched anytime they had sex with white women in the Reconstruction period," he said. "There was no consensual sex that could be had between white women and black men."

Mr. Johnson's wrestler's body — he called himself "Tiger Mandingo" online — was a source of fascination for some of his partners. But when Mr. Johnson tested positive for H.I.V., Dr. Thrasher wrote, he became "the perfect scapegoat."

"It was not that he had no agency or responsibility in the story," Dr. Thrasher said on Thursday, but "he was really holding all of this anxiety and all of this worry about AIDS and stigma and H.I.V. and queerness in America all on his shoulders."

Mr. Lohmar, the St. Charles County prosecutor, said on Thursday that "nothing about the trial was unfair," except for his team's failure to present certain evidence to the defense in time.

Because prosecutors did not disclose some evidence to the defense until the morning of the trial — recorded phone conversations Mr. Johnson made while in the county jail — an appeals court decided to overturn the conviction 17 months after the original sentencing.

Instead of a new trial, Mr. Johnson, who previously had a clean criminal record, accepted a plea deal in which he did not admit guilt but agreed to a 10-year sentence.

Eric M. Selig, the lawyer who negotiated on Mr. Johnson's behalf, said the original sentence was disproportionate to the crime.

"We don't charge people with other incurable diseases, like hepatitis, with a criminal offense for exposing others," he said.

During his incarceration, Mr. Johnson wrote thank-you notes to friends and strangers who had written to him in support, which he said helped him deal with homophobia in prison and self-doubt.

"You lose your confidence," he said. "I kept every single letter."

In theory, H.I.V. exposure laws are meant to encourage H.I.V.-positive individuals to disclose their status before having sex, and to practice safer sex, with the ultimate goal of preventing the spread of the virus.

But there is no evidence that these laws have reduced risky behavior or encouraged disclosure, said Catherine Hanssens, the executive director of the Center for H.I.V. Law and Policy, which provided legal support for Mr. Johnson's case.

In the eyes of the law, an H.I.V. diagnosis is conflated with malice, she added.

"These laws effectively treat an H.I.V. diagnosis itself as evidence that the person acted with bad intentions when sex or other types of physical contact are involved in a crime," she said.

Additionally, many laws do not reflect recent treatment options that can give patients a life expectancy almost as long as the general population. A pill taken daily can almost eliminate transmission, experts say. But there remain large barriers to eradicating the virus, including the high cost of antiretroviral drugs, access issues, medical mistrust and other social barriers in poor and black communities.

While some states, like California, have reduced penalties for H.I.V. exposure, Missouri has one of the most punitive laws in the country. This year lawmakers introduced two bills into the Legislature that would have slightly reduced the penalty, but they never made it to a vote.

Mr. Lohmar said he learned of Mr. Johnson's release after receiving a call from one of the witnesses in the trial, who was upset that he was not notified.

Mr. Johnson said he planned to return to college, learn a second language and share his story through advocacy organizations like the Ryan White Planning Council in Indiana. Younger people especially need to learn about the virus to prevent it from spreading, he said.

"You can't do it without education."

ALAIN DELAQUÉRIÈRE contributed research.

CHAPTER 5

Other Outspoken Athletes, Past and Present

As we have seen, athletes have been especially driven to speak out for racial justice, gender equality and rights for L.G.B.T.Q. people. The articles in this chapter highlight other issues taken on by activist athletes, as well as the work of activist athletes in the past. Athletes have raised controversy for their remarks on religion, gun violence, partisan politics and other topics. We also have an opportunity to learn about outspoken athletes from decades past, as professionals like Kareem Abdul-Jabbar and Muhammad Ali faced familiar struggles generations ago.

Magic Johnson and Public Opinion on AIDS and Sex

BY JOHN SIDES | NOV. 7, 2011

TWENTY YEARS AGO TODAY, Magic Johnson told the world that he was H.I.V.-positive. What had been largely a "gay disease" in the public's mind now had a very different face. Did this make a difference?

Philip H. Pollock III, a political science professor at the University of Central Florida, had an answer, thanks to a bit of good luck: he came upon a November 1991 poll in Florida that included questions about AIDS and, most crucially, he was in the field when Mr. Johnson made his announcement. By comparing the responses of people interviewed before and after the announcement, he could estimate its effect on public opinion about AIDS.

In a 1994 article, he found that Mr. Johnson's announcement changed the underpinnings of opinion. Although views of homosexuals were associated with opinion about AIDS — those with less favorable views of homosexuals were in turn less likely to support spending for AIDS treatment and research — Mr. Johnson's announcement made attitudes toward heterosexual sex a more important underpinning of opinion about AIDS. In particular, those with more conservative values (in this case, those who believe premarital sex is always or almost always wrong) became slightly less supportive of spending to fight AIDS. But those who believed that premarital sex was only sometimes or never wrong became more supportive of AIDS spending — by 15 points, in fact. Mr. Johnson's announcement had shifted the types of values that people drew on when forming opinions about AIDS.

The same finding showed up in a separate 1992 poll in which respondents were asked to name a celebrity with AIDS. Approximately 50 percent named Mr. Johnson. Among these respondents, attitudes toward premarital sex were again associated with attitudes toward AIDS; this association was substantially weaker among those who did not recall Mr. Johnson.

Professor Pollock argues that having a famous heterosexual acknowledge his H.I.V.-positive status changed how the problem of AIDS was "constructed" in the public sphere:

> ...It took dramatic symbolism to communicate this construction of the problem to the public at large, to disrupt the way AIDS was discussed and argued in families, among peers and co-workers, and in other social settings. As we have seen, that was the role — and may define the legacy — of "Magic" Johnson.

What the World Got Wrong About Kareem Abdul-Jabbar

BY JAY CASPIAN KANG | SEPT. 17, 2015

A long, strange day with the least understood basketball star of all time.

IN THE SLEEK, COLD LOBBY of the Langham Place hotel in Midtown Manhattan, one of those thoroughly designed spaces in which one cannot find a right angle, much less a comfortable chair, the 68-year-old, 7-foot-2 former basketball star Kareem Abdul-Jabbar was sitting on a leather bench with his arms draped around his protruding knees. It was a melancholy pose, best suited for the solitude of a beach at night or a rocky summit after a long hike. A U.C.L.A. T-shirt and a pair of jeans hung loosely off his narrow frame. Despite having had quadruple-bypass surgery just a few months earlier, Abdul-Jabbar didn't look all that different than he did during his last days on the Los Angeles Lakers in the late 1980s. The only evidence, really, that he had passed retirement age was a dash of white in his goatee.

"Hi, I'm the reporter who is going to follow you around today," I said, sticking out my hand.

"O.K.," he said. It was clear there would be no handshake.

I sat down next to him. He made no effort to start a conversation, so neither did I. We sat in silence.

Abdul-Jabbar has been in the public spotlight for 50 years, and for almost all of that time, he has drawn the ire of most reporters who have dealt with him. For a black athlete to be accepted by the sports media, especially during the early years of Abdul-Jabbar's career, he had to appear humble and deferential and continually thankful to the white world for giving him a chance to become rich and famous. Abdul-Jabbar, who, like many shy, intelligent people, channeled his innate awkwardness through a hardened mask of superiority, didn't fit the model. And while many of the black athletes who were similarly demonized during

Abdul-Jabbar's time — Curt Flood, Bill Russell, Muhammad Ali — have turned into celebrated figures, Abdul-Jabbar, despite his tremendous accomplishments, has never been widely embraced by fans.

Abdul-Jabbar had agreed to meet with me on the occasion of his new book, a lively if somewhat dutiful reimagining of the life of Mycroft Holmes, the brother of Sherlock, that is due out this month. "Mycroft Holmes," written with a co-author, Anna Waterhouse, is Abdul-Jabbar's first novel, but it will be his 10th published book. His collected works go well beyond the usual jockish hagiographies that litter the sports section of every Barnes & Noble. He has written two unusually candid autobiographies about his playing days, a comprehensive history of African-American intellectual accomplishment, a memoir about growing up in the cultural shadow of the Harlem Renaissance and an admirably researched history of a black tank battalion that fought in World War II. But if he wanted to discuss his writing, his book, his influences or anything at all, he gave no sign. Instead, for the next 15 minutes, he intently studied his fingernails with a mild look of disappointment on his face.

"We are going to have a great time today!"

Our mutual silent treatment was suddenly interrupted by the appearance of Deborah Morales, a bustling dynamo who has been Abdul-Jabbar's manager for over a decade. Abdul-Jabbar stood up, walked wordlessly to the hotel's entrance and peered at the sidewalk.

Morales handles all of Abdul-Jabbar's public engagements with enormous, slightly delusional enthusiasm, as if he were still winning championships with the Lakers. But her hustle has paid off: Over the past several years, Abdul-Jabbar has emerged as a prolific columnist, writing in Time, Esquire and The Huffington Post, while also maintaining a steady presence as a pundit on political talk shows on MSNBC and CNN. In front of a camera, Abdul-Jabbar comes across as a learned rationalist. He quotes liberally from literature, and he tries to wrestle ideas back into their historical contexts; he rarely, if ever, talks about basketball or his playing career.

After scanning the sidewalk for gawkers, Morales ushered us into a waiting car. The radio was on, tuned to talk news. Morales asked the driver to change the channel to jazz.

The day's itinerary, enthusiastically set by Morales, called for a trip to the Bronx Zoo followed by lunch at the Empire State Building. Why Abdul-Jabbar, who grew up in New York City and is famously uncomfortable in crowds, would have wanted to visit two of the most touristy, clogged spots in the city was never explained.

BY 10 A.M., as Abdul-Jabbar moved briskly among the exhibits, the asphalt walkways of the zoo had started to fill up with schoolchildren walking hand in hand in neon T-shirts. The kids stared at the tallest man they had ever seen, and one of their chaperones turned to a colleague and whispered, "That's Kareem Abdul-Jabbar." Abdul-Jabbar strode on, determined to ignore them.

We saw tigers and silverback gorillas, as well as baby goats at the petting zoo. Abdul-Jabbar, looking impassively at the animals, would occasionally recite a fact about their mating habits or natural habitat. "Sea lions and wolves share a common ancestor," he said dryly. He struck me as a man whose preferred mode of communication is a stack of random, verifiable statements.

In the zoo's play area, Abdul-Jabbar, at Morales's urging, lay down on a giant spider web made of ropes for one of dozens of photo ops for his Facebook page. "Look scared!" Morales ordered while pointing her iPad's camera at Abdul-Jabbar.

"But I'm not scared," Abdul-Jabbar said. After some more coaxing from Morales, he opened his mouth, held his hands up by his face and gave a halfhearted look of faux terror.

As we approached the otter exhibit, a man with his young son in tow looked up at Abdul-Jabbar and said, "Hey, that's one of the greatest basketball players of all time!" The father extended his hand toward Abdul-Jabbar and said, "Wow, man. ... Kareem."

Abdul-Jabbar dropped into a hunch and stared miserably off into the space above the man's head. After it became clear that the man and his child were not going to step aside, Abdul-Jabbar offered up a curt nod, turned and stalked off. Morales jogged up to the child and handed him a playing card autographed by Abdul-Jabbar. Gazing after his bowed, retreating figure, the father reached down, grabbed his confused son by the shoulders and slowly walked him toward the next exhibit.

BY ANY MEASURE of accomplishment, whether individual statistics or overall team success, Abdul-Jabbar was an undeniable superstar. His high-school team at Power Memorial, near Lincoln Center, won 71 straight games. At U.C.L.A., Abdul-Jabbar, one of the best players in the history of college basketball, won three national championships and three N.C.A.A. tournament most outstanding player awards. During a 20-year career in the N.B.A., he won the same number of championships as Michael Jordan (six), and bested him by one M.V.P. award (also six). He is the N.B.A.'s all-time leading scorer. And yet discussions of his greatness are usually tinged with annoyance, as if his dominance must be nodded at but not dwelled upon.

He has tried, repeatedly, to register his side of the story by writing. In high school, Abdul-Jabbar took a summer job with a Harlem-based black newspaper and covered the 1964 Harlem riots. His literary ambitions never abated. In the mid-1970s, the writer Gay Talese, while doing research for his book "Thy Neighbor's Wife," ran into Abdul-Jabbar at the Playboy Mansion. Abdul-Jabbar told Talese that when he retired, he wanted to become a sportswriter. "It seemed like such a strange thing to admit," Talese told me. "It almost felt like he wanted to be anyone else. He was caught in this huge body, but his aspiration was to be diminished in terms of ambition: He wanted to be the man in the press box. You don't expect a person with stardom in every muscle to want to become a writer."

Much later, on a trip back to New York City, Abdul-Jabbar accompanied Talese to Elaine's, an Upper East Side restaurant that catered to the city's literary elite. "He wanted to go be with writers," Talese said. "He wanted to see Styron and Mailer. Again, I found it very unusual. It just seemed like there was a part of him that didn't want to be a man of the body."

In 1983, Abdul-Jabbar published "Giant Steps," the first of two engrossing autobiographies. He writes about growing up in the '50s and '60s in the Inwood neighborhood of Upper Manhattan, the only child of a Juilliard-trained trombone player turned transit cop and a stylish woman from North Carolina who demanded that her son receive a proper education. As a boy, Abdul-Jabbar — whose birth name was Ferdinand Lewis Alcindor Jr. — ran around with a diverse, middle-class crew. This innocence was shattered when his best friend, a white boy named Johnny, ultimately betrayed him in the seventh grade by calling him a "jungle bunny" and a "nigger." "I just laughed at him," Abdul-Jabbar writes. " '[Expletive] you, you … milk bottle.' It was the only white thing I could think of."

When he started at Power Memorial, Abdul-Jabbar was already known around the city as an up-and-coming basketball star. He was written up in sports dailies and accosted on the subway. A few weeks after his 16th birthday, Richard Avedon shot his portrait. His coach, with whom he became very close and who shielded him from reporters, was an irascible Irishman named Jack Donohue. The older man would talk to his star about the racism he saw while stationed at Fort Knox in Kentucky. On a trip to North Carolina in 1962, his first time alone in the South, Abdul-Jabbar got to see Jim Crow for himself. "So I knew a little of what Mr. Donohue was talking about," he writes. "He was certain that racism wouldn't die until the racists did, and so was I. What I didn't tell him was that I hoped it would be soon and that if I could help them along, I would be delighted. I wasn't quite ready to pick up the gun, but I was intimate with the impulse." (His close relationship with Donohue was damaged when the coach told his protégé that he was behaving like a "nigger" during a halftime rant.)

The next year, the 16th Street Baptist Church in Birmingham, Ala., was bombed, killing four young black girls and partially blinding another. Abdul-Jabbar's impulse hardened into something stronger. "As I watched the ineffectual moral outrage of the black southern preachers," he writes, "the cold coverage of the white media and the posturings of the John F. Kennedy White House, my whole view of the world fell into place. My faith was exploded like church rubble, my anger was shrapnel. I would gladly have killed whoever killed those girls by myself."

After being recruited by nearly all the major college basketball programs in the country, Abdul-Jabbar landed at U.C.L.A., where he studied history and English, dropped acid and became entranced by "The Autobiography of Malcolm X." After his first season on the court, the N.C.A.A. rules committee outlawed dunking when Abdul-Jabbar netted an average of 29.5 points a game and a 67 percent field-goal percentage. Other players dunked, but none as frequently and as ferociously as he did. The rule change, as a result, was informally known as "the Alcindor rule." "Clearly, they did it to undermine my dominance in the game," Abdul-Jabbar writes in "Giant Steps." "Equally clearly, if I'd been white they never would have done it. The dunk is one of basketball's great crowd pleasers, and there was no good reason to give it up except that this and other niggers were running away with the sport." Abdul-Jabbar's U.C.L.A. team won the national championship again when he was a junior.

That year, Abdul-Jabbar refused to play in the 1968 Olympics because he did not want to represent a country that did not treat him as an equal. The press pilloried him for it. In a much-publicized spot on the "Today" show, Joe Garagiola, a baseball player turned TV personality, asked Abdul-Jabbar why he wouldn't play for his country.

"Yeah, I live here," Abdul-Jabbar said. "But it's not really my country."

"Well, then there's only one solution," Garagiola said. "Maybe you should move."

His relationship with the press only worsened.

In 1969, Abdul-Jabbar was drafted by the Milwaukee Bucks, where he would perfect his signature sky hook — a balletic feat that involves an explosive one-legged leap before flinging the ball into the hoop with one hand — and win three of his eventual six M.V.P. awards. Before games, Abdul-Jabbar read books in front of his locker to avoid engaging with reporters. (On his reading list that year: Sir Arthur Conan Doyle, who reignited his childhood interest in Sherlock Holmes. He admired the detective's ability to synthesize huge amounts of information.) He became notorious for berating reporters who he thought were trying to bait him into a controversial answer.

Basketball, because it is played in shorts and without a helmet or cap, invites a peculiar intimacy that puts each facial expression, each bodily tic, into heightened focus. Michael Jordan, and then Kobe Bryant, were celebrated for the way they set their jaws in determination. Abdul-Jabbar was judged, and is still judged, on his grim game face and the apparently joyless way he ran up and down the court. He was traded to the Lakers before the 1975-76 season, and won two more M.V.P. awards in his first two years. But the team floundered. When Magic Johnson came to the Lakers in 1979, the press regarded him as the team's savior. They loved his radiant smile and cast him as the exuberant, warm foil to Abdul-Jabbar's supposedly arrogant, selfish loner.

Despite being painfully aware of his role in the Magic-Kareem binary, Abdul-Jabbar found himself drawn to the rookie's enthusiasm. He began to open up, in his own peculiar way. He chose to explain himself to the public by writing a book in which he discussed, in grim detail, the anger he felt toward white people and how it informed the choices he made in his youth. He did not apologize.

This is the Abdul-Jabbar paradox: He's a man who cares enough about his legacy to write two memoirs and eight other books, but he refuses to engage in the usual smoothing, sanding and editing that is required of a public persona. He instead asks you to accept his version of his truth, even if the truth is that at 68, he sometimes has a hard time being civil to children and still refuses to shake the hand of a reporter.

ABDUL-JABBAR RARELY stretches out to his full height. Instead, he hunches: His shoulders close on their hinges, and he tucks his chin into his neck. It's a necessary adjustment to a world that is not designed for a man as tall as he is. In the car on the way to lunch, though, he stretched back in his seat, stared out at the passing skyline and tapped his knee to the jazz on the radio. He said that he once hoped to spend some of his retirement in a brownstone in Harlem, but the crowds and the constant attention had forced a retreat back to a suburb of Los Angeles, where he could get around without the hazards of busy side-walks. He is divorced and has five grown children: three with his former wife, Habiba, and two by other women. He lives alone. He talked about his recent emergency quadruple-bypass surgery but insisted that the epiphanies of a life-threatening illness had eluded him.

On Fifth Avenue, we were shepherded into a restaurant on the first floor of the Empire State Building. Abdul-Jabbar folded himself into a corner booth — a process that required him to stick his legs out from underneath the table at a 45-degree angle — and ordered a cheese-burger. When the food arrived, Abdul-Jabbar ate like a bird, all pecks and careful dissections. But his mood had brightened. He chuckled at Morales's giddy stream of non sequiturs, praised her business acumen, even smiled.

He spoke enthusiastically about his admiration for John le Carré and for Edgar Allan Poe's "The Murders in the Rue Morgue" and about his own writing, which he works on for about three hours each morning before, as he put it, "my head gets contaminated with other concerns." When he's writing fiction, he told me, he reads Elmore Leonard and Ross Thomas for dialogue. When he turns his attention to style, he reads writers as diverse as Gillian Flynn, who wrote "Gone Girl," and the offbeat experimentalist Miranda July.

All of Abdul-Jabbar's books have been written with a co-author. He worked with the poet Anthony Walton on the history of the black tank battalion. The process of writing a book with Abdul-Jabbar, Walton told me, involved breaking down boxes of Abdul-Jabbar's research — videotapes, old photographs, contact lists and bibliographies — into a narrative. "I remember when I realized that the story was going to be the story of one platoon," Walton said. "That's one of the oldest stories of all time. It goes back to the Iliad. I remember how excited Kareem was when we talked about that.

"Just imagine what it was like to be him," Walton added. "It was 50 years of him being 18 inches taller than everyone and having the brain that he had. Imagine being this jazz head coming up during black power. This is just a dude who has a different head."

In recent years, Abdul-Jabbar has turned his attention toward the Internet, where he has found an unexpected role among the online commentariat. He has written on Lena Dunham, Ferguson, the body-shaming Serena Williams has endured, the Charleston shootings and Donald Trump. (Trump recently responded to one of Abdul-Jabbar's columns by printing it out and writing across the text with a marker: "Kareem: Now I know why the press always treated you so badly. … You don't have a clue about life and what has to be done to make America great again! Best wishes.") A bit stiff and laden with quotations from Toni Morrison and Ernest Hemingway, the columns demonstrate a change in Abdul-Jabbar's politics: He has become a pragmatist who sees the path toward "racial harmony" as a continuum along which one is either moving forward or moving backward. His column on Rachel Dolezal, the N.A.A.C.P. chapter president who deceived people into thinking she was a black woman, struck a conciliatory tone. "She has been fighting the fight for several years and seemingly doing a first-rate job," Abdul-Jabbar wrote. "Bottom line: The black community is better off because of her efforts."

I found myself wondering what Abdul-Jabbar's career might have been like if it had happened 30 years later. Social media has given athletes a direct avenue to their fans that has cut the sports reporter out of his job as translator, and it has emboldened professional athletes to make political statements they might not have made five years ago. During the Ferguson protests last fall, players for the St. Louis Rams walked out onto the field with their hands raised in protest. In December, during the Eric Garner protests in New York, LeBron James, Kyrie Irving and several other N.B.A. players wore "I Can't Breathe" T-shirts during pregame warm-ups.

These protests were meaningful, but they pale in comparison to the risks Abdul-Jabbar took during his playing career. His refusal to play in the Olympics and his pride in the face of reporters may not be replayed in every Lakers retrospective, but they still linger in the public's memory. By throwing himself straight into the muck of online opinion-making, where his name can be tweeted, shared and liked, Abdul-Jabbar has dusted off his legacy. The odd man with the discomforting, unrelenting opinions seems finally to have found an audience.

ABDUL-JABBAR IS a thoughtful and deliberate dresser. Nearly every piece of clothing he owns must be custom-ordered or tailored. In 1967, Life magazine photographed him being measured at a men's wear shop. The tailor, whose arms are wrapped around Abdul-Jabbar's waist, is standing on a chair. When I met him again at the Langham, about a month after our trip to the zoo, he was dressed for the night in a simple, impeccably pressed white shirt and a pair of narrow-legged black slacks, stomping around the room in search of his blazer. We were about to head to the Village Vanguard, where he was scheduled to meet a film crew that was finishing up a biographical documentary titled, appropriately enough, "Kareem: A Minority of One." Abdul-Jabbar, the basketball player, is from Los Angeles, but Lew Alcindor, the kid who hopped around jazz clubs, played pickup games at the famed Rucker Park in Harlem and hung out at parties with Wilt Chamberlain, is a cosmopolitan New Yorker.

I asked Abdul-Jabbar if he sometimes wished he had played in the era of social media, if Twitter and Instagram might have given him a more ideal way to communicate with fans.

"That would have been great," he said. "It would've been nice to really be able to explain myself in the way I wanted to explain myself."

He began to talk about Magic Johnson, who, despite the years and their divergent paths, is still cast as Abdul-Jabbar's opposite. Where Kareem was dour, Magic was outgoing and friendly. Where Abdul-Jabbar was mechanical, Magic was creative. For better or worse, Abdul-Jabbar, basketball's scarecrow, was uprooted and stored away, forever defined by how much like Magic he wasn't.

"I understood why people liked him," Abdul-Jabbar told me. "He had that great smile, so white people thought his life was O.K. They thought that racism had not affected him. They were wrong, of course. But that's what they saw when they saw him. Magic made white people feel comfortable. With themselves."

I asked Abdul-Jabbar if he regretted the way he had treated the press, if he ever wished that he had humored them a bit more in the hope that they might help the public get to know him.

"Oh, yes," he said. "I just didn't realize back then how much it was hurting me." He turned away. "But it cost me dearly."

JAY CASPIAN KANG is a contributing writer for the magazine. He last wrote about how black social-media activists have built the nation's first 21st-century civil rights movement.

Muhammad Ali, the Political Poet

OPINION | BY HENRY LOUIS GATES JR. | JUNE 9, 2016

A FRIEND ASKED ME the other day to choose my favorite Muhammad Ali fight. "The Rumble in the Jungle," I responded. I was thinking of all the rhymes that accompanied it, from "You think the world was shocked when Nixon resigned? Wait till I whip George Foreman's behind," to the very phrase "rope-a-dope," as he named the strategy he used to defeat a superior opponent in the heat of Kinshasa. It was an athletic event but it was also a linguistic one.

Almost from the beginning of his career, when he was still called Cassius Clay, his rhymed couplets, like his punches, were brutal and blunt. And his poems, like his opponents, suffered a beating. The press's earliest nicknames for him, such as "Cash the Brash" and "the Louisville Lip," derived from his deriding of opponents with poetic insults. When in the history of boxing have critics been so irked by a fighter's use of language? A. J. Liebling called him "Mr. Swellhead Bigmouth Poet," while John Ahern, writing in The Boston Globe in 1964, mocked his "vaudeville" verse as "homespun doggerel." Time magazine, in a particularly nasty triple dig in 1967 over Ali's opposition to the Vietnam War, his embrace of the Nation of Islam and his name change, called him "Gaseous Cassius."

But the same verse can strike one critic as doggerel and another as art, and not everyone missed the power — and the point — of Ali's poetics. Even Ahern admitted that "the guy is a master at rhyming," and The New Yorker editor and Ali biographer David Remnick would eulogize him as "a master of rhyming prediction and derision." Perhaps Maya Angelou, whose own poetry is sometimes labeled doggerel, said it best: "It wasn't only what he said and it wasn't only how he said it; it was both of those things, and maybe there was a third thing in it, the spirit of Muhammad Ali, saying his poesies — 'Float like a butterfly, sting like a bee.' I mean, as a poet, I like that! If he hadn't put his name on it, I might have chosen to use that!"

Edmund Wilson once said that "we have produced some of our truest poetry in the folk songs that are inseparable from their tunes." Likewise, the power of Ali's poetry, often bland on the page, is inseparable from the compelling resonance of his voice.

A century ago, the great literary historian George Saintsbury, in his monumental "A History of English Prosody," defined doggerel "in the worst sense" as "merely bad verse — verse which attempts a certain form or norm, and fails." But Saintsbury maintains that there is another sort of doggerel that "ought never to die."

"This doggerel," he wrote, "is excused by the felicitous result. The poet is not trying to do what he cannot do; he is trying to do something exceptional, outrageous, shocking — and does it to admiration."

If ever there is to be a collection of Ali's verse, Saintsbury's observation is the perfect blurb for the dust jacket.

So many of the deeply moving tributes pouring out in memory of Ali have stressed his centrality in mainstreaming black radicalism, in broadening the appeal and reach of black cultural nationalism. (He also mainstreamed the complexity of being a black human being by trumpeting both his ego and id.) And there is no gainsaying the importance of Ali to our people's embrace of the word "black" as a replacement of Negro, along with the right to change one's religion and one's name: "I am America," he once said. "I am the part you won't recognize. But get used to me. Black, confident, cocky, my name, not yours; my religion, not yours; my goals, my own; get used to me."

The question is: How did Ali help to accomplish this transformation, help to mainstream black radicalism?

The first way was by challenging the Negro establishment with his change of religion, his change of name and then his stance against the war. Two of our greatest athletes, Floyd Patterson and Jackie Robinson, denounced Ali; Patterson for changing his name and religion; Robinson for his anti-war stand. But Ali also helped move black radicalism into the mainstream through his voice, his canny use of rhyme. Black poets had been using rhyme effectively for decades, both formal poets such as Langston Hughes and Countee Cullen, but also, on the streets, anonymous "barbershop poets" engaging in colorful linguistic rituals of insult such as "playing the dozens," "woofing," "capping," all subsets of the language game of "signifying." But Ali used rhyme in powerful new ways.

He was, if anything, a master signifier, the Shakespeare of linguistic pugilism, using his words to counterpunch his opponents, well before they stepped in the ring:

> *Now Liston disappears from view,*
> *The crowd is getting frantic.*
> *But our radar stations have picked him up,*
> *He's somewhere over the Atlantic.*

It would be a mistake to say that Ali made black oral poetry more sophisticated or complex, but he did make it more political. After learning his local draft board had declared him eligible for induction into the Army in 1966, Ali recited this poem:

> *Keep asking me, no matter how long,*
> *On the war in Vietnam,*
> *I sing this song:*
> *I ain't got no quarrel with no Viet Cong.*

When Ali described himself as "the astronaut of boxing," that Joe Louis and Jack Dempsey "were just jet pilots — I'm in a world of my own," he was right at least about the last part: The politics of his change of name, the politics of his religious conversion and the politics of his opposition to the Vietnam War gave his poetry a political context that Ali couldn't have escaped if he had wanted to.

In 1964, Cassius Clay upset Sonny Liston to become the world heavyweight champion, and the Rev. Dr. Martin Luther King Jr. was awarded the Nobel Peace Prize. Who could have imagined that three years later, Dr. King would denounce the Vietnam War just a few weeks before Ali would refuse induction. Dr. King, the resonant voice of the civil rights movement, turned to Ali, the renegade lyrical poet from the ring, to justify his position: "Like Muhammad Ali puts it, we are all — black and brown and poor — victims of the same system of oppression." A saint quoting the words of our most radical versifier.

I'm not arguing that Ali should be added to the next edition of The Norton Anthology of Poetry. But I am arguing his importance to the shaping of the black poetic tradition. There was certainly a direct connection between the politics of Ali's rhyme schemes and spoken word poetry of both the Last Poets group, formed on Malcolm X Day in Harlem in 1968, and Gil Scott-Heron, who recorded his first album in 1970, a hip and a hop between them and the birth of rap music just a few years later.

As George Saintsbury argued back in 1906, there was a kind a doggerel that could achieve for its creator a form of immortality. "Like the other kind, it has never died," he wrote. "And unlike the other kind, it ought never to die."

Perhaps these words anticipate the literary legacy of Muhammad Ali.

HENRY LOUIS GATES JR., a professor of literature at Harvard and director of the Hutchins Center for African and African American Research, is the host and executive producer of the forthcoming PBS documentary "And Still I Rise: Black America Since MLK."

Stephen Curry, on a 'Surreal' Day, Confronts a Presidential Snub

BY SCOTT CACCIOLA | SEPT. 23, 2017

OAKLAND, CALIF. — Stephen Curry of the Golden State Warriors said he awoke Saturday morning to "about 20 text messages" from friends who were expressing their support for him.

At first, he said, he had no idea what they were talking about because he had not checked social media. Then he saw President Trump's tweet.

"Surreal," Curry said.

One day after Curry told reporters that he would rather not accept an invitation to visit the White House because of his objections to the current administration's policies and rhetoric, Trump tweeted that he was revoking any invitation because of Curry's remarks.

"I don't know why he feels the need to target certain individuals rather than others," Curry, a two-time N.B.A. most valuable player, said at a news conference after the team's first practice of the season. "I have an idea of why, but it's kind of beneath the leader of a country to go that route. It's not what leaders do."

The question about whether the Warriors would visit the White House — a tradition for various sports champions — had trailed them since they won the N.B.A. title in June. Many members of the team, including Coach Steve Kerr, have been openly critical of Trump and his policies.

As a player and as a coach, Kerr has visited the White House on several occasions. And despite his well-publicized criticism of the current administration, Kerr said in June that he was open to the idea of the Warriors' visiting the White House as something of a unifying gesture.

"I think we would, in normal times, easily be able to set aside political views, and go visit and have a great time," Kerr said Saturday. "But

After the Golden State Warriors' practice on Saturday, Stephen Curry spoke with the news media about a tweet from President Trump that was directed at him.

these are not ordinary times. Probably the most divisive times in my life, I guess, since Vietnam, when I was just a kid."

He added, "The president made it really, really difficult for us to honor that institution."

On Friday, at the team's annual media day ahead of the start of training camp, Curry said that the Warriors had not decided as a team whether they would visit the White House and that they planned to talk about it at a meeting. But Curry said that if it were up to him, he would not go. That seemed to be the consensus among the players.

On Saturday morning, Trump made the Warriors' decision for them when he tweeted that the invitation had been "withdrawn" because Curry was "hesitating."

As Kerr put it, "He was going to break up with us before we could break up with him."

Kerr said he learned of Trump's tweet when his wife tapped him on the shoulder in bed.

"I was half-asleep," Kerr recalled, "and she said: 'There it is. There it is.'"

Members of the Warriors organization — including executives in the front office — have used their huge platform to speak out about social causes in recent seasons, including gay rights and racial inequality. General Manager Bob Myers said that would continue to be the case.

"We encourage our players to speak their minds," he said.

For his part, Curry said that he had never set out to become a political figure — and that he was surprised that the president had singled him out.

At the same time, Curry said he felt emboldened by the support he had received from friends and fellow athletes, many of whom were vocal on social media.

"We're not trying to divide and separate this country," Curry said. "We're trying to bring everyone together and speak about love and togetherness and equality."

At one point during his news conference, Curry sounded almost nostalgic.

"I've played golf with President Obama," Curry said. "I'm pretty sure I won't get a tee-time invite during this regime."

Etan Thomas: Now a Different Kind of Player

BY SOPAN DEB | FEB. 27, 2018

WITH THE ADVENT of social media, politically active athletes seem more common now than ever before.

Indeed, N.F.L. players kneeling during the national anthem, a movement started by Colin Kaepernick and echoed by others, became a cultural flash point last season after President Trump aimed his ire on the movement, accusing them of disrespecting the troops.

But before Kaepernick, there was Etan Thomas, an N.B.A. forward who played for nine seasons, seven with the Washington Wizards. Thomas built a reputation for himself as a socially conscious activist and poet, including frequently speaking out against the Iraq War and the federal government's response to Hurricane Katrina. (Of course decades before Thomas, there were activist athletes like Bill Russell, Jim Brown and Muhammad Ali.)

In his latest book, "We Matter: Athletes and Activism," due out on March 6, Thomas interviewed a number of basketball staples, including Kareem Abdul-Jabbar and Dwyane Wade of the Miami Heat, about the consequences of publicly voicing opinions off the court or playing field. He also talked to figures like Mark Cuban, owner of the Dallas Mavericks, and Ted Leonsis, who owns three sports franchises, including the Washington Wizards, about their perspectives.

Perhaps most notably, Thomas spoke to family members of Trayvon Martin, Eric Garner, Terence Crutcher and Philando Castile — all victims of shootings that received widespread attention from prominent athletes.

I spoke to Thomas by phone about the recent comments from conservative commentator Laura Ingraham about LeBron James and Kevin Durant, his experience sharing a locker room with Michael Jordan and why he wrote the book. This is an excerpt from that conversation.

What was your reaction to Laura Ingraham's "Shut up and dribble" monologue on Fox News that received a backlash?

I spent quite a bit of time on this exact topic in "We Matter." This is the notion of an athlete's place. Especially a black athlete's place: "You should just be grateful," "How dare you complain," and "Who are you to speak on this subject?" You heard that criticism back in the day with Kareem Abdul-Jabbar, Bill Russell, Muhammad Ali and John Carlos.

You heard it after Colin Kaepernick took a knee. Now you're hearing it with LeBron James and Kevin Durant. It's not just Laura Ingraham who feels this way. There's a large segment she was speaking for. If you look at the words she chose: "barely intelligible" and "ungrammatical." Right there, she was attempting to insult their intelligence as if they don't have the qualifications to speak on this subject.

The line that stood out to me the most was "Must they run their mouths like that?"

Of course. It's the same thing. That's the whole "Shut up and play." This is not a new thing though. She, of course, verbalized it. But this is something that happens whenever an athlete speaks out.

You briefly overlapped with Michael Jordan when he made his second comeback with the Wizards. He is famously reported to have said "Republicans buy sneakers, too," when it came to political activism. Did you clash in the locker room?

Not at all. People have a certain perception of Michael Jordan, and I would just say the perception is not accurate. That's all. Just from being there with him, I never got any type of resistance from him.

That's a phrase that's going to haunt him for the rest of his days, whenever the topic of athletes and activism comes up. He's not quite what people think he is and that's what my interactions with him for two years were as well. We've had great discussions about different things and he respects other opinions. I wish other people could see the Michael Jordan that I saw.

If Jordan were in the league today, would he be politically active?

It's hard to say that because it's a different time. Back then, there was kind of a lull with athletes and activists. People weren't speaking out as much. But then you've seen a resurgence as of late. I think a lot of that has to do with police killings and the things that were visible on social media.

In your book, you encourage athletes to speak out. What was the dynamic with your teammates like? Did you ever receive any pushback?

I tell people all the time: If they would've heard the conversations that we had in the locker room, they would've been surprised. We had so many political conversations around a current event and everybody had opinions. From around the N.B.A., I would get nods of support. I'd be playing against a certain player and they'd be on the free throw line. They'd tell me, "Hey, I read what you said at that rally. That's good stuff!" Some media people didn't like it. It depended on what side of the fence they were on with whatever I was saying. I never got any pushback from management or coaches.

You write about an interesting conversation you had with the sociology professor Michael Eric Dyson comparing activism of athletes from decades ago to now. He suggests that athletes in the past engaged in "social protest," while today the top athletes are more likely to engage in "social charity." Do you agree?

We were going back and forth and came to some common ground. This is the thing. Everybody back in the 1960s was not Kareem Abdul-Jabbar and Bill Russell. There's sometimes been a romanticizing.

There's always a risk when you do speak out. It might be a different type of risk. Back in the sixties, there was a threat to your life on a whole different level. People love Muhammad Ali now. But back then? When he said he wasn't going to go in the Army? He was hated. People think that Colin Kaepernick is hated right now. They can just imagine it times one hundred with Ali.

Do you feel, given the platform, that there is an obligation for athletes to be politically active?

I don't feel that anybody should be forced to do something that they don't want to do. I think it's kind of unfair to tell somebody to take on a fight that isn't their fight or they're not passionate about it. I don't think that's necessarily fair but I do love when athletes speak out, of course, and I think they should get support.

Alejandro Bedoya Spoke Out on Gun Violence. It Helped Make Him M.L.S.'s Player of the Week.

BY VICTOR MATHER | AUG. 5, 2019

The Philadelphia Union midfielder grabbed a field microphone after scoring Sunday night and urged Congress to act to prevent more mass shootings.

ON MONDAY MORNING, Major League Soccer officials met in New York to determine if they should punish a player who had grabbed a field microphone during a national television broadcast on Sunday night and used it to urge Congress to act to end gun violence.

By lunch, M.L.S. had decided that no punishment was merited.

And by late afternoon, the player, Philadelphia Union midfielder Alejandro Bedoya, had been named the league's player of the week.

The honor capped a whirlwind 24-hour discussion of politics, gun control and the place of both in sports that had begun with nine shouted words from Bedoya during a game on Sunday night in Washington.

A former member of the United States national team, Bedoya had scored the opening goal in the Union's 5-1 win over D.C. United and then peeled off toward the sideline, where he celebrated with his teammates. But as the gathering broke up, Bedoya headed toward a television microphone placed on the grass, leaned down to grab it and shouted: "Congress, do something now. End gun violence. Let's go."

The statement was not out of character for Bedoya, who had expressed — in more explicit terms — a similar call to action on social media in the hours before the match. But it created a potentially uncomfortable situation for M.L.S., which has striven, often to the annoyance of its own fans, to keep political symbols and banners out of its stadiums.

An M.L.S. official, speaking after a league meeting on the incident Monday morning, confirmed that Bedoya would not face a fine or a suspension. Hours later, M.L.S. issued a brief statement that acknowledged the right of players to express their opinions. The statement made no mention of Bedoya specifically, or his decision — apparently spontaneously — to broadcast his opinion to a nationwide audience through a live microphone.

"The Major League Soccer family joins everyone in grieving for the loss of lives in Texas and Ohio, and we understand that our players and staff have strong and passionate views on this issue," the statement said.

By then, fans and others had rallied behind Bedoya's sentiment, mounting an ultimately successful campaign to get him voted as the league's player of the week.

Sunday's game was broadcast on Fox Sports 1, and Bedoya's message into the microphone, several of which are positioned around the field at every game to pick up the sounds of the action, could clearly be heard by viewers. It could not be heard in the stadium.

His sentiment was vague, which was understandable given its brevity. But Bedoya's social media account already had made clear what kind of action he was seeking. Bedoya, the Union's captain, had posted on Twitter earlier in the day about the weekend mass shootings that killed 29 people in El Paso and Dayton, Ohio, saying, "We can start with stricter background checks, red flag laws, making a registry for gun purchases, closing gun show loopholes, and taxing ammunition."

Though his on-field message was brief, it nonetheless caused a stir. While some athletes have been outspoken on political issues, and have taken actions as varied as kneeling during the anthem and wearing shirts with printed messages during pregame warm-ups, that activity has seldom taken place on the field of play during a game.

In extended postgame remarks, Bedoya reaffirmed his on-field comments. "It's absurd, man," he said. "I'm not going to sit idly and watch this stuff happen and not say something. Before I'm an athlete, a soccer player, I'm a human being first."

His team and his coach, Jim Curtin, expressed their full support.

"I'm on Alejandro's team on the Philadelphia Union and I'm on Alejandro's team in support of his comments on gun control," Curtin said after the game. Curtin called the number of mass shootings in the United States "outrageous."

Bedoya, 32, is of Colombian heritage but was born in New Jersey and played college soccer in the United States. After spells in Sweden, Scotland and France, he joined the Union in 2016. He was a regular with the United States national team earlier in the decade and represented it at the 2014 World Cup in Brazil.

Last year, after a shooting at a school in Parkland, Fla., near where Bedoya grew up, he expressed solidarity with victims of that attack.

In the hours after Sunday's game, M.L.S. fans rallied in support of his most recent comments, creating several crowdfunding campaigns to raise money to pay any potential fine he received.

M.L.S. has sometimes struggled to deal with political statements by its fans, juggling supporting a right to free speech with taking action against hateful comments and beliefs.

After news emerged that right-wing extremists had been regularly attending New York City F.C. games, M.L.S. Commissioner Don Garber said the league would not bar them pre-emptively because "our job is not to judge and profile any fan." His position was that the league would only attempt to police political behavior and fan misconduct inside stadiums. But after the comments drew widespread criticism Garber clarified his remarks, saying, "Major League Soccer condemns hateful groups, hateful actions and speech."

That incident and others did little to cool a simmering feud between the league and the fan groups it has cultivated as the core of its matchday experience. Before this season, the Independent Supporters Council, a coalition of fan groups, and supporters organizations devoted to individual teams took exception to changes to the league's code of conduct. The revised code barred using "political, threatening, abusive, insulting, offensive language and/or gestures."

The supporters objected to the word "political," and the council said in a statement, "We, as an organization, feel strongly on ensuring that displays of human rights are not mistaken for political statements."

Still, fans in Seattle were barred in July from displaying a flag of the Iron Front, a group that fought the Nazis before World War II. The team said the flag included prohibited political imagery. A team official later apologized for a letter sent to fans that equated antifacist symbols like the one that appeared on the flag with imagery used by violent far-right groups.

On Monday, M.L.S. fans had their say in a different way. In response to a tweet from the league asking fans to choose a player of the week, a decision made collectively in a vote of reporters who cover the league and fan balloting on Twitter, the replies were nearly unanimous. Though Bedoya wasn't one of the listed candidates, by far the most common response was a hashtag: "#VoteBedoya."

Hours later, he had won.

VICTOR MATHER covers every sport, no matter how small.

Kenny Stills Criticizes Dolphins Owner Over Trump Fund-Raiser

BY KEN BELSON | AUG. 7, 2019

The player said Stephen Ross's fund-raiser ran counter to the mission of a nonprofit Ross founded, which aims to use sports to improve race relations.

PRESIDENT TRUMP has not criticized the N.F.L. in recent months, but he is still having an impact on the league.

On Wednesday, Miami Dolphins wide receiver Kenny Stills criticized his boss, Stephen Ross, who owns the team, for hosting a re-election fund-raiser for the president this weekend on Long Island.

Stills said that Ross's support of the president is incompatible with the Ross Initiative in Sports for Equality, or RISE, a nonprofit group founded by Ross to use sports to improve race relations.

"You can't have a non profit with this mission statement then open your doors to Trump," Stills wrote on Twitter.

The group's mission statement says that it "educates and empowers the sports community to eliminate racial discrimination, champion social justice and improve race relations."

A spokesman for the Dolphins declined to comment about Stills's statement on Twitter.

While team owners have been criticized for their political leanings, particularly in the wake of the protests against police violence by Colin Kaepernick and other players, it is rare for players to openly criticize their bosses.

Stills, though, is one of the most outspoken players on social justice issues, and considers Kaepernick a friend. He was one of a handful of players who continued to kneel during the playing of the national anthem last season, long after Kaepernick played his last game. Stills has said he wants to shine a light on police brutality and economic inequality. A hero to some, he has been branded unpatriotic and ungrateful by others.

Many N.F.L. owners, Ross included, have made significant donations to Republican candidates. The owner of the Jets, Woody Johnson, helped Trump raise funds in the last presidential election cycle. Johnson, Jerry Jones of the Dallas Cowboys and E. Stanley Kroenke of the Los Angeles Rams were among the owners who contributed $1 million to Trump's inauguration.

Robert Kraft, the owner of the New England Patriots, is a close friend of the president's, and was recently at a dinner at the White House.

Ross and Trump have known each other for decades. Both are major real estate developers in New York and elsewhere. Both owned teams in the United States Football League, which folded in 1985 after three years.

Stills, 27, started his career with the New Orleans Saints. He has played with the Dolphins the past four seasons.

KEN BELSON covers the N.F.L. He joined the Sports section in 2009 after stints in Metro and Business. From 2001 to 2004, he wrote about Japan in the Tokyo bureau.

CHAPTER 6

Sports Diplomacy in the International Arena

In international sports, such as the Olympics or World Cup, we see familiar activities from activist athletes: taking a knee, raising a fist and other symbolic actions. But such protests often take on an additional character, as they reflect international political issues such as territorial conflict and human rights abuses. Such demonstrations use international sports as an extension of diplomacy. Athletic success becomes bound up in national pride, turning international sports bodies into informal diplomatic channels.

I.O.C. Names New President Amid Concern Over Possible Athlete Protests in Sochi

BY JERÉ LONGMAN | SEPT. 10, 2013

BUENOS AIRES — Shortly after Thomas Bach, a German lawyer, became the first gold-medal winning athlete to be named the president of the International Olympic Committee on Tuesday, he excused himself from a group of reporters.

Russia's president, Vladimir V. Putin, was on the phone.

"We did not discuss the law," Bach, 59, joked later, a reference to legislation viewed as antigay that was recently passed in Russia ahead of the 2014 Winter Games in the Black Sea resort of Sochi.

There are many serious issues facing the Olympic committee, including public unease over the exorbitant costs of the Games. But perhaps the most urgent concern for Bach will be to formulate a plan for how the I.O.C. would handle demonstrations against the Russian law by athletes at the Sochi Games in February.

Gunilla Lindberg, a member of the I.O.C. executive board from Sweden, said, "The I.O.C. has to really have very clear rules on what you can do and not do."

The Sochi Games face potential protests as part of widespread criticism of the law, which bans the dissemination of information to minors about so-called "nontraditional sexual relations."

Russian and I.O.C. officials have said that athletes and spectators in Sochi will not be affected by the law. And athletes will not face punishment if they answer reporters' questions about homosexuality or gay rights, officials have said.

But the I.O.C. has not answered such questions as: Will athletes face expulsion if they demonstrate on the medal stand, or wear T-shirts or rainbow pins or patches on their uniforms? What if someone wears rainbow-colored nail polish, symbolizing the gay pride flag, as a Swedish high jumper did at last month's track and field world championships in Moscow?

Corporate sponsors, particularly those based in the United States, are worried that protests by athletes, spectators and other visitors could overshadow the Games, Gerhard Heiberg, the I.O.C.'s chief marketing officer, has said. He has called for a plan to deal with demonstrations, adding, "I think this could ruin a lot for all of us."

The Olympic charter refers to sports as a human right that should not be abridged by any form of discrimination. But Rule 50 of the charter says that "no kind of demonstration or political, religious or racial propaganda is permitted" at any Olympic site.

On Tuesday, Bach, who won a gold medal in the team foil competition for West Germany at the 1976 Montreal Games, said a plan regarding Sochi would have to be worked out and communicated to Olympic officials of various nations, athletes and the news media.

While athletes should have the right to express their opinions outside the competition, while in the arena, Bach said, speaking in general, "You have to be protected from political controversies."

What that means precisely for Sochi is anyone's guess. And I.O.C. delegates clearly have different ideas on how strictly Rule 50 should be interpreted.

Larry Probst, the chairman of the United States Olympic Committee, who was elected an I.O.C. delegate Tuesday, said, "We will do everything to comply with I.O.C. regulations and the way they intend to handle any protests or demonstrations."

At the track and field championships last month, the Swedish female athlete who wore rainbow nail polish said she was asked by officials not to do it again.

"For me, nail polish is such a stupid thing to react on," Lindberg said.

Asked whether an athlete in Sochi should be disqualified for wearing a rainbow pin, Anita DeFrantz of the United States, a longtime I.O.C. delegate who rejoined the committee's executive board Tuesday, said: "That sounds like it's moving too far. Sometimes, somebody just being alive is a protest against something, so I think we have to be careful regarding what is or is not allowed."

Dick Pound, a longtime I.O.C. delegate from Montreal, said that although he found the Russian law "disgusting," he believed that even rainbow pins should not be tolerated in Sochi.

Pound said he would give this advice to Olympic officials in various nations: "You say to your kids, 'If you screw around with this we'll send you home.'"

Such discipline of an American athlete could cause outrage in the United States, where attitudes toward same-sex marriage and discrimination based on sexual orientation have evolved significantly.

Pound said that athletes and officials should realize they will be in Sochi as guests.

"If there have been lots of warnings, there's no excuse for it," Pound said of athletes wearing rainbow pins. "Then it becomes a provocation."

Wu Ching-Kuo, an I.O.C. delegate from Taiwan who challenged Bach for president, said the athletes should respect rules against demonstrations in Sochi. But, he added, no city with laws that seem to contradict the rights of athletes set forth in the Olympic charter should be allowed to bid on future Games.

"Any city bidding for the Games should avoid to have this kind of legislation," Wu said.

Prince Albert, an I.O.C. delegate from Monaco, said he thought that athletes should not be sent home for wearing pins. "It is a little strict," he said of Rule 50 of the Olympic charter, but added: "There has to be a rule at some point. It is an issue that has never been easy and has never" found a consensus.

"We have to try to find the best solution," he said.

Mandela Embraced the Power of Sports for Resistance and Unity

ESSAY | BY JERÉ LONGMAN | DEC. 5, 2013

HIS LAST PUBLIC APPEARANCE came at the final of the 2010 World Cup in South Africa. Wearing a coat, gloves and a fur hat, Nelson Mandela seemed frail and dressed against something more penetrating than the evening chill.

Still, he waved from a golf cart and stirred a stadium built like a calabash, a hollowed-out gourd meant to symbolize a melting pot of cultures. Acutely, Mandela understood the power of sport to provide dignity and hope in the face of state-sponsored oppression, to undermine discrimination with resistance and to heal and to help unite a society that the racial segregation of apartheid had brutally divided.

"Sport has the power to change the world," Mandela, who died Thursday, was often quoted as saying. "It has the power to inspire. It has the power to unite people in a way that little else does. It speaks to youth in a language they understand. Sport can create hope where once there was only despair."

A boxer, Mandela belonged to a generation that adhered to the amateur ideal of sport, believing it possessed an intrinsic value and offered lessons in fair play, gracious victory and edifying defeat, said Charles Korr, an American historian and a co-author of "More Than Just a Game," a book about soccer and apartheid.

It was not a naïve view, Korr said, but one that was savvy and pragmatic and rebutted the notion that sports and politics should not mix.

Mandela was kept isolated and was not allowed to play in the prisoners' soccer league on Robben Island, a harsh penal colony off Cape Town where he spent 18 of his 27 years in incarceration. Still, he eagerly followed the league results and recognized soccer's value to other prisoners in providing a sense of humanity and defiance.

"The energy, passion and dedication the game created made us feel alive and triumphant despite the situation we found ourselves in," Mandela said in a film sponsored by FIFA, soccer's global governing body.

Robben Island was also where Mandela reinforced his support for the international sports boycott against South Africa, under which the country was banned from the Olympics from 1964 to 1992.

In a sports-obsessed nation, Korr said, Mandela deeply understood the cultural significance of rugby, cricket, tennis and golf to the white minority and how international isolation damaged the apartheid regime's sense of national identity.

Mandela became a huge fan of the activism of Muhammad Ali. A photo of the American sprinters Tommie Smith and John Carlos raising their gloved fists in protest at the 1968 Mexico City Olympics was also smuggled onto Robben Island, further validating for Mandela and other prisoners the value of dissent in sports in bringing social change.

"He definitely believed that sports and politics are entwined," said Richard Lapchick, who was a leading anti-apartheid activist in the United States and is the founding director of the Institute for Diversity and Ethics in Sport at the University of Central Florida.

"You could smuggle in trade, oil and currency, but if you had a sporting event, you couldn't play in the dark," Lapchick said. "He realized this is a sports-mad world, and it was the way that people in various countries learned what apartheid was really about."

On May 10, 1994, Mandela became South Africa's first black president after three centuries of white domination. After his inauguration, he attended a soccer match at Ellis Park Stadium in Johannesburg to see South Africa defeat Zambia. It was time to re-enter international sport, Mandela told the crowd.

Lapchick, who sat in the presidential box, said he asked Mandela why he had chosen to watch soccer — the favored sport of the black majority — instead of attending inauguration parties.

He said that Mandela replied: "I wanted to make sure our people know how much I appreciated the sacrifices made by our athletes during the many years of the boycott. I have no doubt I became president today sooner than I would have had they not made those sacrifices."

A year later, at the final of the 1995 Rugby World Cup held in the same stadium, Mandela made a widely heralded gesture of reconciliation and nation-building that would have once been unthinkable.

Rugby was the preferred sport of South Africa's white minority. For blacks, the springbok, the mascot of the national rugby team, was a symbol of tyranny. While imprisoned, Mandela said, he invariably rooted for other countries to defeat his own.

By 1995, full democracy had replaced apartheid, and although South Africa had but one black rugby player on its roster, the Springboks played the World Cup under the slogan "One Team, One Country."

As the tournament opened in Cape Town, about five miles from where Mandela had been imprisoned, he told the players: "Our loyalties have completely changed. We have adopted these young men as our own boys."

A month later, South Africa defeated New Zealand in the final in Johannesburg. Mandela ignored the counsel of many advisers and handed the trophy to the Springboks' white captain, Francois Pienaar, while wearing a green jersey bearing Pienaar's No. 6. On Mandela, an emblem of repression was transformed into something unifying and restorative.

"He told me thanks for all we've done for South Africa," Pienaar said at the time. "I reciprocated, telling him we could never have done as much as he's done for South Africa."

Mandela's gesture would be commemorated in the movie "Invictus."

"He never showed bitterness; I don't know if I could have done that," said Mark Plaatjes, the 1993 world marathon champion, who left South Africa to escape apartheid's strictures and became a United States citizen. "He knew how pivotal sports were to South African society and how important it was to keep the white people looking forward versus, 'We need to get out of here; this could be bad.' It allayed their fears, gave them hope that this could work."

Mandela later became the godfather of Pienaar's oldest child. It was sometimes said by prisoners on Robben Island that the thing they missed most was the voices of children. Once on a flight from Johannesburg to London, the South African golfer Ernie Els recalled, Mandela showed great interest and delight in his young daughter.

When he won tournaments, said Els, a two-time winner of both the United States Open and the British Open, Mandela often phoned his congratulations before retreating from public view.

"He always felt proud of what the athletes out of South Africa did for the country," Els said. "Very proud."

Of course, the moral persuasion of sport has its limits. Two decades after apartheid, the "rainbow nation" ideal of South Africa remains clouded by unemployment, AIDS and violence. And the country's most visible sporting figure, the amputee Olympic sprinter Oscar Pistorius, stands accused of murdering his girlfriend.

Still, under Mandela's guidance, sport became a confirmation of possibility. It was his authority that landed the soccer World Cup in 2010. The world's most widely viewed sporting event came to South Africa for a month, and as Mandela took his final public wave, satisfaction was surely mixed with farewell.

"In his view, it was validation of the new South Africa," said Korr, a professor emeritus of history at the University of Missouri at St. Louis. "Mandela believed it showed the rest of the world they belonged."

Lapchick said he considered Mandela and Ali perhaps the world's two most beloved and unifying figures. When told that on the day of his inauguration, Lapchick said, Mandela humbly deferred and replied: "If I was in a crowded room with Ali, I would stop what I was doing and go to him. He is the Greatest."

Flying 3 Flags and
Seeking One Banner

BY BILLY WITZ | JUNE 14, 2014

SAN ANTONIO — Benny Mills, it appears, is the type of man who is incapable of speaking without a smile, one that instantly gives his cherubic face an impish glint. His wife, Yvonne, is a more serious study, a woman who chooses her words carefully, as if they are irrevocable, and speaks them with a quiet force.

Taken together, this charming earnestness — or perhaps it is an earnest charm — is readily apparent in their son, Patty Mills, the Australian backup point guard for the San Antonio Spurs whom they prefer to call Patrick.

It is visible when he waves a towel from the bench, exhorting his teammates with a bonhomie that does not feel over the top. It is present when he dives after a loose ball, as he did Tuesday night in Miami, knocking it ahead to a teammate to kick start a fast break, because as the smallest guy on the court at 5 feet 11, what choice did he really have?

Mills is among the many examples of the team-first ethic that the Spurs are being celebrated for as they close in on an N.B.A. championship, leading the Miami Heat by three games to one entering Game 5 on Sunday night.

This inclusive notion, of playing for others, runs particularly deep for Mills.

His turn on basketball's biggest stage is a source of pride for sports-mad Australians, but being the first indigenous Australian to play in the N.B.A. finals — his mother is Aboriginal and his father is a Torres Strait Islander is immensely gratifying for him.

Mills speaks metaphorically of flying three flags: of Australia, the Aboriginals and the Torres Strait Islands, the archipelago off the northern tip of the continent. When he dressed after Game 2, he wore a tie that was adorned with the image of a dhari, the headdress that is the emblem of the Torres Strait Islanders' flag, and a pearl shell, which his grandfather used to dive for.

"My heritage and my culture and where I'm from mean the most to me, more than anything," Mills said.

But questions of culture and heritage — namely, what does it mean to be Australian? — are complicated and deeply personal, and ones that the country continues to wrestle with as it moves slowly toward reconciliation with its indigenous people after generations of marginalization and abuse.

Coming to terms with that history is continuing.

"To be honest, I think I still am," said Mills, who is 25. "There's still stuff I've learned and that obviously surprises me, and that's how it's been since I was young. I learned gradually as I grew up and I understand more. I think it's a long process. Learning about our past is definitely important, not only for Australians but people around the world. It's something that Australia should never be ashamed of. It's part of our history. It's part of us."

Yvonne Mills is a member of the Stolen Generations. That term refers to the indigenous children who were removed from their families and placed with white families as part of a government- and church-sanctioned program that began in the late 1800s. It was not outlawed in all states until 1969.

Born on the rural western edge of South Australia, Yvonne said, she was separated from her brother and three sisters, all of them older, when she was 2 ½ years old. She was placed in an institution before being sent to live with another family.

"I was always told she didn't want me," said Yvonne, who along with her siblings learned otherwise when their family's files were released after a National Inquiry report on the separation of indigenous children from their families was issued in 1997. "I just had a few letters, but my brother had a large stack. She wrote: 'I want my children back. Please give me my children back.' "

Yvonne and Benny, who have lived in the capital, Canberra, since they were married in 1982, have been deeply involved in supporting indigenous programs. Yvonne works for the capital government, developing policy and managing finances for indigenous health and education programs. Benny, who was dissuaded from becoming a pearl diver by his father, was sent to a boarding school in Cairns and has worked on federal assistance programs aimed at Aboriginals and Torres Strait Islanders.

'GIVING PEOPLE A GO'

Benny also helped establish an indigenous basketball program called the Shadows, which provided an opportunity to play for those who could not afford a conventional club. The Shadows was as much a social program as it was about basketball, an opportunity to learn life skills and feel connected.

"Australia prides itself on giving people a go," Benny said, using the phrase that describes opportunity. "Eighty percent of the time it's fine, but the others aren't able to stand on their feet, get a job and have shelter. It's about moving out of depending on the government and giving them the capacity to do it themselves. They need role models on how to do it."

Some Aboriginals and Torres Strait Islanders are old enough to remember an era when they could not sit with whites in theaters or use public toilets. They also lacked the same access to education and health care.

That they often lived on the fringe of towns was an apt metaphor for their place in society.

"They came off missions and reserves; they didn't always have jobs and homes to live in," Yvonne said. "Aboriginal people have this feeling of shame, of being unequal. They've carried this shame all these years, and you can understand why. They don't want to compete against a white person."

Benny and Yvonne made sure Patty would not have any insecurity. He played for the Shadows at age 4, immersed himself in sports like track and rugby, and attended Catholic schools until he turned 15, when he was admitted to the Australian Institute for Sport. There were few other indigenous children, and when racism arose, it was dealt with quickly. If it was on the court, Patty would let his game do the talking. If it was with an adult, his parents stepped in.

"We had to get him to understand he was special," Yvonne said.

Benny added: "We told him, the best thing you can do is walk away. Come and tell us and we'll sort it out. We felt that if he knew about his background and he was confident, he'll put things in context and not back down."

A TURNING POINT

As Patty was growing up, it was a time of great change in Australia. In 1992, Eddie Mabo, a Torres Strait Islander, won a land-rights case against the government, which had dismissed indigenous land claims as being on empty land. Five years later, the National Inquiry findings were issued and the government declared National Sorry Day to commemorate the Stolen Generations, though it was not until 2008 that a prime minister formally apologized.

That served as the backdrop for the 2000 Olympics, where Cathy Freeman, an Aboriginal sprinter, lit the flame at Sydney Olympic Stadium and later delivered a signature moment of those games, winning the gold in the 400 meters and then carrying the Aboriginal flag around the track.

"That moment was — I get shivers just thinking about it," Mills, who had just turned 12, said as he pointed to goose bumps on his forearm. "I ran track, and my pet event was the 400 meters, and I wanted to be like Cathy Freeman. The whole country was on Cathy's back during that race. Everyone was clued in during that race seeing her cross the line and how she handled herself, not only on the track, but before and after, because she had so much pressure."

Mills would like to serve as a similar inspiration.

There is a documentary in the works on Mills, which will focus less on him as a basketball player (he was the leading scorer at the 2012

Olympics) than on his indigenous roots. Some of the film, titled "For My People," was shot on Thursday Island, where his father still has relatives. He often listens to the islands' ukulele-strained music.

"Patty embraces being a role model," said his Spurs teammate Aron Baynes, from Queensland. "A lot of indigenous youth are fighting to get through, so if they can have somebody they can look up to, that's a great thing."

In the United States, Mills, who scored 14 points off the bench in Game 4, is more of a curiosity. He is often assumed to be African-American until he opens his mouth. Even his teammates are getting to know more about him. On June 3, San Antonio Coach Gregg Popovich made a point at a team meeting of acknowledging Eddie Mabo Day. Popovich explained to the team why the holiday is so significant in Australian history and why it means so much to Mills.

It is the type of inclusive gesture the Spurs make a habit in their multicultural locker room. It was charming. It was earnest. And it explains why Mills feels so much at home.

Human Rights and the 2022 Olympics

OPINION | BY MINKY WORDEN | JAN. 18, 2015

THE OLYMPIC SPIRIT has come to this: Two authoritarian countries are vying to host the 2022 Winter Games, competing to endure a huge financial strain for the benefit of burnishing their public image. The withdrawal of Oslo in October left Beijing, China's capital, and Almaty, the largest city in Kazakhstan, as the contenders. They formally submitted their bids to the International Olympic Committee this month.

That helps explain why the president of the International Olympic Committee, the German lawyer Thomas Bach, pushed through landmark human rights reforms at a big Olympic summit meeting in Monaco last month.

For the first time, host countries must sign a contract that requires protections for human rights, labor and the environment. These "international agreements and protocols" are meant to protect against abuses such as Russia's anti-gay law, passed ahead of last year's Winter Games in Sochi, and the labor and human rights abuses before and during the 2008 Summer Games in Beijing. These reforms are about to get a rigorous test in the global spotlight — whether the 2022 Games are in China, which welcomed journalists to Beijing in 2008 with a censored Internet, or Kazakhstan, which locks up critics and closes down newspapers.

Over the past decade, Human Rights Watch has documented how major sporting events are also accompanied by human rights violations when games are awarded to serial human rights abusers. Repressive countries promised to respect media and other rights to secure the events, then reneged and relied on international sporting bodies to stay silent.

As these countries prepare for events, forced evictions without fair compensation free up space for the massive new infrastructure construction that Olympics require. Migrant workers are cheated and labor under long hours and sometimes deadly working conditions. Construction leads to environmental and other complaints. Activists who object are silenced or jailed. Beijing locked up critics of the Olympics. In Russia, an environmentalist drew a three-year prison sentence, and members of the feminist band Pussy Riot were beaten and detained for their protests of the Sochi Games. Given the abuses, is there any hope for change?

If there is the political will to implement them, the contract reforms could improve conditions in countries that host big sporting events. Autocrats are increasingly turning to international sporting events to boost their global standing, so the regulations adopted by their governing bodies might be the only way to make human rights advances in some of the most abusive places.

At Sochi last year, for example, the I.O.C. pressured the Russian government to take action against the theft of wages from workers who helped build Olympic venues and infrastructure. Some 500 companies were investigated, and inspectors found that thousands of workers had been cheated out of more than $8 million in wages. The general director of a top construction company was arrested on suspicion of withholding wages. This action resulted from a specific reform from the 2009 Olympic Congress: a promise that the I.O.C. would intervene in the event of "serious abuses," including abuses of migrant workers.

In Iran, hard-liners and reformists alike cheer the country's volleyball successes. A law student, Ghoncheh Ghavami, was jailed in Iran's notorious Evin prison last year after she protested a ban on women entering a stadium to watch an International Federation of Volleyball World League match. In November, the federation (known as FIVB, the acronym in French) called on the Iranian government to release Ms. Ghavami, and affirmed its commitment to "inclusivity and the right of women to participate in sport on an equal basis." The federation warned that Iran's policy could limit its ability to host international tournaments in the future. Ms. Ghavami was released on bail shortly thereafter, but not before a revolutionary court convicted her

JOÃO FAZENDA

of "propaganda against the state" and sentenced her to one year in prison. She is appealing.

In 2012, Saudi Arabia allowed two women, at the last moment, to compete at the London Summer Games. But it still forbids sports for all girls in state schools and has no women's sports federations. The Saudis should win a gold medal in brazenness for sending a 199-member men-only team to last fall's Asian Games, claiming, "Technically, we weren't ready to introduce any ladies."

Human rights and sports crises are not limited to the Olympics. Russia, despite its record of worker abuse, was awarded the 2018 World Cup. This summer, authoritarian Azerbaijan will roll out the welcome mat for the first European Games in Baku, despite escalating repression, including the December arrest of a top investigative journalist.

As Qatar builds an estimated $200 billion of infrastructure for the 2022 World Cup, hundreds of South Asian migrant workers have died working on construction projects. FIFA, the governing body of world soccer, is ripe for institutional reform. In May, it will hold a once-in-a-generation presidential election, in which the current president, Sepp Blatter of Switzerland, will seek a fifth term against stiff competition, including Prince Ali bin al-Hussein of Jordan, who has championed reforms to advance women's participation. Those candidates should back human-rights-based reforms to the FIFA Charter and set out their position on the human rights, discrimination, corruption and labor crises that have dogged the body.

The Olympic reforms passed in December mean that if future host countries fail in their duty to uphold rights, the I.O.C. is now obliged to enforce the terms of the hosting agreement — including the ultimate sanction of withdrawing the Olympics. And for those who break rules like nondiscrimination, the punishment should be a ban on playing and hosting, as the I.O.C. imposed on apartheid South Africa from 1964 to 1992 and Taliban-run Afghanistan from 1999 to 2002.

Mr. Bach has started the ball rolling, but with abuses mounting around global sporting events, it's time for other sporting federations like FIFA to begin reforms. Fans, corporate sponsors and the general public are increasingly turned off by human rights violations. The I.O.C. reforms aren't a panacea, but they represent an important step forward.

MINKY WORDEN, director of global initiatives at Human Rights Watch, is the editor of "China's Great Leap: The Beijing Games and Olympian Human Rights."

Palestinian Soccer Association Drops Effort to Suspend Israel From FIFA

BY JODI RUDOREN | MAY 29, 2015

JERUSALEM — The Palestinians dropped their bid to suspend Israel from international soccer competition at the last minute Friday, and agreed to instead form a committee of the sport's governing body, FIFA, to handle their complaints of racism and discrimination.

Jibril Rajoub, president of the Palestine Football Association, called for a vote at FIFA's annual congress to ask the United Nations to determine whether five teams from settlements in the occupied West Bank should be allowed to continue to play in Israeli leagues. But FIFA's president, Sepp Blatter, blocked that initiative, and said the new committee would also decide how to handle the contentious question of the settlement teams.

In an emotional speech, Mr. Rajoub said he had been persuaded to abandon the demand to suspend Israel by fellow delegates to the FIFA congress, particularly one from South Africa, who said the vote would be "painful" for the conclave scarred by scandal after Wednesday's dawn arrest of top soccer executives. He accepted Mr. Blatter's proposal for a "peace match" between Israeli and Palestinian teams, but also said it "does not mean I give up the resistance."

"I think it's time now to raise the red card for racism, humiliation and discrimination in Palestine and everywhere," Mr. Rajoub said from the podium, pulling an actual red card from his coat pocket.

He said the Palestinian situation was "even worse than what was in South Africa," which FIFA suspended from the 1960s until 1992. "There they wanted them to be slaves," Mr. Rajoub said, referring to South Africa during the apartheid era, adding, "But here in Palestine, they don't want us to be."

The FIFA campaign, part of a mounting Palestinian effort to press the case against Israeli occupation in international forums, garnered global attention and incited deep concern in Israel's soccer-obsessed society. Israel's Foreign Ministry sent diplomats to Zurich to join sports officials in a blitz to block the proposal, winning the support of European federations that made it all but impossible for Mr. Rajoub to garner the required 75 percent majority.

Mr. Blatter echoed Israelis in describing the proposal as a dangerous politicization of sport, and met repeatedly with Mr. Rajoub and his Israeli counterpart, Ofer Eini, to broker a compromise, including a meeting during Friday's lunch break that ended two hours before the proposal came up for discussion. Mr. Eini said he was "delighted" that Mr. Rajoub had dropped the suspension, and publicly invited him for a handshake, which the two men eventually concluded to great applause.

"Let's leave it to the politicians to deal with politics — you and I together, let's join forces and do the best football we can on both sides," Mr. Eini said, addressing Mr. Rajoub from the podium. "I hope that our cooperation will be the beginning of a process that, maybe, will lead to peace between our peoples, that maybe will bring our peoples together, and football is a uniting element, not a dividing element."

Prime Minister Benjamin Netanyahu of Israel, who said in a Facebook post earlier Friday that the Palestinian proposal "stems from the fact of opposition to our right to maintain our own state," issued a statement after it was dropped, calling it a unilateral "provocation" that he said "will only push peace further away."

The new FIFA committee is to monitor Israeli commitments to ease athletes' travel through checkpoints and border crossings, remove tariffs on the import of sports equipment, and help build fields and facilities in the West Bank and Gaza Strip. Mr. Blatter said it would also "deal with the matter of the Palestinian or Israeli territories," referring to the fate of teams from five Israeli settlements, though he also said FIFA's executive committee had decided this week that it "cannot interfere" in such a dispute.

Yaakov Finkelstein, an Israeli diplomat sent to Zurich for the FIFA congress, said any action on the settlement teams would have been "a deal-breaker for us."

The Palestinians contend the settlement teams violate FIFA rules by, essentially, having one member's teams playing in another's turf. The amended Palestinian proposal, which the congress passed overwhelmingly, calls on FIFA to ask the United Nations for official notification of its 2012 resolution upgrading Palestine to nonmember observer-state status "in order to prove the territorial issue."

Mr. Rajoub has been pressing FIFA to take action against Israel for three years, and said previous committees formed by the organization yielded little. But this year's campaign gained more traction, amid intensifying international criticism of the continuing occupation and a growing movement to boycott Israeli academic and cultural institutions, and companies that do business in settlements.

Zaid Shuaibi, a spokesman for the Boycott, Divestment and Sanctions movement, expressed disappointment with FIFA as well as the Palestinian soccer organization. "FIFA and its membership have delayed the suspension of Israel," he said in a statement, "but they cannot delay the growth of the international boycott of Israel or prevent the continued isolation of Israel because of its human rights abuses and war crimes against the Palestinian people."

Pro-Palestinian protesters camped outside the congress, and two women burst into the hall Friday morning, shouting, "Red card to racism!" before being quickly removed by security guards.

By afternoon, a few dozen young Palestinian players gathered in the West Bank village of Nabi Saleh, carrying soccer balls and the symbolic red cards. Along with international activists, they chanted, "One, two, three, four, occupation no more; five, six, seven, eight, Israel the fascist state," and "FIFA, FIFA, we are pros, FIFA, FIFA, Israel goes," then threw stones at Israeli soldiers, which drew tear-gas canisters in response.

The protesters, some wearing jerseys honoring Barcelona and its Argentine star, Lionel Messi, said the Palestinian push signaled progress regardless of the outcome in Zurich.

"It's important for us as Palestinians to share our struggle for liberation with the entire world," said Marah Tamimi, 14, whose family has led weekly demonstrations in the village for years. "I hope that one day this red card will be used to kick Israel out of our land."

Salam Salah, 9, said he played soccer "in the streets of my neighborhood every day after school, even when it's raining."

"Soccer is my life," he said. "One day I may become a player on Palestine's national team, and I would like to be treated like any athlete from any country in the world. This is a message to the world through soccer that we need our freedom and the harsh occupation must stop."

RAMI NAZZAL contributed reporting from Nabi Saleh, the West Bank, SAM BORDEN from Zurich, and RICK GLADSTONE from New York.

Egyptian Judo Athlete Refuses Handshake After Losing to Israeli

BY VICTOR MATHER | AUG. 12, 2016

RIO DE JANEIRO — An Egyptian judoka declined to shake hands with his Israeli opponent after their match on Friday, eliciting jeers from the crowd.

Or Sasson, the Israeli, defeated Islam El Shehaby, the Egyptian, in a first-round match in the heaviest weight class, over 100 kilograms (about 220 pounds).

After a moment of prayer, El Shehaby got up and seemed reluctant to perform the traditional bow to his opponent. Eventually, he gave a quick nod and left the mat. A judge and a referee urged him to return. Sasson then approached El Shehaby with his hand extended, but El Shehany backed away.

Throughout the competition, as at all judo matches, opponents have bowed to each other, often multiple times. To decline a handshake is a serious breach of judo etiquette.

"That is extremely rare in judo," the American coach Jimmy Pedro said. "It is especially disrespectful considering it was a clean throw and a fair match. It was completely dishonorable and totally unsportsmanlike on the part of the Egyptian."

A judo federation spokesman said in an email to The Associated Press that a bow was mandatory but that shaking hands was not. He said El Shehaby's "attitude will be reviewed after the Games to see if any further action should be taken."

Before the match, El Shehaby had faced pressure on social media not to show up, the news site NRG reported. "You dishonor Islam if you lose to Israel," he was told. "How can you cooperate with a killer?"

There is a history of animosity between Israeli and other Middle Eastern athletes at the Olympics, including in judo.

Egypt's Islam El Shehaby, right, with Israel's Or Sasson after their judo match Friday.

Israeli and Lebanese athletes got into a dispute about sharing a bus to the opening ceremony last week. The Lebanese team admitted preventing Israeli athletes from boarding, but said it was because the bus had been reserved for the Lebanese athletes.

When a Saudi judo player forfeited a match on Tuesday, the official reason was that she was injured, but the Israeli news media claimed it was because she would have faced an Israeli in the next round.

At the 2004 Athens Games, Arash Miresmaeili, a gold medal favorite in judo, was disqualified for showing up over the weight limit for his first-round match against an Israeli. It was reported that he had gone on an eating binge to intentionally forfeit, and he said, "I refused to fight my Israeli opponent to sympathize with the suffering of the people of Palestine, and I do not feel upset at all."

Under Fidel Castro, Sport Symbolized Cuba's Strength and Vulnerability

BY JERÉ LONGMAN | NOV. 27, 2016

ON JULY 24, 1959, months after coming to power, Fidel Castro took the mound at a baseball stadium in Havana to pitch an exhibition for a team of fellow revolutionaries known as Los Barbudos, the Bearded Ones.

He pitched an inning or two against a team from the Cuban military police and, by some accounts, struck out two batters.

"He threw a few pitches, people were swinging wildly and letting themselves be struck out by the Leader," said Roberto González Echevarría, a native of Cuba who is a literature professor at Yale and the author of "The Pride of Havana: A History of Cuban Baseball."

Mr. Castro, who died Friday at 90, also avidly followed Havana's Sugar Kings of the International League, a Class AAA team in the Cincinnati Reds' farm system from 1954 to 1960. He went to some games because he was a fan and "he liked being on TV," Mr. González Echevarría said.

The persistent notion that Mr. Castro's fastball had made him a potential big league prospect has long been debunked by historians. By many accounts, his primary sport as a schoolboy was basketball. He was tall, at 6-foot-2 or 6-foot-3, and he told the biographer Tad Szulc that the anticipation, speed and dexterity required for basketball most approximated the skills needed for revolution.

Yet it was primarily baseball, along with boxing and other Olympic sports, that came to symbolize both the strength and vulnerability of Cuban socialism.

Successes in those sports allowed Mr. Castro to taunt and defy the United States on the diamond and in the ring and to infuse Cuban citizens with a sense of national pride. At the same time, international isolation and difficult financial realities led to the rampant defection of top baseball stars, the decrepit condition of stadiums and a shortage of equipment.

The former Soviet bloc and China also acutely understood the value of sporting achievement as propaganda, but there seemed to be some fundamental differences in Mr. Castro's Cuba.

For one thing, Cuba under Mr. Castro promoted mass sport, not simply elite sport. About 95 percent of Cubans have participated in some form of organized sport or exercise, from children who start physical education classes at age 5 to grandmothers who gather to practice tai chi, said Robert Huish, an associate professor at Dalhousie University in Halifax, Nova Scotia, who has studied Cuban sport, health and social programs.

Secondly, "I think Fidel Castro legitimately liked sports," said David Wallechinsky, the president of the International Society of Olympic Historians. "One got the sense with East Germany, for example, that it really was a question of propaganda and that government officials didn't have that obsession with sport itself that Fidel Castro did."

Whatever hardships they endured, Cubans could take pride in their sports stars.

As Javier Sotomayor, the only man to clear eight feet in the high jump, soared to his records in the late 1980s and early 1990s, Cubans for a time marked the height of his jumps in their doorways, according to Mr. Huish.

"There was a real effort to connect nationalistic pride to athletic achievement," said Mr. Huish, who was scheduled to make his 42nd trip to Cuba on Monday. "Boxing became a really important factor in that. You would hear how it was connected to revolution and how socialism and having universal access to sport meant that the victory of the boxer is really everyone's victory."

Teófilo Stevenson, a three-time Olympic heavyweight boxing champion from 1972 to 1980, once famously explained why he had turned down a chance to sign a professional contract and perhaps to fight Muhammad Ali, saying, "What is a million dollars' worth compared to the love of eight million Cubans?"

The idea that sports "were healthy and good for developing bodies," Mr. González Echevarría said, derived from the American role in helping to establish Cuba's educational system while occupying the country from 1898 to 1902 after the Spanish-American War.

In "Castro's Cuba, Cuba's Fidel," a biography by the American photojournalist Lee Lockwood, Mr. Castro spoke little of baseball, instead stressing his long love for basketball, chess, deep-sea diving, soccer and track and field. "I never became a champion," he told Mr. Lockwood, adding, "but I didn't practice much."

In 1946, an F. Castro was listed in a box score as having pitched in an intramural game at the University of Havana, where Fidel Castro attended law school, though González Echevarría said he could not confirm it was the future leader.

The only known photographs of Mr. Castro in a baseball uniform were taken while he played for Los Barbudos, the informal revolutionary team, Mr. González Echevarría said. Mr. Castro was never scouted by the major leagues, Mr. González Echevarría said, and the notion that Mr. Castro was once a promising pitcher "is really a lie."

Instead, Peter C. Bjarkman, a baseball historian, argues that Mr. Castro's post-revolutionary identification with baseball derived from two factors: One, an acknowledgment of the entrenched popularity of a sport played in Cuba since the 1860s and as popular there as soccer was in Brazil. And two, a stoking of revolutionary zeal at home and a forging of propaganda victories abroad.

While Mr. Castro staged some exhibitions and played some pickup games after coming to power, a primary objective was to bedevil the United States in a "calculated step toward utilizing baseball as a means of besting the hated imperialists at their own game," Mr. Bjarkman wrote in an article for the Society for American Baseball Research.

Mr. Castro banned professional sports in Cuba in 1961, and several years later, said, "Anybody who truly loves sport, and feels sport, has to prefer this sport to professional sport by a thousand times."

His strategy worked for decades as Cuba played baseball against mostly amateur competition, or non-major leaguers, winning 18 championships in the Baseball World Cup from 1961 to 2005 and three Olympic gold medals from 1992 to 2004.

But the collapse of the Soviet Union (and later Venezuela's oil economy) cost Cuba its financial benefactors. And its dominance began to ebb amid rampant defections of top Cuban players and the growing inclusion of professionals from other nations in international baseball tournaments.

Cuba won only one of the three Olympic tournaments held after 1996, before baseball was discontinued for the 2012 London Games (it will return at the 2020 Tokyo Olympics). And Cuba has yet to win the World Baseball Classic, a quadrennial tournament that began in 2006 and features major leaguers.

Meanwhile, the American trade embargo, still in place even though the two countries have begun to normalize relations, has left Cuba with poor sports facilities, including some pools with no water; fewer night baseball games because of the cost keeping the lights on; games halted in some stadiums until fans can retrieve foul balls; and a leaky roof and soaked mats at the national wrestling center.

In 2013, Cuban officials took a more pragmatic approach to professionalism, allowing athletes to compete for earnings and to play in other countries (though not in Major League Baseball). Cuban coaches are also being exported to other countries in exchange for hard currency. The athletes keep 80 percent of their winnings and agree to compete for Cuba in international competitions.

Antonio Castro, a son of Fidel Castro and a vice president of the International Baseball Federation, told ESPN in 2014 that Cuban players should be permitted to play in the Major Leagues and be able to return to Cuba "without fear."

"Then no one loses," Antonio Castro said. "And they don't have to be separated from their family, from their friends."

But after President Obama attended an exhibition baseball game in Havana in March as the first sitting American president to visit Cuba since the 1959 revolution, Fidel Castro threw a brushback pitch.

In a column, he criticized renewed relations between the two countries, writing, "We don't need the empire to give us anything."

Pan Am Games Protesters Get Probation. Olympians Get a Warning.

BY JERÉ LONGMAN | AUG. 21, 2019

Two athletes who protested the national anthem at a recent competition were placed on 12 months' probation. But stopping other competitors from making political stands at next year's Tokyo Olympics won't be easy.

THE 2020 OLYMPICS in Tokyo will take place amid sagging credibility of the Olympic movement itself and ahead of a divisive American presidential election. The Games will occur during awakenings to gender equity and sexual abuse. They will happen during a rise of nationalism around the world. And they will come at a time when athletes seem to have more willingness and access than ever to express their thoughts on politics, social issues and human rights.

So when the top United States Olympic official on Tuesday sent letters to two American athletes who protested the national anthem at the recent Pan American Games in Peru, placing both on 12 months' probation, she also included a warning to prospective Olympians about making political gestures at the Summer Games next year. But trying to silence athletes in Tokyo might be futile when some feel more emboldened than ever to speak out.

The letters sent this week, from the chief executive of the United States Olympic and Paralympic Committee, Sarah Hirshland, went to the hammer thrower Gwen Berry, who raised her fist during the national anthem, and the fencer Race Imboden, who knelt on the medal podium.

Such wrist slaps might become more consequential if repeated, Ms. Hirshland suggested in her letters, which seemed intended for a broader audience.

"It is also important for me to point out that, going forward, issuing a reprimand to other athletes in a similar instance is insufficient," Ms. Hirshland wrote in the letters, which were first obtained and reported by The Associated Press.

But this is a far different environment from 1968, when the American sprinters Tommie Smith and John Carlos were sent home from the Summer Olympics in Mexico City after making a gloved-fisted protest against social inequality on the medal stand.

President Trump could respond with vitriol to any criticism of him during the Olympics, as he did in a Twitter spat with the American soccer star Megan Rapinoe during the recent Women's World Cup, but "much of the country is going to be much more sympathetic" now than in 1968, said David Wallechinsky, the president of the International Society of Olympic Historians.

Today's athletes can build support through social media and, in some cases, are buoyed by their coaches and companies like Nike. There also are many more avenues to convey their thoughts beyond silent gestures of protest. In interviews, Gregg Popovich, the coach of the San Antonio Spurs, who will lead the United States men's basketball team in Tokyo, has been highly critical of Mr. Trump.

"I feel there is a group of people who are always going to think that standing up for the many is more important than the repercussions for themselves," Mr. Imboden said.

Douglas Hartmann, the chairman of the sociology department at the University of Minnesota, who has studied Olympic protests, said, "I think more athletes are more inclined to speak out on social issues than any moment probably since the '60s." But, he added, "I'm pretty sure they are not inclined to do that during the actual competitions and ceremonies."

An athlete who makes a political gesture on a medal stand, or in a uniform, or after scoring a goal or winning a race, would be violating the Olympic Charter, and risks ejection from the Games, not to mention public excoriation and the loss of financial opportunity, if not the medal itself.

But such public gestures are precisely what the International Olympic Committee "is terrified about," Mr. Hartmann said.

If any large-scale protests — from Americans or athletes from the world's other hot spots — took hold and found public sympathy during

EZRA SHAW/GETTY IMAGES

Gwen Berry of the United States, pictured competing in Lima, Peru, on Aug. 10, protested on the medals stand at the Pan American Games last week.

the Tokyo Olympics, Mr. Hartmann said, they could provide a transformative moment and undermine the Western view of sport as being "sacred, purely fun and an inherently positive social activity."

The I.O.C. takes an often contradictory position, discouraging political activity but also supporting it if it portrays the Olympic committee as a positive moral force. For instance, the Ethiopian marathon runner Feyisa Lilesa was not penalized for crossing his arms above his head as he reached the finish line in second place at the 2016 Rio Olympics, protesting the treatment of his ethnic group, the Oromo people.

"They want credit for everything good and want to run from everything controversial," Mr. Hartmann said of the I.O.C.

What gets tricky, Mr. Hartmann said, is when "athletes take on causes or issues that to most observers seem not political but within their rights, as moral causes."

So what would happen if, say, an American athlete protested

silently at the Tokyo Olympics, as Mr. Imboden, the fencer, did at the Pan Am Games? He said his decision to kneel was over what he considered "shortcomings" in the United States like "racism, gun control, mistreatment of immigrants and a president who spreads hate."

Surely, some people would consider that a moral act, and many would be in agreement with Mr. Imboden's stance on those issues. But many others would disagree, and might consider any athlete who took a similar action as unpatriotic.

Ms. Hirshland, the chief executive, wrote in letters to Mr. Imboden and Ms. Berry, the hammer thrower, that: "The goal of a Games that are free from political speech is to focus our collective energy on the athletes' performances, and the international unity and harmony each Games seek to advance. When an individual makes his or her grievances, however legitimate, more important than that of their competitors and the competition itself, that unity and harmony is diminished. The celebration of sport, and human accomplishment, is lost."

In truth, though, sports and politics are inextricably linked.

Harry Edwards, a sociologist who counseled Mr. Smith and Mr. Carlos and the former N.F.L. quarterback Colin Kaepernick on their protests, said of the Tokyo Games, "The chance of no athletes protesting is zero."

The key to the impact of any protests, he said, would be how they are framed leading to the Games. The International Olympic Committee and the United States Olympic and Paralympic Committee are "morally bankrupt" and particularly vulnerable to challenges to their legitimacy by athletes, Mr. Edwards said, given endemic corruption and indifference to protecting athletes from sexual abuse in gymnastics and other sports.

If numerous athletes protested against the very organizers of the Games, while also taking political stances, Mr. Edwards said, "the I.O.C. and the U.S.O.C. can't win both of those fights."

JERÉ LONGMAN is a sports reporter and a best-selling author. He covers a variety of international sports, primarily Olympic ones.

Glossary

agency The state of having freedom or control in one's actions.

antitrust A category of law intended to discourage monopolies and promote competition.

apartheid A system of racial segregation that existed in South Africa from 1948 to 1994.

collective bargaining When employees negotiate wages or benefits as a group, rather than as individuals.

contentious Controversial or highly disputed.

criminal justice reform Proposed changes in the criminal justice system, typically involving proposals to reduce mass incarceration, as well as to combat racial disparities in arrests and sentencing.

doggerel Rhyming poetry considered to have poor meter or to be unserious in tone.

draft A system in some professional sports leagues that distributes players among teams.

exhibition game A professional sporting event outside of standard competitive play.

extrajudicial killing A killing outside the bounds of the law, typically used to refer to people killed by police.

free agent An athlete who is not contractually bound to a team.

gender dysphoria A state of distress caused by a non-alignment of gender identity and sex assigned at birth.

hagiography A biography that presents its subject in an overly flattering light.

homophobia Fear of or hostility toward gay or lesbian individuals.

incarceration Imprisonment or jailing.

indigenous Native to, or an original inhabitant of, a place.

intersex A condition of variance from one or more biological sex characteristics.

lockout A bargaining tactic where an employer closes out employees until they agree to the employer's terms.

microcosm A person, place or thing whose elements reflect a larger whole, system or process.

panacea A remedy that can resolve any illness or problem.

pragmatic Emphasizing practical results over theoretical or ideological factors.

revenue sharing The distribution of revenue, such as that between owners and employees. Revenue sharing is often discussed in professional athlete union contracts.

salary cap A limit on the maximum salary an employee can earn. This term often appears in professional athlete union contracts.

surreal Unreal, dreamlike or unexpected.

testosterone A hormone appearing in varying amounts in all humans, associated with the development of male secondary sex characteristics.

Title IX A section of the Education Amendments Act of 1972, which barred sex discrimination in any educational program receiving federal funds.

transgender When a person's gender identity does not align with the sex they were assigned at birth.

Media Literacy Terms

"Media literacy" refers to the ability to access, understand, critically assess and create media. The following terms are important components of media literacy, and they will help you critically engage with the articles in this title.

angle The aspect of a news story that a journalist focuses on and develops.

attribution The method by which a source is identified or by which facts and information are assigned to the person who provided them.

balance Principle of journalism that both perspectives of an argument should be presented in a fair way.

bias A disposition of prejudice in favor of a certain idea, person or perspective.

byline Name of the writer, usually placed between the headline and the story.

chronological order Method of writing a story presenting the details of the story in the order in which they occurred.

credibility The quality of being trustworthy and believable, said of a journalistic source.

editorial Article of opinion or interpretation.

feature story Article designed to entertain as well as to inform.

headline Type, usually 18 point or larger, used to introduce a story.

human interest story Type of story that focuses on individuals and how events or issues affect their life, generally offering a sense of relatability to the reader.

impartiality Principle of journalism that a story should not reflect a journalist's bias and should contain balance.

intention The motive or reason behind something, such as the publication of a news story.

interview story Type of story in which the facts are gathered primarily by interviewing another person or persons.

inverted pyramid Method of writing a story using facts in order of importance, beginning with a lead and then gradually adding paragraphs in order of relevance from most interesting to least interesting.

motive The reason behind something, such as the publication of a news story or a source's perspective on an issue.

news story An article or style of expository writing that reports news, generally in a straightforward fashion and without editorial comment.

op-ed An opinion piece that reflects a prominent individual's opinion on a topic of interest.

paraphrase The summary of an individual's words, with attribution, rather than a direct quotation of their exact words.

quotation The use of an individual's exact words indicated by the use of quotation marks and proper attribution.

reliability The quality of being dependable and accurate, said of a journalistic source.

rhetorical device Technique in writing intending to persuade the reader or communicate a message from a certain perspective.

tone A manner of expression in writing or speech.

Media Literacy Questions

1. "When a Players Union Doesn't Help the Players" (on page 10) is written by sports agent Arn Tellem. How does Tellem's background inform the arguments he makes in the article?

2. What is the meaning of the headline "Players Hold Power Over the N.C.A.A., if They Feel the Hunger" (on page 33)? Compare the headline with the contents of the article's earliest paragraphs.

3. "The Awakening of Colin Kaepernick" (on page 44) is a feature story. What personal details in Kaepernick's life does the author explore?

4. "In a Busy Year, Malcolm Jenkins Raised a Fist and Checked All the Boxes" (on page 67) includes quotations from a variety of sources. What are the motives of these different sources?

5. "Billie Jean King Understands Colin Kaepernick" (on page 87) is an interview story. What kinds of questions does the interviewer ask Billie Jean King? What perspective does King bring to contemporary athlete protests?

6. "For Megan Rapinoe, Boldness in the Spotlight Is Nothing New" (on page 108) includes both quotations and paraphrased statements from various sources. What kinds of quotations were chosen for inclusion, and what information was paraphrased instead?

7. "Sprinter Dutee Chand Becomes India's First Openly Gay Athlete" (on page 135) includes an account of a dispute over hormone testing. How does the author maintain the journalistic principle of balance when reporting on this dispute?

8. What is the intent of "He Emerged From Prison a Potent Symbol of H.I.V. Criminalization" (on page 144)? Consider the experiences of the subject, Michael L. Johnson, as you form your response.

9. What is the tone of "What the World Got Wrong About Kareem Abdul-Jabbar" (on page 151)? As you form your response, consider the headline, article introduction and descriptions of Abdul-Jabbar's demeanor.

10. The author of "Muhammad Ali, Political Poet" (on page 162), Henry Louis Gates Jr., is a scholar of African-American literature. How might the author's background inform the angle of the article?

11. "I.O.C. Names New President Amid Concern Over Possible Athlete Protests in Sochi" (on page 179) is written in the inverted pyramid style. Compare the earliest paragraphs with the last paragraphs in the article. How did the author determine which information was most important?

12. "Under Fidel Castro, Sport Symbolized Cuba's Strength and Vulnerability" (on page 202) draws on sources that include historians and Cuban officials, among others. What makes these sources especially reliable?

Citations

All citations in this list are formatted according to the
Modern Language Association's (MLA) style guide.

BOOK CITATION

THE NEW YORK TIMES EDITORIAL STAFF. *Activist Athletes: When Sports and
Politics Mix*. New York Times Educational Publishing, 2021.

ONLINE ARTICLE CITATIONS

ARATON, HARVEY. "From the N.B.A., a Cautionary Tale on National
Anthem Protests." *The New York Times*, 6 Nov. 2017, https://www.nytimes
.com/2017/11/06/sports/basketball/anthem-nba-abdul-rauf-kaepernick
.html.

BELSON, KEN. "In a Busy Year, Malcolm Jenkins Raised a Fist and Checked
All the Boxes." *The New York Times*, 25 Jan. 2018, https://www.nytimes
.com/2018/01/25/sports/football/malcolm-jenkins-eagles-super-bowl.html.

BELSON, KEN. "Kenny Stills Criticizes Dolphins Owner Over Trump
Fund-Raiser." *The New York Times*, 7 Aug. 2019, https://www.nytimes
.com/2019/08/07/sports/football/kenny-stills-dolphins-trump-ross.html.

BISHOP, GREG. "A Pioneer, Reluctantly." *The New York Times*, 10 May 2013,
https://www.nytimes.com/2013/05/13/sports/for-transgender-fighter
-fallon-fox-there-is-solace-in-the-cage.html.

BRANCH, JOHN. "The Awakening of Colin Kaepernick." *The New York Times*,
7 Sept. 2017, https://www.nytimes.com/2017/09/07/sports/colin-kaepernick
-nfl-protests.html.

BRANCH, JOHN. "N.F.L. Prospect Proudly Says What Teammates Knew:
He's Gay." *The New York Times*, 9 Feb. 2014, https://www.nytimes
.com/2014/02/10/sports/michael-sam-college-football-star-says-he-is
-gay-ahead-of-nfl-draft.html.

CACCIOLA, SCOTT. "Stephen Curry, on a 'Surreal' Day, Confronts a Presidential Snub." *The New York Times*, 23 Sept. 2017, https://www.nytimes.com/2017/09/23/sports/stephen-curry-trump-nba-.html.

CAULEY, KASHANA. "Football Players Are Protesting Police Violence, Not the Anthem." *The New York Times*, 25 Aug. 2018, https://www.nytimes.com/2018/08/25/opinion/football-protests-police-violence-anthem.html.

COX, ANA MARIE. "Billie Jean King Understands Colin Kaepernick." *The New York Times*, 13 Sept. 2017, https://www.nytimes.com/2017/09/13/magazine/billie-jean-king-understands-colin-kaepernick.html.

DEB, SOPAN. "Etan Thomas: Now a Different Kind of Player." *The New York Times*, 27 Feb. 2018, https://www.nytimes.com/2018/02/27/books/etan-thomas-atheletes-as-activists.html.

GATES, HENRY LOUIS, JR. "Muhammad Ali, the Political Poet." *The New York Times*, 9 June 2016, https://www.nytimes.com/2016/06/09/opinion/muhammad-ali-the-political-poet.html.

GOODMAN, LIZZY. "The Best Women's Soccer Team in the World Fights for Equal Pay." *The New York Times*, 10 June 2019, https://www.nytimes.com/2019/06/10/magazine/womens-soccer-inequality-pay.html.

HAUSER, CHRISTINE. "High Schools Threaten to Punish Students Who Kneel During Anthem." *The New York Times*, 29 Sept. 2017, https://www.nytimes.com/2017/09/29/us/high-school-anthem-protest.html.

IVES, MIKE. "Sprinter Dutee Chand Becomes India's First Openly Gay Athlete." *The New York Times*, 20 May 2019, https://www.nytimes.com/2019/05/20/world/asia/india-dutee-chand-gay.html.

KANG, JAY CASPIAN. "What the World Got Wrong About Kareem Abdul-Jabbar." *The New York Times*, 17 Sept. 2015, https://www.nytimes.com/2015/09/20/magazine/what-the-world-got-wrong-about-kareem-abdul-jabbar.html.

KEH, ANDREW. "At World Cup, U.S. Team's Pride Is Felt by Others, Too." *The New York Times*, 29 June 2019, https://www.nytimes.com/2019/06/29/sports/womens-world-cup-lgbt.html.

KLEIN, JEFF Z. "In N.H.L. Negotiations, Union's Good Ideas May Not Matter." *The New York Times*, 16 Aug. 2012, https://slapshot.blogs.nytimes.com/2012/08/16/in-n-h-l-negotiation-the-unions-good-ideas-may-not-matter/.

LEVIN, DAN. "Athlete to Activist: How a Public Coming Out Shaped a Young Football Player's Life." *The New York Times*, 1 Dec. 2018, https://www.nytimes.com/2018/12/01/us/jake-bain-gay-athlete-isu.html.

LONGMAN, JERÉ. "For Megan Rapinoe, Boldness in the Spotlight Is Nothing New." *The New York Times*, 27 June 2019, https://www.nytimes .com/2019/06/27/sports/megan-rapinoe-trump-world-cup.html.

LONGMAN, JERÉ. "A Giant Leap for Women, but Hurdles Remain." *The New York Times*, 29 July 2012, https://www.nytimes.com/2012/07/30/sports /olympics/despite-gains-for-female-athletes-fight-for-true-equality -remains.html.

LONGMAN, JERÉ. "I.O.C. Names New President Amid Concerns Over Possible Athlete Protests in Sochi." *The New York Times*, 10 Sept. 2013, https:// www.nytimes.com/2013/09/11/sports/olympics/bach-takes-over-as-head -of-olympics.html.

LONGMAN, JERÉ. "Mandela Embraced the Power of Sports for Resistance and Unity." *The New York Times*, 5 Dec. 2013, https://www.nytimes.com /2013/12/06/sports/nelson-mandela-resistance-and-healing-through -sports.html.

LONGMAN, JERÉ. "Pan Am Games Protesters Get Probation. Olympians Get a Warning." *The New York Times*, 21 Aug. 2019, https://www .nytimes.com/2019/08/21/sports/olympics/pan-am-olympic -punishment.html.

LONGMAN, JERÉ. "Under Fidel Castro, Sport Symbolized Cuba's Strength and Vulnerability." *The New York Times*, 27 Nov. 2016, https://www .nytimes.com/2016/11/27/sports/under-fidel-castro-sport-symbolized -cubas-strength-and-vulnerability.html.

LONGMAN, JERÉ. "Understanding the Controversy Over Caster Semenya." *The New York Times*, 18 Aug. 2016, https://www.nytimes.com/2016/08/20 /sports/caster-semenya-800-meters.html.

MATHER, VICTOR. "Alejandro Bedoya Spoke Out on Gun Violence. It Helped Make Him M.L.S.'s Player of the Week." *The New York Times*, 5 Aug. 2019, https://www.nytimes.com/2019/08/05/sports/alejandro-bedoya-mls-gun -violence.html.

MATHER, VICTOR. "Egyptian Judo Athlete Refuses Handshake After Losing to Israeli." *The New York Times*, 12 Aug. 2016, https://www.nytimes.com /2016/08/13/sports/olympics/egyptian-refuses-israeli-handshake-or -sasson-islam-shehaby.html.

MERVOSH, SARAH, AND CHRISTINA CARON. "8 Times Women in Sports Fought for Equality." *The New York Times*, 8 Mar. 2019, https://www.nytimes .com/2019/03/08/sports/women-sports-equality.html.

THE NEW YORK TIMES. "Playing College Football Is a Job." *The New York Times*, 27 Mar. 2014, https://www.nytimes.com/2014/03/28/opinion/playing-college-football-is-a-job.html.

NOCERA, JOE. "College Athletes' Potential Realized in Missouri Resignations." *The New York Times*, 9 Nov. 2015, https://www.nytimes.com/2015/11/10/sports/ncaafootball/missouri-presidents-resignation-shows-realm-where-young-minorities-have-power.html.

NOCERA, JOE. "Unionized College Athletes?" *The New York Times*, 31 Jan. 2014, https://www.nytimes.com/2014/02/01/opinion/nocera-unionized-college-athletes.html.

POWELL, MICHAEL. "A Threat to Unionize, and Then Benefits Trickle In for Players." *The New York Times*, 12 Jan. 2015, https://www.nytimes.com/2015/01/13/sports/ncaafootball/with-threat-of-union-comes-a-trickle-of-benefits-to-college-football-players.html.

RUDOREN, JODI. "Palestinian Soccer Association Drops Effort to Suspend Israel From FIFA." *The New York Times*, 29 May 2015, https://www.nytimes.com/2015/05/30/world/middleeast/palestine-palestinian-fa-soccer-israel-fifa.html.

RUEB, EMILY S. "He Emerged From Prison a Potent Symbol of H.I.V. Criminalization." *The New York Times*, 14 July 2019, https://www.nytimes.com/2019/07/14/us/michael-johnson-hiv-prison.html.

SANDOMIR, RICHARD. "Players Show Solidarity With Lockout Looming." *The New York Times*, 23 June 2011, https://www.nytimes.com/2011/06/24/sports/basketball/nba-players-show-solidarity-with-lockout-looming.html.

SIDES, JOHN. "Magic Johnson and Public Opinion on AIDS and Sex." *The New York Times*, 7 Nov. 2011, https://fivethirtyeight.blogs.nytimes.com/2011/11/07/magic-johnson-and-public-opinion-on-aids-and-sex/.

STEVENS, MATT. "Gabby Douglas Says She Also Was Abused by Gymnastics Team Doctor." *The New York Times*, 21 Nov. 2017, https://www.nytimes.com/2017/11/21/sports/gabby-douglas-sex-abuse.html.

TELLEM, ARN. "When a Players Union Doesn't Help the Players." *The New York Times*, 7 May 2011, https://www.nytimes.com/2011/05/08/sports/football/08tellem.html.

TRACY, MARC. "Inside College Basketball's Most Political Locker Room." *The New York Times*, 16 Nov. 2016, https://www.nytimes.com/2016/11/17/sports/ncaabasketball/wisconsin-badgers-nigel-hayes.html.

TRACY, MARC. "Players Hold Power Over the N.C.A.A., if They Feel the Hunger." *The New York Times*, 8 Apr. 2019, https://www.nytimes.com/2019/04/08/sports/final-four-ncaa-amateurism.html.

WITZ, BILLY. "Flying Three Flags and Seeking One Banner." *The New York Times*, 14 June 2014, https://www.nytimes.com/2014/06/15/sports/basketball/the-diverse-heritage-of-san-antonio-spurs-patty-mills.html.

WORDEN, MINKY. "Human Rights and the 2022 Olympics." *The New York Times*, 18 Jan. 2015, https://www.nytimes.com/2015/01/19/opinion/human rights-and-the-2022-olympics.html.

Index

A

Abdul-Jabbar, Kareem,
9, 64, 149, 151–161, 169,
170, 171
Abdul-Rauf, Mahmoud, 63,
64, 65
Ali, Muhammad, 9, 149,
152, 162–165, 169, 170,
171, 184, 186, 204
Alms, Paige, 93
Araton, Harvey, 63–66
athlete/players unions,
10–13, 14–15, 16–18, 19–21

B

Bach, Thomas, 179, 180,
181, 192, 195
Bain, Jake, 129–134
Bass, Michael, 15
Bedoya, Alejandro, 173–176
Belson, Ken, 67–72, 177–178
Bender, John, 48
Berry, Gwen, 207, 210
Bettman, Gary, 16, 17, 18
Bishop, Greg, 113–122
Bjarkman, Peter C., 204
Blatter, Sepp, 195, 196, 197
Branch, John, 44–59,
123–128

C

Cacciola, Scott, 166–168
Carlos, John, 74, 170, 184,
208, 210
Caron, Christina, 90–94
Carroll, Helen, 117, 119

Castro, Antonio, 205–206
Castro, Fidel, 202–206
Cauley, Kashana, 73–75
Chand, Dutee, 135–137
Chastain, Brandi, 99
Collett, Wayne, 74
Colter, Kain, 19, 20, 24–27,
31, 34
Cox, Ana Marie, 87–89
Curry, Stephen, 65, 166–168

D

Davis, Wade, 54
Deb, Sopan, 169–172
DeFrantz, Anita, 181
Dégommeuses, Les,
138–143
Dolan, Sean P., 60
Douglas, Gabby, 85–86
Duggan, Meghan, 92

E

Edwards, Harry, 44, 52,
210
Eini, Ofer, 197
Ellis, Jill, 96, 102, 111, 138
Emmert, Mark, 35
Ernst, Chris, 91

F

Fehr, Donald, 16, 17, 18
Fisher, Derek, 14
Foudy, Julie, 96, 112
Fox, Fallon, 113–122
free agency, 10, 11, 17, 34
Freeman, Cathy, 190

G

Garnett, Kevin, 14, 15
Gates, Henry Louis, Jr.,
162–165
Gold-Unwude, Ros, 36
González Echevarría,
Roberto, 202, 204
Goodell, Roger, 49, 69, 70
Goodman, Lizzy, 95–107,
110
Griffin, Blake, 14

H

Hartley, Chad, 48
Hartmann, Douglas, 208,
209
Hauser, Christine, 60–62
Hayes, Nigel, 8, 37–43
health care/health
insurance, 12, 13, 20, 23,
25, 26
Hegerberg, Ada, 94
Heiberg, Gerhard, 180
Hill, Jordan, 37–43
Hirshland, Sarah, 207, 210
Horan, Lindsey, 96, 102,
104, 105, 106
Huish, Robert, 203
Huma, Ramogi, 20, 25
Human Rights Watch, 77,
192
Hunter, Billy, 14, 15

I

Imboden, Race, 207, 208,
210

Ives, Mike, 135–137

J

Jenkins, Malcolm, 67–72
Johnson, Magic, 145,
  149–150, 157, 161
Johnson, Michael L.,
  144–148

K

Kaepernick, Colin, 7–8,
  37, 40, 44–59, 61, 63, 64,
  68–69, 73, 87, 99, 110,
  169, 170, 172, 177, 210
Kang, Jay Caspian, 151–161
Keh, Andrew, 138–143
Kennelly, Keala, 93
King, Billie Jean, 87–89, 91
Klein, Jeff Z., 16–18
Koenig, Bronson, 37–43
Korr, Charles, 183, 184, 186
Kruse, Kevin, 74

L

Lapchick, Richard,
  184–185, 186
Levin, Dan, 129–134
Lindberg, Gunilla, 180, 181
Lloyd, Carli, 96, 98, 101,
  103, 104–105, 107
Lohmar, Tim, 145, 147, 148
Longman, Jeré, 76–79,
  80–84, 108–112, 179–182,
  183–186, 202–206,
  207–210
Lurie, Jeffrey, 70, 72

M

Major League Baseball,
  34, 124, 205
Major League Baseball
  Players Association,
  10, 12
Major League Soccer, 98,
  100, 125, 173–176

Mandela, Nelson, 183–186
Marshall, Brandon, 45, 49,
  55, 59
Mather, Victor, 173–176,
  200–201
Mervosh, Sarah, 90–94
Miller, Marvin, 10–13
Mills, Patty, 187–191
minimum salaries, 10, 13
Moller, Andrea, 93
Morales, Deborah, 152,
  153, 154, 158
Morgan, Alex, 95, 96, 98,
  101, 102

N

Napier, Shabazz, 33, 36
Nassar, Lawrence G.,
  85–86
national anthem protests,
  7–8, 37, 44–45, 54–55,
  60–62, 63–66, 67, 68–69,
  71, 73–75, 110, 169, 177,
  207
National Basketball
  Association (N.B.A.), 11,
  12, 13, 14–15, 16, 18, 35,
  63–66, 93, 124, 125, 154,
  166, 169, 171, 187
National College Players
  Association, 20, 25
National Collegiate
  Athletic Association
  (N.C.A.A.), 19, 20, 22–23,
  25, 27, 29, 32, 33–36, 48,
  119, 120, 131, 154, 156
National Football League
  (N.F.L.), 7, 9, 11, 12, 13,
  16, 18, 24, 25, 35, 45, 49,
  50, 55, 57, 59, 61, 63,
  67–72, 73–75, 123, 124,
  125, 169, 177, 178
National Hockey League
  (N.H.L.), 15, 16, 18, 124

National Labor Relations
  Board (N.L.R.B.), 19, 20,
  21, 22, 23, 26, 34
Netanyahu, Benjamin, 197
Nevius, Tim, 35–36
Nocera, Joe, 19–21, 28–32

O

Ogundimu, Olumide, 44,
  46, 49

P

Paul, Chris, 14
Pichon, Marinette, 139, 142
Plaatjes, Mark, 185–186
Players Coalition, 67–72
Pollock, Philip H., III,
  149–150
Pound, Dick, 181, 182
Powell, Michael, 24–27
Probst, Larry, 181
Pugh, Mallory, 96, 102, 106

R

Rajoub, Jibril, 196, 197, 198
Rapinoe, Megan, 8, 55, 78,
  79, 96, 98, 99, 101, 102,
  103, 105, 107, 108–112,
  139, 140, 142, 143, 208
revenue sharing, 10, 11, 16,
  17–18
Roberts, Michele, 64, 65,
  66
Robinson, Jackie, 34, 74
Rome, Marine, 138–143
Ross, Stephen, 177–178
Rudoren, Jodi, 196–199
Rueb, Emily S., 144–148
Russell, Bill, 64, 152, 169,
  170, 171

S

salary caps, 11, 12, 15, 18
Sam, Michael, 123–128, 131
Sandomir, Richard, 14–15

Sauerbrunn, Becky, 96, 101

Semenya, Caster, 8, 80–84, 137

Sherman, Richard, 74

Shuaibi, Zaid, 198

Sides, John, 149–150

Smith, Tommie, 74, 184, 208, 210

Solo, Hope, 101

Stevens, Matt, 85–86

Stills, Kenny, 177–178

student athletes, 7, 10, 19–21, 22–23, 24–27, 28–32, 33–36, 37–43

Switzer, Kathrine, 90

T

Tellem, Arn, 10–13

Thomas, Etan, 169–172

Thrasher, Steven, 146, 147

Tracy, Marc, 33–36, 37–43

Trump, Donald J., 44, 45, 61, 64, 65, 68, 70, 71, 73, 108, 109, 131, 159, 166–168, 169, 177, 178, 208

U

U.S. women's national hockey team, 92

U.S. women's national soccer team, 76, 90, 95–107, 108–112, 138–143

V

Valenti, Bianca, 93

W

Wallechinsky, David, 203, 208

Wambach, Abby, 95, 97, 100, 103, 110, 138

Wilcke, Christoph, 77–78

Williams, Buck, 63, 64–65

Williams, Serena, 99

Williams, Venus, 92

Witz, Billy, 187–191

Wolfe, Tim, 28–32, 34

Women's National Basketball Association (W.N.B.A.), 76, 93–94

Worden, Minky, 192–195

World Surf League, 93

Y

Yee, Don, 34, 35

This book is current up until the time of printing. For the most up-to-date reporting, visit www.nytimes.com.